S0-BEZ-462

Transcendental
BASKETBALL
BLUES

BY
MIKE PEMBERTON

"For the strength of the Pack is the Wolf...and the strength of the Wolf is the Pack."
Rudyard Kipling, The Jungle Book

Born to run

Jack Henderson's seam splitting shoulders sagged when he saw the family's tarnished, silver Chevrolet Caprice station wagon.

It was the fall of 1978, and Jack, a seventeen-year-old high school senior on an English class field trip, had wedged his lanky body into a folding chair on the top floor of the state university library when he spotted the car crawling along the street six stories below. Even through the first frost of fall on the library's windows, he could see it was Mary Lou, could tell by the way the Chevy lurched, how she punched then paused on the accelerator, incapable of producing a steady, smooth pace, the Caprice herky-jerking toward the interstate and the open road. Leaving.

That was what she did. She left. The destination never mattered as long as the road took her away from Plainview-St. Jude, the twin cities in Illinois that the Hendersons called home.

As the silver Caprice melted into the gray October sky, he wondered where his father, Sam, and the police would catch up with Mary Lou this time. Because it did not matter where she drove, they would find her. And they would bring her back.

Jack closed his eyes, buried his brown, long-haired head into slim hands—"piano playing hands," Mary Lou told him; "basketball player's hands," Sam said—and wished he could escape the reality of his family's life. But the image of his father, who ran an engineering firm when not serving as mayor of St. Jude, kept returning to his mind: Lucky Strike dangling from his lip, phone crooked beneath his chin, and a fresh scotch and water in one hand as he asked Chief Royal to issue a missing person bulletin. Soon after he would be jumping into a squad car with the bald-headed, antacid-popping chief and driving to the bus station, diner, or greasy truck stop where Mary Lou sat sipping hot Lipton tea, hair tied into a bun, brown eyes vacant yet wary, her heart fluttering as Sam enters and slips into the chair across from her.

"Leave me be," she would say. "Go home. To your other home. You know, the blonde and your bastard children you keep across town. I'll come to my home when I'm ready."

"Mary Lou, you stopped taking your meds, honey," Sam would whisper. "There's only one family, one home."

And when she said no, Royal would barge through the door, and she would shriek and curse as Sam yanked her hands across the tabletop, and the chief slapped handcuffs on her thin wrists, all the while assuring the wide-eyed diners that everything was OK.

The bulky cop would then jerk Mary Lou to her tiny feet, separating her kicking and screaming from the white Formica tabletop, and rush her to the back seat of the squad car. Sam would drive her Caprice, while Royal, cherries rolling, took the interstate to St. Jude, where Mary Lou would be checked into the psychiatric wing and pumped full of Haldol, the drug of choice for treating a paranoid schizophrenic. There she would lie in the steel hospital bed, leather restraints across thin arms and legs, as the drug-induced calm took over, her fingers drumming the stiff mattress, playing an imaginary piano, her voice bluesy and ragged as she whispered to herself, to everyone, to no one, "Damn it all, damn it all, damn it all...."

Surrender, Surrender

As Mary Lou's Chevy lurched toward the horizon, Jack turned away from the window to see a library geek, a cute library geek, talking. Braided blonde hair, blue eyes framed by granny glasses, with long legs flowing from the hem of a knee-length denim dress, interrupted by an apple-shaped rear. The girl put a quick stop to his wandering thoughts.

The cute geek talked about methods of researching a seminar paper. Their teacher, Ken "Dipshit" Dunham, made the assignment the previous week, not so they could learn to write a paper, but so Dunham, having lost control of the class, could kill one day a week by bringing everyone to the library for research.

Not that Jack cared about any of it, except for the library girl's body.

As a rule, Jack did not give a damn about high school or senior year or graduation or homecoming or prom or anything except slamming a few brews on Friday night with his buddies, listening to AC/DC or Cheap Trick and hoping that, by the grace of God, he would get laid for the first time. Saturday morning, still not laid, he would rejoin his friends at the Roundhouse, the old grade school gym they snuck into to play basketball. Slipping and sliding on the beige linoleum floor, while Snake, the Lord-knows-how-old hippie turned janitor, whooped and hollered from the four-foot-high stage running alongside the court, his dreadlocked, bleach-blond hair flopping about like the mop he never used as Snake enjoyed the occasional doobie and watched the boys play. Streaking up and down the floor, they sweated out the beer, the smokes, and all the high school bullshit they absorbed the previous week, soaking the floor with it all, until, after a couple of hours, the linoleum grew too slick to navigate, and they collapsed onto the stage, lean bodies cleansed, lungs sucking in the stale gym air and second-hand pot smoke, drained and refreshed at the same time, hungry and ready to party again on Saturday night.

Jack sat in the back row at the library so as not to block anyone. A warm afternoon sun emerged from behind grey clouds, shone through the tall windows and made him sleepy. He didn't hear what the girl said, only stared drowsily at her body as she spoke, stared until even her exquisite figure could not hold his attention, and his head began to dip.

He woke to a smack across his head and a hand clenching the back of his neck. "Wake up, Henderson!" Dunham hissed.

Jack gagged at the stench of cigarettes, coffee, and antacids spilling from Dunham.

The young librarian stopped speaking and everyone turned.

Blood surged to Jack's cheeks, he jumped to his feet, knocking his chair and Dunham's hands away with a swing of his right arm that sent the teacher and his toupee flying.

"Henderson!" Dunham shouted as he crawled on his knees, scrambling to find his hairpiece. "Henderson!"

Jack glanced down at Dunham's pale scalp then past his classmates and the librarian, toward the ribbon of road down which Mary Lou's Caprice had disappeared. The class burst into nervous laughter. The girls, especially the "good girls," like Miss-Teen-America-in-the-making, Sandy McCarty, scrunched pancake-powdered faces at Jack and whispered. "Wouldn't you know Jack'd do something like this."

Many of the boys pointed and snickered at Dunham. But Randy Jenkins and Frank Connolly, two hotshot basketball players, came to his aid. The boys were reverse images of each other: Jenkins a blond, fresh-faced, rawboned country kid and Connolly a dark-skinned Irish. Both wore their blow-dried hair feathered and parted down the middle, and both were the type who wore their letter jackets even while inside. But they didn't come to help Dunham out of any concern for the teacher. They despised him as much as anyone else did, but they despised Jack more. Being a standout basketball player who chose not to play varsity, Jack's absence from the team was a bigger source of conversation than their presence on it. His aloofness cheapened those prized letters stitched to their jackets, and Jenkins and Connolly hated him for it.

As they flashed your-ass-is-grass grins at him, Jack saw the librarian take a half step forward, her arms spread and palms up, like a minister calling a congregation to prayer, lips parted to speak, to help. But his stare stopped her.

"Henderson!" Dunham said, clutching the tangled toupee as he struggled to stand. "Henderson, this time you're done. This time I got you. You can't hit a teacher. This time it's expulsion, Henderson. Henderson?"

But Jack was on his way out the door, two bony middle fingers thrust high over his head and waving like miniature flags at a Fourth of July parade. Long strides carried him out the door and down the winding steps away from Dunham, Jenkins, Connolly and the librarian, down to the main floor, where he found the exit and, once outside, sprinted for the alley behind the library.

Out of sight, chest heaving, he dropped to his knees, but the cold concrete offered no respite. He gasped and groaned. Numbed by the tired pattern of his mother's abandonments, he had stopped crying over her loss long ago. It was as if she had died, and the mourning period that allowed for tears had passed into depressed reflection. All cried out, as the old folks said.

Chilled by the frost, Jack rose, rubbed his dry eyes, and walked home.

Days of September

"Look at the score, Jack... Try not to bang the keys, Becky... Slow down, Maggie... Tempo... go with the flow of the music... Don't fight it... embrace it," Mary Lou would instruct Jack and his two younger sisters.

A music major at Smith College, Mary Lou had declined an invitation to audition with the Chicago Symphony. Instead, eager to start her family, she played with the St. Jude Symphony and gave lessons to neighborhood children. She taught her own children to play and sing as soon as they were old enough to sit at a piano. At the end of their lessons she would lead them through her childhood favorites, songs from Mary Poppins, The Sound of Music, any Judy Garland or Wizard of Oz song. Her music made the cookie-cutter house in the pre-patterned subdivision a home.

Often she played after putting the children to bed. Lying in his bedroom, door closed, Jack heard the muffled sounds of the piano beneath the carpeted plywood floor. He was too young then to know the songs by name: classical music like Mozart, Beethoven and Chopin, nostalgic pop tunes like "Days of September," "Sunrise, Sunset," or a modern classic like Gershwin's "Rhapsody in Blue" with its rousing opening Daaaaaaaah... da-da-da-da-da-da-da-da-da-da... da ... DUMMMMMM. Jack's heart jumped with the notes. The songs revealed a disturbance in his mother's comforting aura, a feeling Jack could not give voice to and which Mary Lou acknowledged with a light brush of his little-boy-blond hair when they knelt to pray at the end of the day or with a wistful gaze as she tucked him in.

Some evenings, with Sam's snores the only sound upstairs, Jack sneaked from his room in Batman pajamas and bathrobe, perched on the staircase, and watched his mother play. Her straight back facing the stairwell, she rarely used any sheet music, being more comfortable with memory and emotions than paper and ink. The ability to read music, as she saw it, was merely a means to the end of mastering a piece and making it her own. "If you don't play with feeling," she told the children, "why play at all?"

He watched his mother's silhouette sway from side to side, fingers plugged into the piano as if it were the source of her life force, energizing and enervating her. A silent audience of one, Jack balanced on the edge of the stair, determined to scurry away when the music stopped before she could detect him. Yet somehow he would always awake the next morning with no memory of returning to bed, the scent of his mother's Chanel No 5 clinging to his PJs.

Before she ran away the first time, Mary Lou had been dicing onions in the kitchen and sliced off the padded part of her left thumb, the blood streaming and drip-drip-dripping a burgundy polka-dot pattern on the white linoleum floor.

"Damn it all," Mary Lou muttered.

A chunk of thumb gone, Jack had thought, and even then only a faint damn escaped. Damn: a word people uttered when watching a figure skater fall— "Damn, that must've hurt."

Sam rushed her to the emergency room, the chunk of skin still on the bloodied cutting board looking like a pale piece of chicken. Jack wiped it into the trash and scrubbed the board clean.

Four weeks passed where Mary Lou could not play the piano, a prison sentence without parole, but she never complained. Then, thumb healed, she ran away.

Hotel California

Yeah, Jack thought, as he walked home, he remembered her from before. But he knew her now, too. He recalled the last visit in the mental hospital that fall. Used to be, Chanel No 5 made him think of his mother. Now, hospital stench did.

Hospitals were lousy places even when seeing someone with a minor problem, like a broken leg. After numerous visits to Mary Lou, Jack decided it was the smell: that antiseptic, mothball, kitty-box, stinking stale odor that emanated from the buckets and mops, the spray bottles and cloths of the janitors who struggled to neutralize the stench of piss, puke, and shit. Rather than fight it, he dealt with the foulness by breathing it in, embracing it, immersing himself. Total immersion the key. The reason why people think their own shit does not stink. After a few minutes the olfactory senses are surrounded, and the stink becomes the norm.

But the stink in the mental ward, or at the hospital or nursing home, is the worst. It is not yours, it is not theirs, it is everyone's. The mental patients urinate and defecate on the floor, wiping feces on anything they can reach until the staff cleans it up, slaps on the restraints, and the patients start to spit, curse, piss, and crap all over again, the whole process repeating itself. The stink never leaves the air. Once someone has smelled that odor they never rid themselves of it. They carry it with them forever, and whenever they get a whiff— no matter when or where—they flash back.

Resigned to this inevitability, Jack clutched the construction-paper get-well cards from Becky and Maggie and took a deep gulp as he entered the ward. He invited the stink to sink into his lungs, to filter through his pores, hating the vision of his mother as paranoid schizophrenic that the stench evoked, yet surrendering to its truth, to the fetid fact of mental illness.

Mary Lou sat in the recreation room, strapped into a padded, beige wheelchair facing a window screened with meshed white wire. A bright sun cast a polka-dot pattern across her. The faded leather restraints dangled from the arms of the chair, wrists so petite the staff cut an extra hole in the strap to keep her from slipping free. They tied her ankles down as well. She drummed her fingers in a halting beat, keeping time with a song only she could hear. They administered Haldol, attempting to tame the wild thoughts schizophrenia thrust upon her. But the drug did not calm so much as dull; the errant thoughts muted but still present. Her face looked pale and delicate under the harsh fluorescent lights: dark shadows pooled beneath high cheekbones, brown eyes glassy, fragile beauty still present but frozen, like a well made-up corpse. If not for the drumming fingers and the milky dribble at corner of her mouth, she might have been dead.

There was a single door, meshed white metal grate from top to bottom, like the window, and one other patient, an older woman with a shock of grey hair, frayed tips jutting at all angles. The woman whispered and danced at a languid pace, unaware of Jack and Mary Lou's presence. In a corner of the room stood an upright piano, its oak finish scuffed and scratched, ivory keys yellowed and black keys faded. A TV hung from the ceiling in another corner, the volume muted, a black-and-white version of the Andy Griffith show flickering. Brown-stained wooden tables and unmatched chairs stood scattered about as if a party had just ended, everything discarded and in disarray. Jack snagged a heavy chair and dragged it across the gray-and-white-checked linoleum. He raked his fingers through tousled hair and folded his lean frame into the narrow seat, angling it towards Mary Lou, their knees bumping when she tilted forward.

The grey-haired woman flitted and floated around them in a zigzagging orbit.

"Hi, Mom," Jack said, trying to make eye contact with Mary Lou to gauge the effect of the Haldol. He always looked in her eyes, searching for signs of life, trying not to take it personally when she failed to respond.

"How you doing, Mom?"

"Did your father send you to check on me, Jack?" Mary Lou said, voice flat and hard, words slipping from pursed lips in time with her finger tapping as she stared out the caged window. "See if I was still here?"

"No, Mom, I asked if I could come by myself, like I always do."

"Well, tell your father I'm here. He should be happy. Him and Chief Royal. I know what they're doing. I know what they're about. They can't fool me. I know."

"I just came to see how you were feeling, Mom."

"I'm not feeling anything. They won't let me play the piano. Let me loose, Jack. Let me play the piano...like last time."

"Uh...I don't know, Mom," Jack said, squirming. "Last time I did that, that head nurse, Decker, was ticked. Said she'd tell Dad. Not let me visit on my own anymore. 'Sides, you can play all you want when you get home. When do you think you'll be ready to come home, Mom?"

"Home? Which home, Jack? You know your father has two, right?"

And there it was.

She had not been on the Haldol long enough, her speech still staccato and sharp, mind racing. Jack started to respond, started, like a crazy man, to argue with a crazy woman. But he stopped and let her spew. She had to, she had to set him straight so he would know nothing was wrong with her. It was everybody else who had the problem.

"You know about his other wife, right, Jack? That blonde. Your father never did like me as a brunette. But that's how God made me. What am I supposed to do? Never good enough. Like my breasts. I know he'd like them bigger. Like that Nordic whore he's sleeping with. It's never good enough for your father. Never. So your father got another wife, another family. They live across town, you know. Everybody knows. Grandma Henderson, my sister. They all know, have known for years, but never told me. Betrayed me. Of course, I can understand my sister not telling me. She has her own lies to hide. Sleeping with Sam herself. And I can understand Grandma, Sam is her son. But what about the people at church, Father McIntire? They all knew, and they kept it from me. But then I realized... Your father, your father... They were afraid of your father. That's why he's mayor. To intimidate people. Keep them quiet. And it worked, for a while. And they thought I didn't know. Thought I didn't know about the blonde—'What Mary Lou doesn't know won't hurt her'—I'm sure that's what your father told people. 'Mind your business, or I'll send the chief of police after you.' And he would do it, too. Does it to me when I leave. Because I know, now. I have known. For longer than they think. But I didn't say anything. Didn't want to ruin your kid's lives. Have you think less of your father. So I let it go. Let him have his second family. Sleep with your aunt. The damn blonde. All the rest. And I acted like Miss Happy Homemaker. Let him think, let them all think I didn't know. But I did know. I figured it out. I'm not dumb. Not an airheaded housewife with nothing but brownies and meatloaf on my mind. I have a college degree. I could've been a great musician. I am a great musician. Oh, yes, I figured it out. But I let it be. As long as he kept it out of my house, I let it be. But then he brought Basker to the house. The Hound of Baskerville, he told you kids. Thinking he's so goddamn clever and cute about naming that dog. Said he got the dog from the Humane Society of all places, that bastard of a father of yours—"

"He did get it from the Humane Society, Mom," Jack said, unable to stop. "I was with Dad when we picked Basker out. Me and the girls. We chose Basker. We named him Basker because Becky was reading that Sherlock Holmes book at school. You remember, don't you Mom, Becky reading that book?"

"I remember what I need to remember," Mary Lou said, then tilted an ear toward the ceiling as if something spoke to her.

"I know, I know," she said, nodding, then turning to Jack. "I know what I know. I have sources you don't have Jack. People you don't know. They tell me these things, Jack. I don't blame you. Of course you believe your dad. It's not your fault he's a lying, conniving, sonuvabitch. He took that dog away from the blonde's house because she was allergic to Basker's long fur. Had to get rid of him to please her. So your dad brought that mutt to the pound. Let you kids think you picked him out. That's what happened, Jack. And I told him so. Told him I knew where that dog came from. I knew about the second family. About my sister. Knew it all. I was told by reliable sources. Reliable sources, I told him. And when I saw the way he looked at me, I knew I'd better leave, better get out of the house, out of town—"

"Mom, the dog came from the Humane Society. The girls've been wanting a dog for a long time. You know that. They felt down when you were, uh… gone…. Dad was trying to pick up their spirits. Give 'em something to take their minds off things. The guy who runs it told us Basker's owner died. There was no one to take him. They were going to put him to sleep, Mom. That's what happened. There's no second family. Dad isn't doing anything with your sister. He's not a conniving SOB. It's all in your head."

"That's right Jack. It's all in my head. I'm sure your father tells you how ill I am. Paranoid schizophrenic. I know. I know. That's what they do, men like your father, Hitler, Stalin. I read Solzhenitsyn. No news to me. The powers that be always stick people like me, people who know the truth, stick them in places like this. Dope us up. Keep us out of sight and out of mind so we can't tell what we know. Can't label them for the hypocrites they are. Expose them for their crimes. We're a danger to them. Like Christ was to the Romans. A revolutionary. So they crucify us. But they can't nail people to a cross anymore. So they put them in hell-holes like this—for their own good… Oh, I know what they're doing. Nobody's fooling me. You tell your father I know what's going on. Go ahead. You tell him. Tell him I know. I know everything."

"OK, Mom, fine. I'll tell Dad. Becky and Maggie say hello and they love you." She stared ahead.

"They're fine, by the way," Jack said, voice catching for a moment, then clear-ing. It always did, as he knew it would, the scene a reenactment of so many. "I'll tell them you asked. What's another lie gonna hurt? Here, they made these for you."

He tossed the rainbow colored cards onto the nearest table.

"Oh, I'm sure your father's taking care of you kids. You're his legacy. You and the blonde's bastards. I'm the odd one out. Because I know. I know everything. I know all about—"

Jack jumped from his seat, scooted the chair away with a squeak and stepped behind Mary Lou. He took a deep breath, rested his hands on her shoulders and kissed her cheek, the skin icy and brittle to the touch despite the bitter eruptions of anger.

"I'll see you in a couple days, Mom."

"Aren't you going to untie me? Let me play?" she said, eyes wide, as if the preceding rant had never happened.

Jack sighed, he gripped the handles of the wheelchair and hung his head.

She started again to curse Sam, her sister, the Catholic Church, the CIA, the Nazi's, the Jews, her voice turning low and guttural.

"Tell your father I know about that blonde. Tell him I know, Jack. I know about it all—"

"Enough, Mom," Jack said, shaking the chair until it hopped, Mary Lou clutching the arm rails. "Stop it, goddamn it. Stop."

The grey-haired woman's slippers shuffled across the linoleum.

"Let me loose, Jack," Mary Lou whispered. "Let me play. The voices go away when I play."

Jack leaned his weight on the wheel chair. "Screw it," he said. He knelt in front of his mother, putting a finger to pursed lips, his other hand on her lap.

"Promise to be quiet?"

Mary Lou nodded.

Behind her the grey-haired woman stopped.

Jack undid the straps on Mary Lou's ankles and looked at his mother again. She nodded.

He released her hands, disengaged the brakes on the wheelchair and rolled Mary Lou to the piano, the grey-haired woman scampering behind.

"Give me a sec', Mom, to get the door… then play away."

Mary Lou sat up straight and adjusted the white hospital gown as if intro-duced to an audience, her freed hands hovering above the worn keys, awaiting her cue from the maestro.

Jack slid the chair to the door and stepped into the hallway, looking for nurses and orderlies. Seeing none, he pulled the door to, tipped the chair, and poised it beneath the knob. With a final glance around the hallway, he let go the chair, pulled the door swiftly shut, and felt the chair wedge beneath the knob on the other side.

Within seconds the first bluesy bars of "Over the Rainbow" squeaked from the out-of-tune piano. Jack stopped and watched his mother through the iron screen, her pale hands shaking, her drug-saturated mind retrieving the notes from hazy memory. The grey-haired woman danced in disjointed rhythm.

"Oh, Christ almighty… Henderson… I'm calling your father, Henderson. I'm calling your father."

Jack turned to see the squat, stomach-churning Nurse Decker, white shoes thumping, stubby arms pumping.

Jack smiled and walked the opposite way, a dozen long strides separating him from the pissed-off nurse who slammed her shoulder against the blocked metal door, jerking and twisting the jammed knob.

"I'm calling your father!" Decker shouted at Jack, before turning her attention to Mary Lou and the grey-haired woman. "You two stop that! Open this door! You know you're not supposed to play in the recreation room."

Mary Lou's ugly diatribe, the blues-tinged music, the nastiness of the ward, and Nurse Decker's shouting floated around Jack, but none of it fazed him. Instead he was saved that day, as he had been on other days, because his survival mode had kicked in. Granted by the grace of God, or Buddha, or Mohammed, or whatever, a protective barrier formed around him, allowing him to weave through the mental ward without screaming, allowing him to breathe the stench of that hospital, his life, his mother's life, his family's life, and to convince himself that none of their shit stank.

But this defense disintegrated as Jack emerged from the phosphorous glare of the sanitarium. He squinted in the bright October sun and spotted a young couple strolling hand-in-hand with their fair-haired toddler, the parents laughing, the boy lapping up affection, the certainty of that affection yet to be tested. Jack's guard dropped altogether when the crisp autumn air caught in his throat and bent his six-foot-four frame in half. He coughed like a coal miner arising from the depths, hacking and spitting until, lungs cleared, he righted himself. Shoulders squared, his mind readjusted to the open-air world. Inhaling the cleansing breeze, he plunged forward.

Total immersion the key.

Dream Weaver

A thirteen-year-old Jack dribbled a red, white, and blue striped basketball to a staccato beat. A subconscious mantra, the beat built with the first thump vibrating through his fingertips and flowed up thin, adolescent arms, surging into heart and brain, rising and roaring like timpani approaching crescendo.

Jack faced the hoop from the top of the key, juking from side to side, black Chuck Taylor high-top sneakers squeaking, ball bobbing like a yo-yo on an invisible string, hands shifty-quick like a sideshow shell game hustler.

Thump-thump-thump, squeak-squeak-squeak, left-right-left-right-left-right, thump-squeak-left-thump-squeak-right.

Almost. The rhythm not there yet, momentum building. Wait for it, wait, wait. THUMP-SQUEAK-LEFT, THUMP-SQUEAK-RIGHT-THUMP-LEFT-THUMP-THUMP-THUMP-SQUEAK-RIGHT—THUMP!

The ball rose with his hands to shooting position—right underneath, left on the side—his thin legs flexing then extending, arms rising above his head, body trailing. At the height of his leap, he fired the ball toward the orange rim with a flick of the wrist, right arm extended, fingers pointed to the sky, hand dipping on the follow-through as his body descended. Landing on the balls of his feet, Jack gazed as the ball back-spun toward the hoop, a tricolor rainbow arcing across a robin-egg-blue spring sky. Taught to follow his shot, assume the miss, Jack stutter-stepped forward, ready to snatch the rebound and slash to the hoop or time his leap for a tip-in. But the ball settled in the net, dropped to the concrete and returned to him.

Jack jabbed, cut, jumped, and spun, launching shot after shot. He slowed after a miss, slapping the ball to the pavement, knees bent, crouching, dribbles low and hard, desperate to retrieve the beat. Sometimes standing straight, dribble deliberate and high, shoulders squared, he strutted, prowling the perimeter like a tiger circling prey, the loop tightening, pace quickening.

T H U M P - T H U M P - T H U M P - T H U M P - T H U M P - THUMPTHUMPTHUMP—QUICKSTEP-THUMP-QUICKSTEP—LEAP.

Jack attacked the basket, ball cradled in upturned right hand, arm raised, lower legs dangling like a kid perched on a dock. At full ascension, he stretched and banked the ball off the sun-faded backboard, the vinyl dimples rubbing against the nylon net with a soothing swish. He batted the ball, the drumbeat dribble enveloping him in an endorphin trance, the world outside the court banished.

The sound of rubber tires sliding on gravel broke the spell. Sam arrived home from work in a cloud of dust, brand new 1974 gold Plymouth purring. Breathless, sweat rolling down blue-veined arms, eyes wide, Jack focused on nothing and saw everything, like a young Indian brave emerging from the ritual sweat house, the visions vivid.

Sam tossed his grey and white plaid sport coat to the concrete and called for the ball. Blue-striped tie askew, Lucky Strike dangling from his bottom lip, close-cropped hair faintly recalling a tinge of red, Sam bounced the ball and moved laterally, searching for his own rhythm, seventeen again.

Sam picked up the dribble twenty-five feet from the hoop and stood at a forty-five degree angle from the backboard. Right foot forward, two hands on the ball, he released a high, arcing shot that banked off the board and slipped through the basket with a ripple, an improbable, awkward, even ridiculous-looking miracle of a kiss shot. Yet he made more than he missed.

"Right off my nose. I still got it baby!" Sam shouted.

Jack's metronome of a dribble sputtered. He picked up the scent of supper from his mother's kitchen.

Jack saw Becky and Maggie laugh as they stepped out the screen door to join Sam on the court. A bluesy version of "Over the Rainbow" drifted through the living room windows: Mary Lou playing the piano and singing while supper simmered, her classically trained voice a husky drawl, the melancholy music flowing as if she had the blues herself.

Jack tossed up a few more shots, not stopping until he swished three in a row. He let the ball bounce off the court after the final swoosh, watched it roll through the thick green grass of his father's manicured lawn and settle next to the rock border of Mary Lou's flower garden. A scented sea of jasmine, lavender, ivory, burgundy, hot pink, and gold blossoms lapped a grassy ridge on which a ruby red rose bush towered over white roses on either side. The center branches of each rose bush tied to fresh pinewood stakes, hammered snug into the coal black dirt to prevent the plant from collapsing under the weight of its own petals. Not a weed grew in the garden, where nurture triumphed over the natural tangle of wild growth.

VROOOOOOOM! VROOOOOOOM! VROOOOOOOM!

The silver Caprice roared as it raced around the corner, fish-tailed in the gravel and zoomed onto the court. Mary Lou was behind the wheel, a wicked grin cracking her porcelain face, black hair shocked straight. The car lurched right, left and barreled at the family.

Jack jumped.

"Jeezus," he shouted, sitting bolt upright in bed.

The glowing green digits of his alarm clock read 3:12 a.m.

Jack shoved off the bed spread and swung bare feet onto the floor, head throbbing from the Old Milwaukee he tossed back with his buddies after stalking out of the library.

He went to the bathroom, but paused on the way back, light leaking from his parent's bedroom, no snores from Sam. Jack crept downstairs.

The piano stood in silent abandonment, the TV flickered from the den. Slumped in his easy chair, a crumpled pack of Luckys on the end table next to a half-empty bottle of scotch, Sam's snores accompanied the static white noise whooshing from the fuzzy screen.

Jack grabbed a red plaid blanket from the couch and covered his father.

Living for the City

Later that morning Jack slouched next to Sam in the small waiting room outside Principal Frank Locke's office with a fidgety Dunham parked across from them. Sam smoked Luckys like a kid popping sugar cubes—Mary Lou was still missing. Seated next to Dunham, legs crossed, smiling as he chitchatted with Sam, was Reggie Collins, the dean of boys. Collins had become a local basketball hero while playing at the university and now was in his second year as head coach of the varsity boys' basketball team at St. Jude High. Nothing extraordinary about that, except that Reginald Cornelius Collins was black. He was the first black high school varsity coach in the state of Illinois outside of Chicago or East St. Louis, and that gave Collins a high profile. He accepted the fact that his presence on the sidelines jarred people. Someone had to be first. And while central Illinois in the seventies was not Birmingham, Alabama, in 1963, Collins had lived in Plainview-St. Jude long enough to know its racist history. Long enough, for instance, to know that, prior to the end of WWII thirty-five years earlier, blacks sat in the balcony at the St. Jude movie theater. "Nigger heaven," the whites called it.

Long enough to know the story of two Afro-sporting Army veterans who walked into Stumpy McMillan's barbershop in downtown St. Jude on a grey December day less than fifteen years ago to get a haircut. One tall and lean, the second short and stocky, they unzipped faded green Army jackets with American flags sewed to the sleeves and took seats against the wall. All the bullshit and yackin' that goes on in a barbershop stopped. The black guys picked up copies of Sports Illustrated, one with Bill Russell on the cover, the other Mickey Mantle, and struck poses as cool as the outside air. Stumpy stopped cutting a customer's hair, smiled, and said:

"Somethin' I can do for you boys?"

"Just a haircut," said the tall one.

"Well, I'd love to help you, but I don't cut Negroes hair."

"Excuse me?" said the tall one.

"Nothin' personal. Don't know how. You boys be better off going down to Division Street in Plainview, see Chester Washington. He's a friend of mine. Tell him I sent you. He'll do you right."

"Friend of yours, huh?" said the tall one. "Lookee here, Division is at least three miles away. It's freezin' outside, we don't have a car, and there ain't no buses in this town. Why should we walk all the way down to Division for a haircut when there's a barber shop right here?"

"Because," said Stumpy, smile gone, "I don't cut Negroes hair...and I think you know that."

The tall one rolled the Russell SI up like a stick, stood, and took two steps toward Stumpy. But as he did, the short one slipped in between, putting his hands on his friend's chest, talking low and slow. Several of the white guys getting haircuts rose, white cotton barbershop sheets hanging loose, clenched fists hidden.

The tall black man scanned the room, staring at each white man.

"We're gonna be back," he said. "Every Saturday. 'Til you give us a haircut like you're doing for every other man in this room."

The two black men zipped their coats and stalked out the door, the bell hanging from the top jangling.

"Uppity niggers," they heard Stumpy mumble as they stepped outside.

They kept walking, outnumbered and sure to be arrested if they raised a ruckus. But they returned every Saturday, bringing more men, then a reporter from the *St. Jude Harbinger*, until Stumpy, concerned about the unwanted publicity, relented and allowed a barber to cut their hair.

Collins had his own story. As an undergrad in the early seventies, he had worked part-time in the planning commission office at the St. Jude City Hall, a job his college basketball coach had arranged with Sam Henderson's help. One day he was filing manila folders containing property tax bills behind a six-foot-high ivory-colored partition which separated him from the main desk. At the front of the office, a sixtyish white woman named Swoozie perched behind the front counter, seated sideways to Collins, her gray hair tied in a bun, bifocals dangling around her thin neck.

"We were told this is where we could come to see the master plan for zoning," Collins heard a man's voice say. "We were curious about plans for subsidized housing."

Collins stood on his toes and glanced over the partition to see a fair-haired young man and woman.

"Building a new house?" Swoozie said placing the glasses on the tip of her nose.

"Yes, yes we are," said the man, focusing on the clerk, not noticing Collins.

"Where?"

"North of St. Jude, near Heavenly Hills."

"You'll be fine," said Swoozie, either forgetting about Collins or not caring. "There's no government housing planned for that area and the existing is miles away. Besides, the minorities prefer to live on the south side. They'll be nowhere near your property."

"Hold on," the man said, the pitch of his voice changing. "We're not interested in the race of the people. We're concerned about the subsidized housing. A house is a big investment."

"Of course it is," said Swoozie flashing a Poly Grip smile. "And you want to know who your neighbors are going to be, right?"

"Well, yes, I guess," the man said to Swoozie and his wife. "But it's not like you...."

"It's OK," Swoozie said. "I understand. It's like I tell my husband. We love our grandchildren, but we don't want them bringing friends. We gotta take care of our own, but not everyone else's. That's all I meant."

Collins could not resist the urge. He dropped down from his toes and walked out from behind the partition.

"Hey, Swoozie," he said, eyes down, pretending to read a property tax receipt, "this can't be right. A Musaffah Mohammad is listed at 403 Heavenly Hills Lane. We all know there ain't no black folk allowed in—" Collins stopped and looked up in mock surprise at the presence of the young couple. "Oh, excuse me, Swoozie, I didn't realize you had someone with you. I'll get with you when you're done."

Swoozie glared at Collins, who returned a smile. The young couple's jaws dropped as they stared at the black man standing stark against the ivory partition.

"Well, OK, then," said the man offering his arm to his wife. "We can see you're busy. Thanks for your help."

A few years later the local government erected signs at the town limits of Plainview-St. Jude with the word *Racism* crossed out and a line beneath that read, *NOT IN OUR TOWN*.

Problem solved by official proclamation.

But Collins also remembered the day he read in the *St. Jude Harbinger* that Sam Henderson had recognized his hire as the St. Jude basketball coach at a city council meeting, working it in on a discussion of civil service jobs for minorities. Collins's situation had nothing to do with city business, and people wondered what Sam was thinking. But Collins knew. Since his days as an undergrad at city hall, Collins had seen how Sam talked to the garbage men and sewer workers, always using the same respectful and friendly tone he used with businessman, university leadership, and so-called mover and shakers. No surprise Sam was serving his third term as mayor with no serious challengers on the horizon.

By acknowledging the hire of the first black basketball coach at St. Jude, Henderson was doing what he always did: taking a stand where others would not. From before and after the Nigger Heaven days, from the sixties when a black man could not get a haircut in downtown St. Jude, to the seventies when the name and location of a subdivision carried more than one meaning, Sam knew blacks were mistreated. By recognizing Reggie he was acknowledging a new day and signaling he was not a go-along-to-get-along-politician, but a leader. As a coach, a leader himself, Collins respected Sam Henderson for that.

"Coach," Sam said as they sat outside Locke's office that day, "how's the team shaping up this year?"

"Pretty good I think, Sam, but you never know. Depends on who shows up to play. I think Tim Brewster might get a college scholarship if he has a good year and Jenkins looked strong in the summer Y league. But that doesn't mean anything come March and tournament time."

Collins noticed Jack jerk his head up at the mention of the Y-league and Jenkins. Collins had been at the Y-league tournament game last summer when Jack and his team, the Running Rams, beat Brewster, Connolly, Jenkins, and the varsity ballplayers. He recalled when Jack slammed a breakaway dunk that ricocheted off the hardwood and smacked Jenkins in the face.

"The Connolly boy's dad and I played together," Sam said. "If he's as tough as Frank, Sr., he may be a player."

"True enough. Be nice if all the boys played as hard as their dads. I hear you had quite a team."

"We made a run in the tournament, that's for sure. Five hundred team during the season, but made the Sweet Sixteen. And those were the days before they separated the big schools from the small. No Class A, AA. You played whoever came your way. Nobody told us we didn't have a chance. We just wanted to play. See how good we really were."

"That can make all the difference," Collins said, glancing at Jack.

Jack rolled his eyes and then closed them, slumping further into the chair, legs spilling into the middle of the room. Dunham shook his head at Jack as he gave Collins a "what-are-you-gonna-do-about-these-kids?" glance. Sam and Collins talked basketball for a few more minutes, two ex-jocks swapping stories, while the chubby Dunham squirmed, nothing to contribute. When the conversation hit a lull, Sam fired up a Lucky and stared into a gray haze.

Collins, who had as a good a feel for people as he did for the game, stayed quiet. As he looked at Jack, he could not help but think of his older brother Rudy. Same long legs and big, flat hands, same coat-popping shoulders framing a lean, V-shaped torso that flowed into a tapered waist and non-existent hips. A basketball player's body, for sure. And Rudy, like Jack, was a great streetball player.

Yeah, Collins thought, a lot like Rudy. Right down to the same screw-the-world, I-don't-give-a-damn attitude.

An insincere attitude, Collins bet, a manufactured defense in order to be perceived as cool. He had watched Jack play numerous times, and he always played hard. He did give a damn. The kid might not like high school or teachers or adults or whatever it was that teenagers didn't like at any given moment when emotions and hormones run high, but he did give a damn about basketball. You could see it by the way he prowled the court, a big cat marking his territory.

Rudy had given a damn, too, and not just about basketball. He'd just been afraid to admit it. Doing so would have exposed vulnerability, revealed hidden hopes and dreams that already had been pissed on from a young age by an absentee father, a forever-working single mom, food stamps, life in the projects, and dyslexia that had gone undiagnosed until Rudy was twelve. The South Side Chicago public schools slapped the slow-learner label on Rudy and relegated him to the dumb kids classes, the classes where students were passed for showing up and graduated to create space for the next wave.

As a teacher and coach now, Collins understood the pressure and challenges faced by public schools. But it repulsed him to see teachers, administrators, and school boards all patting themselves on the back, telling the taxpaying public how great their schools were because they hit graduation targets. The least educated, neglectful people in the district knew it meant nothing if the kids could not read or complete a job application. The South Side parents knew it was bull and cursed the arrogant so-called educators who sent their own kids off to Catholic schools or private academies on the North Side.

By the time Reggie turned twelve and Rudy sixteen, their mother, Harriet, gave up on their MIA father and married a respectable, church-going man named Roosevelt "Rosey" Coombs. Rosey had graduated from a trade school at twenty-one and built a plumbing business that afforded him a small home in a secure neighborhood for Harriet, the boys, and their younger sisters. Three square meals, a stepfather who took an interest, a mother who did not work sixteen hours a day, it all made a difference for the younger kids.

When Reggie turned twelve he started seventh grade at a North Side academy. Each school day, the gray-haired, black ticket agent punched Reggie's good-for-a-month public transit ticket with a smile and a "How we doin', young man?" Reggie hopped on the northbound train (hair cut short, pressed white shirt, black tie, belt, socks, shoes, and slacks) for the hour ride that transported him to the other side of the city and a world that was a rumor to kids like his older brother. Reggie sang in the choir, read every book he could get his hands on at the school library, and learned to play chess, the trumpet, and basketball. In high school he earned academic and athletic All-American honors and punched the final and most important ticket upon graduation, a full-ride scholarship to a state university. During those four years in which he enjoyed the luxury and freedom to think and find himself, he realized he wanted to teach and coach young people.

Life had offered Rudy less. A lost academic soul by the time Rosey arrived on the scene, Rudy refused Rosey's offer to go with Reggie to the North Side academy, not wanting to leave his friends for a school where he would be ridiculed for "bein' stupid" by a new group of kids. After high school, Rudy worked at a factory that made aluminum can lids, taking the train south to an industrial park. In the evenings after his shift, when the weather permitted, he swapped steel-toed work boots for black Converse high-tops and played streetball until the sun went down or the street lights came on. He played in Y leagues on the weekends and in winter, where he dominated regardless of the competition. College scouts scouring the South Side neighborhoods in search of basketball talent drooled at his physical ability. For kicks, the six foot four Rudy would palm a basketball in either hand and dunk both at the same time, head level with the rim. But despite the scouts' own tricks for making academically challenged kids eligible to play, the scouts could never get Rudy past the board of admissions. "Too dumb," a young Reggie heard one of them whisper.

So Rudy worked, played ball, chased girls, and cheered for his little brother. He never did drugs or drank. Never caused Harriet or Rosey any trouble. Never said anything bad about anyone, not even those who called him dumb. "Shiiiiit," he said to Reggie, laughing, "guess I ain't done nothin' to prove 'em wrong."

If only a few things had been different, Reggie thought, as he sat looking at Jack, looking at Rudy, at all the young boys who got lost along the way. A couple of people taking an interest, even one, it could make a difference. Reggie knew, because it did for him. But it never happened for Rudy. Not in time, anyway.

When Rudy graduated from high school, Vietnam raged. Healthy, with no college deferment, the draft board called three weeks shy of his nineteenth birthday. Six months later he landed in Vietnam. Two months after that, he returned to the States in a black vinyl body bag.

Blown to pieces by a North Vietnamese land mine, the Army said.

After dodging a few hundred on the South Side of Chicago, Reggie Collins thought, eyes focused on a dozing Jack.

The Boys Are Back

Jack stirred and saw Collins staring. Sam noticed nothing, his Lucky smoldering, his thoughts adrift with the smoke. Jack glared at Collins then shut his eyes again.

What a weirdo, he thought. What the hell's he looking at? Who cared if Collins liked him. He wasn't interested in playing varsity, just like he wasn't wowed by Collins like Jenkins and Connolly were.

Collins was a low-scoring, defensive-minded point guard whose game, Jack joked, resembled a corn-fed white guy's more than a Chicago-bred playgrounder. He did not fit the black or jock stereotype academically either. Majored in English literature, quoted poetry in practice, minored in religious studies. Always polite and cool, and dressed liked he stepped out of the pages of *Ebony*.

Jack had heard mixed reviews of Collins around St. Jude. "Tryin' to be white," the black kids at the Y said. "An educated, God-fearin' man," a weathered, white farmer said one day at the counter of B&W's Diner, where Sam and Jack ate breakfast on Saturday's. "You gotta respect that."

Maybe there was truth in both sentiments, but Jack's seventeen-year-old brain did not care if Collins was white, black, brown, or purple. He was still a point guard turned coach-slash-teacher-slash-preacher with a Napoleon complex and an over-developed vocabulary.

Reggie Collins, Mr. All-American-free-ride-jock-suck-up. A gentleman and a scholar? An Uncle Tom or the Jackie Robinson of St. Jude? Who gives a damn? What does this guy know about me or my situation?

Jack had his own problems. For one, expulsion, now glaring at him from a plastic chair in the form of one Dipshit Dunham. But, somehow, he felt fine. Maybe it was the pale lime color of the concrete block walls. Psychologists said lime was a calming color. The public schools concurred. Every principal's office Jack had visited, and there had been many, bore the same lime shade.

Jack chalked up his calmness to fatigue, namely the hangover he carried after partying with the Rams last night at Luke Davis's off-campus apartment. Even though in trouble for flipping off Dunham, Jack knew Sam would be preoccupied with finding Mary Lou and that Grandma Henderson would be watching the girls, same as she always did when "Mom went on a trip." Reaching home after the library incident, Jack had scarfed down a turkey sandwich, gulped two glasses of milk, run up to his room to get cash, and left a note in the kitchen that he was at Luke's. His cash he'd taken to keeping in a hiding place where Mary Lou would not find it. Once Sam had removed her name from the bank accounts and credit cards, she had begun stealing from the kids to finance her escapes.

Grandma Henderson and the girls were in bed when Jack stumbled home at ten, entering through the back door to hear Sam talking on the phone in the den. A half-hour later when Sam opened his bedroom door, Jack pretended to be asleep, and Sam acted as if he believed him.

Despite his father's smoldering quiet that morning outside Principal Locke's office, Jack smiled at the thought of Luke and the rest of the Rams. They'd all grown up in the same neighborhood, where they had played ball together since grade school. Why the group of them—Jack, Luke, his little brother, P.K., Jeff Gudman, Eliseo "Cheyo" Jackson , and Jimmy "Kip" Keino—called themselves the Running Rams, none of them could remember. Something to do with basketball, a beer bottle logo, and the hyped-up imagination and energy a close group of teenage boys generates.

Running Rams was a contradiction in terms. Rams do not run away from a fight. They dig into the dirt, jaws tucked into their chests, then charge and butt heads until the stronger ram prevails and the weaker turns tail. But Running Rams was their summer league team name. "Old Black Betty, Bam a Lam" by Ram Jam became their theme song. Barney Fife, Jethro Bodine, and the spaghetti western star Clint Eastwood were their patron saints. A general "Party on, but let's not screw up our chances to get into a good college" was their motto.

Jack stole a glance at Collins. The combination of the *Jenkins looked strong* comment and Jack's hangover reminded him of the night the Rams had gathered at Luke's apartment a few months earlier to celebrate the victory over the varsity in the summer Y league.

Jimmy and Gudy rustled about in the kitchen, scrounging frozen pizzas to toss in the oven, while Jack, Cheyo, P.K., and Luke sprawled on the cheap, orange and black plaid cushions of Luke's garage sale furniture. Posters plastered the walls: Jimi Hendrix, the Who, Charlie's Angels, Charlie Daniels, and Jack's personal favorite, Jim Morrison. A red, white, and blue neon Pabst Blue Ribbon sign flashed on and off in the kitchen, and the Doors "Roadhouse Blues" thumped from the stereo, as the boys sipped beers and settled in for a bullshit session.

Luke, stout and shirtless, ensconced in the brown, corduroy Lazy Boy recliner he retrieved from the curb on garbage pickup day a year earlier. One man's trash another's treasure, he had carried the chair four blocks and up two flights of stairs to its present location, where it had not budged since. Sporting a farmer's tan from July corn detasseling—table leg arms tan up to the bicep, face burnt, beer keg of a chest and sturdy legs white—he laughed about a bone-crunching pick he'd applied to Jenkins in the first minute of the game. Smothering a long neck bottle of Old Milwaukee with one meaty hand, he brushed his flattop haircut with the other and laughed as he recalled the look on a gasping Jenkins face. Luke wrestled light heavyweight in high school and college, and his hair, build, and never-say-die attitude earned him the nickname *Sarge*. But Jack called him Luke. They had known each other so long, it would have been like calling a brother by a nickname his friends had given him.

His younger brother, Paul Kennedy "P.K" Davis, named after a pope and a president, resembled Luke around the eyes, dark brown and intense, but that was where the resemblance stopped. P.K. stood five feet eleven inches and carried one hundred fifty pounds on a distance runner's frame, his dishwater blond hair flowing when he raced up and down the court. An excellent ball handler and passer who shared his wrestler-brother's fearlessness, P.K. became the Ram's point guard, penetrating the paint with controlled aggression. Able to dish off to a Ram for a basket while opposing teams smacked him to the floor, P.K. always bounced up, ready for more.

As for Luke and basketball, the pick on Jenkins summed up his contribution. Luke played the role of the enforcer/garbage man/sixth man who came into the game to give the guys a break. He rebounded well, took up space on defense, shot the ball when wide open and under the hoop, and stayed out of the way. What Luke loved, what he lived for on the basketball court, was a collision: a charge, a pick, a takedown on a breakaway, not undercutting the guy, but tackling and wrapping him up, sending him to the free throw line to *earn* the two points. But the ultimate thrill for Luke was a good hard screen, the gasp slipping from opposing player's lungs as they bounced off his rock-ribbed chest.

"Perfect pick," he said, thinking of Jenkins.

"Sweet," P.K. said.

"Pinche gringo," the half-white, half-Mexican Cheyo said from his spot on the orange and black plaid couch. "Makes you wonder if Jenkins teammates hate his ass. Nobody called out the screen. Nobody."

Cheyo, "as in 'DAYO'" he told teachers calling roll at the beginning of each school year, slapped his chest with almond colored hands and laughed. Cheyo had the whitest teeth east of Hollywood, and when he smiled those teeth split the coal black whiskers encircling his mouth, giving his half-man, half-boy face the look of a crazed bandoleer from a spaghetti western. Cheyo's dad, Robert, a tall, dark-haired Scot-Irish Catholic, was a soft-spoken Illinois grad who returned to St. Jude to practice law. He met Cheyo's mom, Vita, a second-generation Mexican-American from the barrios of Chicago, in college.

Cheyo resembled Robert, but inherited his mother's boisterous personality and energy. Although only six foot one—"Whaddaya mean *only*?" Cheyo would say, "That's tall for a Mexican!"—he played forward for the Rams. An early bloomer who shaved at thirteen, he weighed one hundred seventy pounds and had finished growing at fifteen. By eighteen he was buying beer without an I.D. Like Luke, he enjoyed the rough and tumble play on the frontline. A scrappy guy on the court, who always guarded one of the opponent's top scorers, Cheyo trash-talked a mix of English and Spanish—"Not today vato, no mas, no mas!"—pestering opponents into turnovers and fouls. Never interested in offense and an average ball handler, Cheyo got points off hustle, put-backs, and free throws.

That day in the Y game, Cheyo guarded Connolly. The varsity player's frustration was palpable as Cheyo held him well below his scoring average. Carrying four fouls into the fourth quarter, Connolly fouled out after Cheyo stole the ball and streaked down the court for a breakaway layup. Pissed, Connolly had clipped him at the knees and flipped Cheyo onto the hardwood, preventing the basket and clearing the benches.

"Temper, temper, amigo," Cheyo said with a smile to the cursing Connolly.

After the refs restored order, Cheyo made two free throws and the teams shot technical fouls, Jack sinking one for the Rams, Jenkins missing for the varsity, giving the Rams a two-point lead.

"Yeah, well," Luke said, referring to the pick on Jenkins, "you paid for it later. Connolly cheap-shotted you but good, man."

"Forget about it, mano. We won. That's all that matters," Cheyo said, then pointed at the muted TV. "Hey, turn it up. *Jeopardy's* on, and they got a category on Elvis."

Luke raised the volume over the stereo.

"What is 'Jail House Rock'?" Luke and Cheyo shouted at the TV.

"What is 'Jail House Rock'?" a black-tied guy with granny glasses responded. "Elvis for 400, Art."

"Song from Elvis first movie," said Art Fleming the host of "Jeopardy."

"What is 'Love Me Tender'?" said Luke.

"What is 'Are You Lonesome Tonight'?" said the TV.

"Wrong, you lame ass, Coke-bottle-glasses nerd!" Luke yelled at the screen.

"Sorry," Art said. "What is 'Love Me Tender'."

"Man," said Luke. "How can you grow up in America, go to college, and not know crap about the King. Unbelievable."

Luke and Cheyo, like the rest of the Rams, were Elvis fans. The Rams dug the Stones, Led Zeppelin, Cheap Trick, Jimi, the Doors, Pink Floyd, AC/DC, all that stuff, but they knew that in his day Elvis was the baddest rock 'n roller of all. The Rams were not build-a-shrine-in-your-house, Elvis-in-black-velvet type fans, but admirers of the Elvis of the 1950s to the 1968 comeback TV special, before fried peanut butter and banana sandwiches and a handful of pills became his diet, and he bloated up like a Thanksgiving Day parade float. Bouncing around the stage, Kung Fu fighting, a parody of himself, the King had died long before they found him crumpled on the bathroom floor, pants around his ankles, bottles of uppers and downers on the shelf.

Being surrounded by sycophants was what killed Elvis, the Rams agreed. Past a certain point, nobody told him *no*, and everybody needs somebody not afraid to say no. The Rams had their folks and each other. They drank, and when they drank too much it bit them in the ass, but no pills, no hard drugs. Listening to Jimmy Morrison howl and smoking the occasional Marlboro while swigging an Old Milwaukee long neck was about as crazy as it got. No harm, no foul.

"Can you believe that geek?" Luke said. "'Are You Lonesome Tonight'? You got to be kidding me. You can't understand this country if you don't know your Elvis. Don't have to like him, mind you… although if you don't that makes you suspect in my book. But if you don't know Elvis, you don't know America. I don't give a damn how many freakin' PhDs you get. It's impossible. Your education is incomplete. Remember…"

"*Before anyone did anything, Elvis did everything!*" Cheyo, Luke, Jack, and P.K. shouted in unison, slapping hands and giggling.

"Ah, man," Jimmy Keino said as he walked in from the kitchen with Gudy, a fresh brew in his hand. "Drinkin' beer and talkin' trivia about Elvis. Won't be too long before Luke starts wavin' the Confederate flag."

"Now, you know, Jimmy," Luke said. "The Civil War wasn't about slavery. It was about individual state rights. And what the hell do you care, anyway? You weren't even born here."

"I knew it, I knew it," Jimmy said laughing as he sat down on a chair next to Luke. "Elvis always gets you goin'."

Jimmy "Kip" Keino was an honest-to-God-African-American-via-Kenya who was so black he looked blue, whose real name was not Jimmy, and whose Kenyan name was not Kip. Kip was the name of a miler who'd won an Olympic gold medal in 1968, but even his folks called him Jimmy or Kip.

At six foot three, Jimmy played forward, joining Cheyo and Jeff Gudman on the front line. Like Jack he could create his own shot, using a fast first step to get to the hole and jumping-jack leaping ability to finish. Unlike Jack he lacked a good jump shot and so, even though the shorter of the two, Jimmy played forward.

"Jimmy, you're always stirrin' shit up, lookin' to argue," Luke said and laughed, slapping Jimmy on the knee. "Doesn't matter whether you're speaking English or that Kenyan tribal rap with your parents when you don't want us white folk knowin' what's up."

"Guilty as charged," Jimmy said, who scored a thirty-two on his ACT and hoped to use that and a high grade-point-average to gain acceptance into the prelaw curriculum at Georgetown. "Comes from being the product of two parents with PhD's," Jimmy continued, "who don't let me talk enough around the house because they're busy impressing each other with their big brains. And reminding me they are descended from royalty and to act accordingly."

"Yeah," said Luke. "We know all about your royal lineage. All you guys from Africa are descended from royalty. Not a peasant in the bunch. Your parents remind me of these reincarnation believers. None of those bastards say, 'I was a shitkicking shepherd.' No, every last one of 'em was a Roman Emperor or a member of a royal court. Not a shitkicker or a whore in the bunch. Maybe that's Africa's problem, got so much royalty ain't nobody left to work."

"Excuse me?" said Jimmy. "You gonna start with your lazy-nigger-societal-theory-from-the-perspective-of-an-Elvis-lover rap?"

"Hey man, I didn't say that," Luke said, face red. "Why is it you and Richard Pryor can rip honkies, but we make one joke and y'all get on your high horse and start screamin' racism?"

"We're all prejudiced," Jimmy said. "It's just a question of degree and whether we choose to admit it, try to rise above it."

"Ah, Jesus H. Christ, Jimmy," Luke said. "Now you gonna get all philosophical on us. I was just havin' fun with you. Sometimes, man, I feel like…"

"Like what? Kickin' my uppity ass?" Jimmy said rising.

"Well, now that you mention it," Luke responded leaning forward.

"Hey, fellas," Gudman said with a laugh as he plopped onto the couch and pulled Jimmy down with him. "What is this, an after-school special on race in

America? We kicked some major varsity ass, and you guys are startin' in on that crap? Give it a rest, man. Give it a rest."

Jimmy waved his hand and sank into his chair. Luke, jaw grinding, muted the TV. Jack, P.K, and Cheyo stopped talking and took swigs from their beers.

Gudman was the one guy beside their dads or Jack who could shut up Jimmy and Luke. All the boys looked up to Gudy, a walking, talking blond-haired, blue-eyed billboard for the All-American boy. Straight-A student, star pitcher on the baseball team, class president, dated all the best looking girls, never made fun of kids but liked to drink beer and hang with the guys as much as anybody. The most popular kid in school, hands down. Everyone loved Gudy, the Golden Boy they called him, and not behind his back with a smirk and a wink but with admiration. As Jack's little sister Becky once said with a sigh and a roll of her eyes, "He's so cool."

But on the court, the easy going Gudy became a fierce competitor. When Connolly took Cheyo down, Gudy, taking a breather on the bench, leapt into the middle of the fray, and came face to face with Timmy Brewster, the black, six foot eight, two-hundred-twenty-pound starting center for the varsity, who'd knocked Jack away from Connolly with one swipe. Even at six foot four, one ninety, Gudy looked small next to Brewster. But Gudy did not give an inch and shoved Brewster like he was firing a cross-court chest pass. The big man tumbled to the floor, the ref and Y staff stepping in before Brewster retaliated.

When the game resumed Gudy checked in for Luke and called for the ball in the post. Back to the basket and Brewster, who banged him with a forearm to the spine, Gudy took the inbound pass with his right hand and pivoted the same direction, giving a quick head and shoulder fake. Brewster, amped from the shoving, took the bait and leapt. Gudy reversed direction, ducked around the big man's body, took two hard dribbles and soared to the hoop, jamming the ball with his right hand as Brewster fell away to the left.

The crowd roared and the Rams exchanged high-fives as they raced back to play defense, never to surrender the lead.

But, now, a few hours removed from the win, they sat in silence.

"Gudy's right," P.K. said, ever the point guard, directing traffic, kicking butt when needed, praising when deserved. P.K. raised his beer. "A toast to the Rams."

"To the Rams," Jack and Cheyo said, bumping bottles with P.K.

"What is this half-ass shit?" P.K. said and stood up, lifting his Old Mil high. "Running Rams! Running Rams! Running RAMS! RUNNING RAMS!"

All the boys stood and chanted, Jimmy and Luke cracking grins as they jumped up and down, anger fading as fast as it emerged.

Like a family around the kitchen table telling stories from back in the day, the boys lingered at Luke's and talked about the game:

There'd been the varsity boys bickering after Cheyo's breakaway and Gudy's dunk, as they sensed the game slipping away, their first string about to get beat by a beer-drinking, college-prep, mish-mash of neighborhood kids. The crowd was one of the biggest for the tournament, with high school and younger kids ringing the court, a few parents, coaches, and college scouts in the stands, as well as the team from Blooming Grove who the Rams would meet the next day in the finals, led by All-State player Hassan "Go-Go" Jones, a jet-black, six foot six superman, who seemed to never tire or slow down during a game, his engine running on ten cylinders to everybody else's eight. There'd been the deer-in-the-headlights look on Jenkins's face when Jack slammed the ball. Jack going airborne eight feet from the hoop, the crowd rising with him, even Go-Go Jones, gazing as Jack's right arm extended high, the brown leather ball suction-cupped to his hand as Jack froze in midair for a split second, bent knees even with Jenkins eyes, before descending and driving the ball through the rim so hard it smacked the hardwood and ricocheted off Jenkins's left cheek. The gym exploded, kids ringing the court hooting and hollering, Jones and his all-black team laughing, exchanging high-fives, coaches and scouts, hands on hips or arms folded across chests, nodding, grinning, exchanging knowing glances. Then, after the game, the junior college scout who approached Jack and asked for his phone number.

"That's gotta feel good," Gudy said, tipping his Old Mil Jack's way.

"Ah, to hell with that. I ain't goin' to a JC to play ball."

"Bull, Jack," Cheyo said. "I saw you give him your phone number."

"No, you didn't" Jack said, laughing. "You saw me give him the number to the police station. I got it memorized from the list of emergency numbers posted by our kitchen phone. First number we call when Mom's on the run. Guy's gonna be talkin' to the police dispatcher."

The boys laughed and exchanged high fives.

Empty brown Old Milwaukee bottles lined and then fell from the plywood-and-concrete-block "coffee table," clinking on the floor when the boys kicked them out of the way as they rose for another round from the fridge or to take a leak, the curling smoke of Marlboros overhead as Jimmy Morrison and the Doors roared. Bullshit thickened the air, choking the boys with laughter, cheeks stinging from constant smiling, not wanting to go, but curfew creeping close, beer yawns spreading, finally heading for home, leaving Luke stretched out on his recliner, clicking the remote control.

Jack and P.K. were the last to leave. As they stumbled toward the door they listened to Luke mumbling at a flickering image of a singing Andy Gibb, the latest in a long line of wavy-haired, teen heartthrobs.

"Pathetic wannabe," Luke grumbled, "not even good enough to be an honest-to-God Bee Gee, whatever the hell that is. There's one King, goddammit, and his name is Elvis. That's the TRUE gospel according to Luke…. 'Amen,' said the choir."

As Andy Gibb disco danced across the shimmering screen, Luke went dark, sound asleep. Jack and P.K. giggled as they shut the door behind them.

The next day, hungover and outmanned, the Rams were blown out by Hassan Jones and his team as the St. Jude varsity players sprawled around the court, cheering for Blooming Grove and jeering the Rams.

Wayward Son

"Jack," Sam said, shaking his arm, jerking Jack's thoughts to the present.

Dunham glared at Jack like gum stuck to his shoe.

Principal Locke stood next to the open door and motioned everyone to enter. Locke, bald as Dunham, did not bother with a toupee. A strip of close-cropped black hair ran around the back of his head from temple to temple then spilled down the sides of a thin face and merged into a matching beard. Jack followed Sam into the office and there, sitting in a straight back chair, knees together, sporting a navy blue suit, blonde hair in a ponytail, sat the sexy librarian.

"Ken," Locke said to Dunham, "I believe you know Miss Linda Stevens."

"Ms. Stevens, please," she said with a smile as she rose, towering over the pear-shaped Dunham in her platform shoes.

"Mizzzz Stevens, I'm glad you're here," said Dunham, one eye twitching.

"Ms. Stevens," continued Locke, motioning Dunham to the side, "this is Sam Henderson, Jack's dad, and Reggie Collins, our dean of boys, and, of course, the subject of our meeting, Jack Henderson."

Sam and Collins shook Ms. Stevens's hand. Jack did, too. Her fingers gave his a gentle squeeze, lingering for a moment. Jack's palms began to sweat as the calm from the hallway vanished.

"Ms. Stevens is pursuing a Masters degree at the university," said Locke after everyone sat, "and was guest speaker at the library yesterday when the incident between Mr. Dunham and Jack occurred." Locke paused and turned to Dunham.

"Ken, to get right to the point, Ms. Stevens saw things differently than you related them to me."

"Different how?" said Dunham. "The kid went off after I shook him awake. Blew like a rocket. Knocked me down, made an obscene gesture, and skipped school for the rest of the day. What else is there?"

"Well, Ken—" said Locke.

"The *else* is," Ms. Stevens said, turning towards Dunham. "I saw you sneak up behind this boy, and choke him. If somebody did that to me, I think I might jump up and push them away."

"Look, Ms. Stevens," said Dunham, "with all due respect, you haven't been teaching for thirty years. You haven't had to deal with kids like this. And you don't know this one. Falling asleep in class is typical. I finally had enough. I wanted to get his attention."

"Well, you got it," said Ms. Stevens. "And you're correct, I'm not a teacher. But I know teachers aren't supposed to choke students. And, in my opinion, this boy showed the type of restraint that you, the teacher, did not. I'm amazed he didn't hit you. You choke him anywhere else, and a lot of people would say he'd be within his rights to hit you as an act of self-defense."

"Oh, please," said Dunham, the color racing from neck to brow. "Frank, I know this young lady means well, but c'mon, you know Henderson. You know what I'm dealing with here. If anyone ever needed a kick in the ass, it's him."

"Wait a minute," Sam said, turning towards Dunham. "I'm not going to sit here and say there aren't times Jack could use a swift kick. I know my son. He can be headstrong and a smart alec. But it isn't your job to kick him in the butt. You have a problem with Jack, you let me know, and I'll take care of it. And anybody who knows me and knows what I'm all about, knows that's a fact. You know it, Ken... I mean, what the hell? What were you thinking?"

"So, Ken," said Locke nodding, "do you want to amend your original report of this incident? Did you, in fact, choke Jack?"

"Ah, for chrissakes. How are we supposed to discipline kids like this?"

"I'll take that as a *yes*," said Locke standing. "Ms. Stevens, I want to thank you for taking it upon yourself to come in and clarify this situation. Ken, you and I will need to visit later this afternoon. Now, if you will both excuse us, Reggie and I need to discuss this further with Sam and Jack."

"That's it?" said Dunham. "This kid knocks me down, skips school, and I'm the one in trouble?"

"That's it for now, Ken," said Locke, dismissing Dunham and Ms. Stevens with a wave toward the door. "We'll talk this afternoon. Thanks again, Ms. Stevens."

Jack grinned and gawked at Ms. Stevens' ass as she left. No one noticed, except for Reggie Collins, his brown eyes catching Jack's and staring him down.

He Ain't Heavy

"Jack," P.K. said dropping a barbecued soy burger onto his Calvin Klein designer jeans. "What the hell. Whatta you doin' here? I thought you got expelled this morning?"

"No such luck," Jack said, dragging a chair from a nearby table and squeezing in between Gudy and Cheyo. "Pass the salt, will you Jimmy?"

"Soon as you tell us how you managed not to get tossed," said Jimmy rolling the white shaker in his palms. "What gives?"

"I go out for the basketball team, I stay in school. Now give me the salt so I can choke down this crap before I dissect a frog in Bio and hork it all up."

The boys looked as stunned as a pig on nut-cutting day.

"Jimmy, salt."

Jimmy slid the salt.

"That's your punishment?" Cheyo said.

"Yup."

"But you knocked Dunham on his ass," said Gudy, "flipped him off, and skipped school. And you don't even get a suspension?"

"In-school suspension, all zeroes for this week," Jack said chewing on the tough barbeque and sucking down warm milk. "Plus, the way Collins sees it, me bein' the bad ass streetballer I claim to be, a little on-court discipline is the perfect antidote for my anti-social behavior. Work release, boot camp punishment, high school style. Dad loves it. Thinks it'll do me good. Besides, there were Extenuating Circumstances yesterday."

"Such as?" said P.K.

"Such as, the school district doesn't want to risk getting its ass sued, but they've got to punish me somehow."

"Come again," said P.K.

"Remember that hot librarian I told you about? She showed up at the meeting with Locke and Collins and said Dunham choked me, and he was lucky I didn't hit 'em. Said I showed more restraint than the teacher, and I was within my rights to defend myself by putting lardass on his ass."

"She said that?" said Cheyo.

"Not word for word, Cheyo. I'm paraphrasing for chrissakes, but that's the gist of it. So, Locke said we have Extenuating Circumstances, tells Dunham he's up shit creek for choking a student. Next Collins tells me my ass is his, and here we are. I'm going to b-ball tryouts on Monday."

"Cool," said Gudy. "You screw up, you get cut, and you're home free. You can salvage your grades by doin' well on the finals. It won't affect your getting into the schools we want to go to anyway. You're golden."

"That's what I was thinking. But Collins tacked on conditions. If he thinks I'm loafing or not trying, expulsion could be back on the table. If I make the team…"

Everyone laughed.

"Anyway, if I make the team, I have to attend every practice, every game, even if I never play. Support my teammates, show a good attitude, you know, all that rah-rah stuff. If I don't do that to Collins's satisfaction, he can recommend expulsion. And you know as well as I do that whatever he and Locke recommend to the school board, the board will do. They always support the administration. And, once I'm expelled, Collins said, he will notify any colleges I've been accepted to of my gettin' the boot."

"What'd Sam say?" asked Jimmy. "Does he think it's fair?"

"You guys know Sam. Doesn't matter whether we think it's fair or not. You break the rules, you pay the price. I didn't have to react to Dunham the way I did. Had a lot of options besides jumpin' up and flippin' everybody off, blah, blah, blah."

"He's got a point, I guess," said Gudy.

"Yup, I screwed up. Gave Dunham exactly what he wanted. An excuse to torture my ass. Except Collins is the torturer."

"Looks like you're gonna have to play ball, Jack," said Gudy.

"Well," said Cheyo, "we'll be there for you. Might even listen to parts of the games on the radio when I'm driving to the convenience store to get more beer."

"Knew I could count on you, Cheyo."

"Hey, Jack," said Jimmy, "it won't be that bad. I mean, hell, you're a great ballplayer. Why not let people know?"

Jack shrugged and threw pieces of soy burger on the yellow plastic plate. His stomach churned from the meeting and the cafeteria's fake burgers, nasty even for a starving guy.

"How 'bout morning and afternoon practices, Jimmy," said P.K. "Runnin' bleachers, defensive drills, washboards, all that crap. Don't let all that talk of Collins recitin' poetry and spouting John Wooden homilies fool you. When it comes down to it the guy's a hard-ass. A basketball lifer. I hear his practices are brutal. Who needs that? 'Sides if Jack wants to play organized ball he can always go to JC next year. Plenty of 'em would take him. They know who he is. What's the point of high school ball at this point, for Jack?"

"Still, it can't hurt," said Jimmy.

"Then why don't you join him, Jimmy" said P.K. "You could make the team."

"Well…"

"Well, what?" Jack said to give Jimmy grief. "If it's a good thing for me, ought to be a good thing for you. Hell, for all y'all. You could all make varsity. Make it a lot better team, that's for sure."

"Hold on, hold on," said Gudy. "You serious? You askin' us to join you?"

"Relax, Gudy, I'm just givin' Jimmy grief. I know you guys don't want to get dragged into this. Party on. Just call me from time to time and let me know what's happening. I'll be tied up for the next four months."

"Why not?" said Jimmy, leaning forward and looking each Ram in the eye.

"Why not, what?" said Cheyo.

"Man, you're a dense mother sometimes," said Jimmy, shaking his head. "Why play ball? What else we got to do? We play four, five times a week anyway. Let's keep Jack company. Why not take the Runnin' Rams off the street and onto the sports page? Think about it. We could ruin the season for all these letter-jacket-wearin', gym rat, senior-year-get-their-moment-in-the-sun jerks like Jenkins and Connolly. Sit them on the bench and let the Rams run wild. It'd be perfect."

"I can dig it," said Gudy.

They turned and looked at Cheyo and P.K.

"Oh, man, c'mon," said P.K. "No way, Jose. Senior year. Party hearty. Score chicks, chill on the books, hang at my brother's. Now y'all want to get up at 5:30 to play ball? Then turn around and do it again at 3:30 instead of heading home? All 'cause Jack got his ass in bind? I mean, Jack, I love you, but senior year, man?"

"P.K., your brother wrestled and threw back plenty his senior year," said Gudy. "I play baseball every spring. Basketball'll be over by March. Right after we win the state championship. We'll find time to party."

"Ah, man," said Cheyo. "Jack, you serious about this?"

"I'm not asking, amigo. Your compadres are."

Cheyo and P.K. looked at each other.

"It's up to you, bubba," said Cheyo.

"Christ Almighty," said P.K. crossing himself like the altar boy he was. "OK, I'm in, but, Jimmy, you're the first one I puke on at practice."

Big Balls

Jack was 99% certain he would make the team, but having the Rams along would make it easier to go up against Jenkins, Connolly, and the rest. And who knows, Jimmy and Gudy might be right, they might be a great basketball team come March when the state tournament rolled around. Not all the jocks were assholes or bad ballplayers.

As long as none of the Rams got arrested, Jack thought.

Thanks to a misdemeanor "illegal transportation of alcohol" beef involving Gudy and Cheyo, the Rams had caught the attention of the local police. Gudy and Cheyo paid a fifty-dollar fine and agreed to perform community service, picking up trash at local parks for four Saturdays. The court treated the boys as juveniles and placed no permanent mark on their record. Their parents kept the boys grounded for another month, but in the eyes of the law, the whole thing never happened. Except the incident put the Rams on the cops' radar.

And now they were on the jocks'.

Word spread after lunch that the Rams were going out for varsity. Jenkins, Connolly, Brewster and four or five players, surrounded Jack's locker after school.

"So," said Jenkins, the son of a farmer, slotted as starting point guard, "I hear Daddy bailed you out of an expulsion and got you playin' real ball. Old ballplayer like Sam must be happier than a pig in shit."

"I thought it was 'a pig in slop'" Jack said, "but, hey, whatever. But you know, Jenkins, next time you're gonna confront me, think about what you're gonna say the night before. Hell, take a week. Take the stress off your brain. Run it past Connolly first. Word is he does your homework, anyway."

"Screw you, Henderson."

"See what I'm sayin'?" Jack said turning to Connolly and Brewster. "He's your buddy, work with him for chrissakes. He's an embarrassment to your kind."

"Looks like you're our kind, now," said Connolly who was Jack's height, but thicker through the chest, shoulders, and legs, bright blue eyes betraying a good nature not to be concealed even at tough-guy-moments like this. "If you make the team."

Jack smiled.

"Look here, Jack," said Brewster's dumpster-deep voice as he shoved Jenkins and Connolly aside. Separated from the group, the Chief, as the local sportswriters dubbed him, stood in front of Jack like a giant mahogany statue, face all angles and shadows. He raised a blue-veined hand.

Silence reigned.

"It makes no difference to me who goes out. You and the Rams want to bring it, then bring it. But let's be clear. You make the team, you best play hard. I gotta lot ridin' on this year. I don't get a scholarship, I don't go to college. So I ain't interested in a bunch of beer-drinkin', don't-give-a-shit-about-nothin'-cause-my-Daddy-can-always-bail-me-out preps gettin' on this team and then bailin' when times get tough 'cause they did it for the helluva it. You play, you play hard. You hear?"

Jack knew Brewster respected his game and, as a center, did not feel threatened by Jack like Jenkins and Connolly. Jack figured Brewster was happy the Rams were coming on board. But he knew Brewster could not turn on the crowd he hung with by jumping up and down like a cheerleader. He had to be loyal. Jack understood all that. But he played second fiddle to no one, nor would he be intimidated.

"Look, big man." Jack jabbed a finger into Brewster's thick chest and stared up into his eyes, trying to look as fierce as a not-quite-filled-out seventeen-year-old-peach-fuzz-white-kid can when facing down a chiseled black kid with four inches, forty pounds, and a full beard on him. "Don't you worry 'bout me and the Rams. We're comin' to play. You just make sure these jagoff buddies of yours don't do anything that's gonna make problems when they come to the unhappy realization that they ain't gonna be getting as much playin' time this year. If they make the team at all."

Brewster's eyes gleamed, ready to laugh or stuff Jack into the locker.

"Alright, alright," a voice said behind Brewster as the small knot of jocks broke up. Stepping out from behind the massive Brewster stood Coach Collins.

"Since when do you boys hang around school after the bell rings? Jenkins, Connolly, Brewster, the rest of you, go home. Go on, now. Tryouts are 5:30 a.m., Monday morning. Save your energy. You're going to need it."

The group broke with a grumble. Brewster raised a fist like a Black Panther power salute from the sixties, before he turned and walked away. For a second Jack thought about flashing one in return, but caught himself. He hated that bogus crap. White guys acting black. Grain fed boys who have been no closer to a ghetto than Rockefeller, talking jive, soul shaking, curling and perming straight hair into half-assed Afros and playing the fool. So Jack nodded and thanked God for giving Brewster a calm disposition and the ability to see through face-saving bull.

"You too, Henderson," said Collins. "By the way, I heard about your buddies. You make sure your Rams understand the deal. I'm not putting up with any stuff from you or your boys. If any of them cause problems, you'll be going down with them. Understood?"

Jack nodded to Collins, like he had to the Chief.

"You best get your rest too, Henderson. You haven't been worked the way I'm going to work you."

Hands on hips, Collins stared at Jack for a moment, then turned away.

Jack thought about what Collins must have been as a point guard coach-on-the-floor-type, trying to control everything.

"Goddam points are all the same," he mumbled as he snatched his backpack and slammed the locker.

Little Sister

Getting rest would not be an issue. Jack was grounded for the next two weeks.

Seventeen and grounded. What bullshit, he thought as he walked home.

But then again, Jack knew Sam had no choice. Even though Sam cut him slack because of Mary Lou, he knew not to push the old man too far. It was his parent's house, their rules. And despite Jack's boozing and truancy, he respected that. Besides, even though he was a war hero, an elected official, a devoted family man, and an all-around respected guy who played by the rules and raised his kids to do the same, Sam was not a total hard-ass.

When Sam was a teenager, he fought in WWII. Honest to God combat, watching buddies like Ollie Ollafson, a big, gentle Swede from Wisconsin, get wounded. When he was nine years old, Jack had met Ollie, and he remembered it vividly, Ollie letting him rap his fist on the metal plate that replaced the piece of his skull shattered by shrapnel.

Kentuckian Kenny Carlson had not been as lucky.

Sometimes, after a couple of scotches, Sam talked about the day Kenny died. Sam and Kenny had been walking side-by-side into a small village in Germany when—BAM!—a single shot from a Kraut sniper in a church steeple ripped across Carlson's face, his nose bouncing off Sam's chest, his blood splatter stinging his eyes.

"Sometimes," Sam said, "the Nazi's left a sniper behind to slow us down, inflict some pain. A suicide mission really, 'cause eventually we'd kill 'em. It was senseless. But sense has nothin' to do with combat."

When Carlson got hit, Ollie, Sam and the rest of the platoon took cover. They hustled toward the church, slapped a shell into the bazooka that Ollie had been carrying since the guy who'd been trained on it had been killed two days earlier. They half-ass sited the barrel on the steeple and blew both it and the sniper to pieces, brass church bells banging and clanging, toppling to the cobblestone street below. Once they cleared the town, they dug Carlson's grave, burying the bayonet of his M-1 into the dirt, helmet perched on the butt. Before laying him to rest, Sam cut a lock of Carlson's blond hair, removed letters and photos from his family and girl, and slipped off his dog tags. He mailed it all to Carlson's mother. Ollie said a few words, and the platoon—now down to ten from the original forty—trudged on through town.

They banged on the door of a wealthy Burghmeister and took food and wine without raising a gun barrel, the shaking, old German all but throwing it at them in his haste to get them on their way. As they passed the silenced sniper and church bells a few of the GI's spat on the soldier, already stripped to the waist by the town people, boots gone, upper body pale and luminous against the dark cobblestones, gray eyes adrift on a dewy face.

"He couldn't've been more than fifteen," Sam said. "But what the hell, I was eighteen. It didn't matter. They killed us or we killed them. Nobody checked ID's."

So, although Jack knew Sam did not like him drinking beer, smoking Marlboros, skipping school to play pool, and doing dumbass things, a father's disapproval was nothing compared to combat. Besides, Jack had heard stories about his Dad. St. Jude was a small town. Sam had done his share of hell-raising both before and after the war and still managed to become a solid citizen.

"Hey, Jack. Wait up."

Jack stopped walking, turned and smiled.

Katy O'Brien, red hair cut in a Dorothy Hamill wedge, grinned back.

"So," Katy said, green eyes dancing, "I hear Jack Henderson, the great street baller is playing *Organized Basketball*. The world must be coming to an end."

"Wow, news travels fast. I suppose you and your fellow point guard Collins are already making plans on how to corral me? Goddam points want to run the world."

"I take issue with that remark, Mr. Henderson. I'm a female point guard and as such, already run the world."

"My apologies, Miss O'Brien," Jack said with a mock bow.

"Ms. if you don't mind. I am woman, hear me roar."

Jack laughed out loud.

"C'mon, let's go," he said.

They ran across a four lane street in silence and zigzagged across parking lots and lawns before reaching the sidewalk leading to their subdivision, Katy's house just two doors down from the Henderson's. Jack and Katy had been friends since they were toddlers. *Two peas in a pod*, Sam said. They saw each other almost every day of their lives until junior high when school, extracurricular activities and part-time jobs sent them different directions. Yet they retained a strong bond. The traffic noise dimmed.

"So you ready for Monday?" Katy said.

"Nope. Expect it'll *feel* like the end of the world running wind sprints at 5:30 a.m. Jeezus."

"Well, I'll be at the other end of the school doin' the same thing. Coach Schmidt follows Collins's lead."

"Bookend masochists. What're the odds?"

"Other teams are doin' the same, Jack. Gotta compete."

"If that's your thing."

Katy reached up and slugged Jack in the arm.

At five foot eight and a toned one hundred forty five pounds, she was tall and strong, but looked petite next to Jack.

"Damn, Katy. I think you're gonna be a coach."

"There's worse things."

"I'll check with you at the end of the season."

A crisp fall breeze ruffled their hair and Katy stuck her hands into the pockets of her bell bottom blue jeans.

"So what do the jocks have to say? I saw them at your locker."

"Nothin' welcoming."

"Can't blame 'em."

"No, I suppose not," Jack said, ducking his head as they turned the corner onto their block. "What about the Lady Hilltoppers? How they looking?"

Katy furrowed her brow.

"Pretty good, I think. Brewster's little sister, Anna Lee, is going to be tough. A few of the other girls are coming along. And, of course, we have a great point guard. We won't be as good as you guys could be, though."

"*Could*, being the operative word."

"Oh, I almost forgot. We've also got new uniforms thanks to your mom. Man, she was something else at the school board meeting."

Jack had not attended, but knew when Becky made the junior high girls team the previous year Mary Lou discovered the administration had not allocated money for uniforms. The teams wore old, oversized boys' jerseys and shorts.

"Yeah, your mom stood there and said: 'You gentleman have heard of Title IX?' They ducked their heads or looked away. 'I'll take that as confirmation. I'm willing to give you the benefit of the doubt this year in regard to not ordering new uniforms for the girls. But as we, their parents and other supporters, indicated to the superintendant, you either order uniforms next year for all the female athletic teams or be prepared to go to court. Since you're familiar with Title IX, I'm sure you realize such an outcome will prove embarrassing to the district. Certainly none of us wish to see that occur. Thank you for letting me speak.'"

"So this year," Katy continued, "brand new uniforms. Pretty cool."

"Yeah, well, I guess when she's with it, she can be a force," Jack said.

He glanced at Katy, regretting the snap in his voice.

"Jack," Katy said, nodding toward his driveway.

The silver Caprice was parked in the gravel next to Grandma Henderson's blue Buick.

"Dad and Chief Royal found her quick," Jack said, as they stopped in front of Katy's house.

"Well, that's a good thing, right? Get her home."

"She's not home, Katy," Jack said, staring at the Caprice.

Katy's eyes went flat.

"Maybe I'll see you Monday," Katy said, touching his sleeve.

"Yeah, sure."

Jack watched Katy disappear into her house.

"Hey, girls," he hollered to Becky and Maggie as they played on the driveway. Becky shot baskets while Basker, the mixed-breed mutt, part Golden Retriever, rest unknown, from Sam's "other family" according to Mary Lou, chased the ball. Maggie circled the outer edge of the concrete on a tangerine-colored bike with white-walled wheels, a gift from Mary Lou and Sam for her sixth birthday. She pedaled like a Tour de France competitor climbing the Alps, face wrinkled with concentration.

"Mom's back," Becky said, blonde hair flopping as she shot a lay-up. At thirteen, Becky's game was taking shape. "Back at the hospital, I mean."

"Jackie," Maggie hollered, ringing the bell on the bike and racing to him so fast he jumped away to keep his toes from getting smashed.

Jack lifted Maggie from the white plastic seat and tossed her in the air until she laughed so hard he thought she might gag. Maggie's hazel eyes widened each time he sent her airborne and closed as she fell into his arms, a gleaming gap-toothed smile splitting her lips, as certain Jack would catch her as she was that Santa Claus would be coming at Christmas.

"Daddy said Mommy's takin' a rest at the hospital again," Maggie said when Jack caught her the last time. He brushed red hair away from her freckled face. "She needs her rest after her trips, you know."

"Yes she does, Mags. She wasn't gone long this time, though, so maybe she won't need as much rest."

"I don't know about that," said Becky.

Jack frowned and nodded toward Maggie.

"I mean... I don't know," she said. "You better talk to Dad, Jack."

Jack set Maggie back on the bike. Despite the morning frosts, the late afternoon sun radiated Indian summer warmth. Maggie pedaled away, resuming her orbits as Becky practiced first a left, then a right-handed layup. Jack stood at the back door and watched her, determined in a way he would never be. The game did not come as easily to her as it did to him. Nothing did, Becky said when pissed.

Maggie tooted her horn and Jack grinned and waved as she passed. He lingered by the screen door, thinking he might go help Becky with her shot, chase Maggie around the driveway, but Sam and Grandma Henderson's voices drifted from inside. He'd better check in. He waved at Maggie one more time, petted Basker, sitting by the door wagging his tail, and stepped into the house.

Boys Don't Cry

"Sam," Grandma Henderson said, "maybe it's time to consider commit—"

"Jack," Sam said from the kitchen table, a three-quarter-full bottle of scotch to his right, a highball glass about to touch his lips, and the smoke from an ever-present Lucky Strike curling up from the clay ashtray that Jack made in grade school.

"Oh, hi, killer-diller," Grandma Henderson said.

Oretta "Etta" Henderson was the only grandmother Jack had known. Mary Lou's mother and father both died before Jack was born. He had nobody to compare her to, but talking to his friends about their grandparents, many of whom they never saw because they lived in Florida, Jack knew she was cool. Etta took a special shine to Jack because he resembled John Henderson, her first husband, who died young. Later in life, after Sam and his two younger brothers were grown, she had married a hearty, leather-skinned farmer named Roger Bauer.

Etta liked and respected Roger, but when she spoke of John Henderson her hazel eyes sparkled.

She took Roger's name when they married because that is what women of her generation did, but the kids called her Grandma Henderson, and nobody, Roger included, corrected them.

"You're just in time," she said to Jack. "Supper will be ready in a half hour. Fried chicken, mash potatoes, and corn, your favorite. I hear you're going to play basketball? I think that's wonderful. Your dad is so excited."

Jack looked at Sam, who took a deep drag, squinted through wire rimmed bifocal glasses, then blew a gray stream of smoke into the middle of the room and took a sip of scotch. Sam nodded like Jack had to Becky a moment before.

"Yeah, Grandma," Jack said with a hug. "I'm gonna play ball. Follow in the family tradition."

"I think that's super duper. We'll all be at your games cheering you on. I loved going to your dad's and his brother's games. High school basketball makes the winters bearable."

Jack wondered if she included Mary Lou when she said "all."

OK, that may not be fair, he thought, but his Grandma and Sam contemplating Mary Lou's commitment chafed him. He loved his grandmother, but at times she lived in a parallel universe. She was cooking supper because Mary Lou lay in a psychiatric ward pumped full of mind-altering drugs. Jack was joining the basketball team to keep from being expelled for knocking down a teacher and flipping off his class. And Sam may have been excited about Jack playing ball, but not for the reason it came to pass.

Yet Grandma Henderson stood there ramrod straight, blue-white hair clipped short, with a resolute chin signaling her rigid standards—except when it came to her grandchildren—acting like all of it happened for the best of reasons. The top political spin-doctors could take lessons from Grandma Henderson when it came to shining a positive light on a negative situation.

Jack figured it came from surviving the Depression, being a farmer's daughter, raising three sons as a single parent, learning to *make do* as she said. She did not lecture the kids about how tough things were when she grew up, but when they complained about this or that she told stories of how she treasured receiving a single doll for Christmas, or how her mother, Great Grandma McLanahan, made her four brothers' and three sisters' clothes by hand and turned a dinner of potato pancakes into a four-star meal. She talked of the three-day trip to St. Louis for her honeymoon with John, eating dinner the last night at the hotel restaurant and leaving with a dollar after paying the bill.

"Thank God we'd bought round-trip train tickets."

Jack listened to the stories and knew his Grandmother had grown up without much. But that was her childhood, not his. Jack had all the material crap anyone could ask for, but no Mom at home to turn potato pancakes into an occasion.

"Dad," Jack said with one arm still around Etta, "Mom hates that hospital."

"I know, Jack."

Sam sucked smoke deep down into his lungs as the coal of the cigarette glowed red, then blew it out like a geyser spewing steam. Sam's Lucky Strikes never smoldered in the ashtray, enjoying a slow burn. They went to the ashtray to die, after the last bit of tar and nicotine had been leeched free, the burning end smashed flat, the crushed white cylinders stacked like firewood, until Sam fired up again a few minutes later and set about rearranging the pile of dead soldiers.

But that day, facing the prospect of committing Mary Lou to a place that, if she was not already crazy, would seal the deal, Sam removed his glasses and inhaled those coffin nails like a Rastafarian smoking joints. Jack noticed the deep vertical lines running down his father's face, the puffy, black circles under the eyes, the trembling right hand as he raised the cut crystal glass, and realized his father, the captain of the basketball team, the war hero, the mayor, was beat.

"Look, Dad, I know I haven't been helping the situation," Jack said, sitting down. He faced Sam across the round kitchen table that Mary Lou and Jack had painted forest green, Sam's favorite, the summer before her illness started.

"It's OK, Jack," Grandma said as she put her hands on his shoulders.

"No, it's not OK, Grandma," Jack said, speaking harder than he meant. "Everything's all screwed up and you know it. We all know it. Even Maggie."

"Jack," Sam said.

"Dad, don't keep Mom in that hospital any longer than you have to, OK? I mean, I know she's sick. I know you're tryin' to do what's best. But don't do that. It's killin' her."

Jack's voice wavered, but his eyes held steady with Sam's.

Sam stamped out the cigarette and patted Jack's hand, then slid a Lucky into his lips, flicked a silver Zippo lighter with a practiced click, and forced a tight smile from his weathered face.

"We'll get her home as soon as we can. I promise. But you promise me something, Jack."

"What?"

"You do the best you can, Jack. And don't blame yourself or your mother or anyone else for what's going on here. None of this is anybody's fault. Your mom's mind isn't working right, like people's hearts don't work right. We're going to do our best to get it fixed, but, your mind, when it goes bad, it's not like a heart, not like you can have an operation...." his voice floated away with the exhaled smoke.

Jack knew his father had slept only a few hours since Mary Lou had left. He had not slept much the previous three years, worrying when she would run away or attack him for the various crimes the voices convinced her he committed. As Jack looked at Sam, his sympathy for Mary Lou slipped away. Seeing Sam suck on those Luckys made Jack hate Mary Lou, hate her screwed-up mind, her running away.

Jack took a deep breath. What was wrong with him? Begging for mercy for his mother, yet hating her. Worrying about Mary Lou when it was clear she cared about no one but herself. Clear she wanted to be anywhere but with them. He should be acting like a man, helping his father and grandmother with Becky and Maggie, keeping his own act together instead of making things more difficult.

"We go from here," Sam would say after any major or minor setback, "onward and upward."

But the commotion in Jack's mind did not propel him forward; it paralyzed him. He knew the truth: His life came to a halt, or at best turned sideways, when Mary Lou's spun out of control. And so he sat frozen at the forest-green kitchen table he painted a few years before with this mother because it was his father's favorite color, watching Sam smoke Luckys and sip scotch, wondering for the first time if Sam might leave too.

Grandma Henderson gave Jack's shoulders a squeeze and turned to the splattering chicken.

Sam slipped his glasses on, grey eyes staring into the ashtray as if it were a crystal ball that revealed a fatal future. He tapped off a half inch of ash and gulped the glass of scotch, eyes flickering to life.

"I'm glad you're playing ball, Jack. It'll be good...for all of us."

You Can't Always Get What You Want

Six huge, green, empty plastic trash buckets, lined with shiny black lawn bags held in place by strips of silver duck tape stuck to the rims, stood like ominous, immobile sentinels as Jack, the Rams, and the rest of the varsity basketball wannabes arrived for practice at five-thirty Monday morning.

"Look P.K.," said Jimmy. "They got puke buckets. They must've heard you were tryin' out"

"Don't worry," said P.K., "first hork's still got your name on it."

Like many high school basketball gyms, the Albert J. Reckner Memorial Gymnasium, "the Wreck," housed three full-size basketball courts, two with concrete floors under the wood bleachers on each side of the main hardwood court. The full-size courts had baskets at opposite ends and on either side of the half court so six cross-court games could occur at one time.

On that day, and every day that fall and winter, one side of the gym had the bleachers pushed against the wall. That court, plus the hardwood, would be for the basketball team. The other had a portion of the bleachers retracted with the rest of the concrete court covered by blue wrestling mats. The wrestling coaches, thick, bulky men with mustaches, beards, or Fu Manchus, sweat circles pooling under bulging biceps, whistles blowing, patrolled the concrete edge alongside the hardwood, screaming at any kid who lagged behind: "I *know* you didn't take a seat. I know you didn't just do that. Give me twenty-five pushups and don't leave your feet unless you're wrestling!" On the hardwood, Collins and his assistant coaches, lean and clean-shaven, huddled around a clipboard and murmured.

"The Wreck" was partitioned like a miniature UN peacekeeping zone, and for good reason. Jack respected wrestlers' work ethic, but like most basketball players he figured they wrestle because they cannot do anything else athletic. The hand eye coordination gene lost. He knew from Luke that wrestlers thought basketball players were weak.

And so, due to this shared disdained, the Wreck stood divided.

A whistle screeched.

"Over here, boys." Collins stood in the center of the hardwood court, flanked by his two assistants, "Scooter" Havlik and Gene Lane. Despite his nickname, Scooter was in his early fifties but looked forty, black hair clipped short, jaw as stiff as the tip of a surfboard, shoulders broad, waist tapered, a physical fitness freak who ran as much as the players.

"Little hustle, boys," Scooter hollered, clapping his hands, short, hairy legs chopping across the half-court line. "Let's go, let's go." Next to him, Lane, long and lean, his beach-boy bleached hair thinning on top, blue eyes floating in blood-shot whites, stood almost motionless, the occasional sip from a white Styrofoam cup among the few signs of life. In his thirties, Lane looked rode hard and put away wet. A booze-and-babe hound of the first order, he had dragged himself to practice after four hours sleep.

At twelve, "Radar Gene the Shooting Machine" Lane, had discovered he could shoot a basketball better than 99.9 percent of humanity. And in basketball-crazy Midwest America, that was all a guy had to do. Hung-over, Lane could beat any-one on the court in H-O-R-S-E, including Collins, his opponent lucky to hang an *H*. Except for Sam's team, Lane's was the only St. Jude squad to advance to the Sweet Sixteen. And it was because of Lane, who could flat fill it up. Senior year he averaged thirty-nine points a game and earned a full ride to the University of Southern California, where the LA press lauded him as the missing "Beach Boy." True to the appellation, Lane partied with the Beach Boys, even smoked a joint with a mild-mannered hanger-on named Charlie Manson. But Lane blew out his right knee in his sophomore season and returned to St. Jude within a year. The injury cost him a step, and without it he could not get his shot off if guarded. Left open, he was money, but opposing teams do not leave guys named Radar

Gene the Shooting Machine open. At twenty-two, Radar Gene's basketball career was over.

After six years of partying, Lane managed to get a PE degree from the university. He had been at St. Jude ever since as a PE/Driver's Ed teacher and assistant basketball coach. But his fame as the local golden boy who, for one near-perfect season, almost took the town to the Promised Land, gave him special dispensation for all sins. The drinking, the womanizing (to his credit he never knowingly involved himself with a married woman—but unknowingly and drunk, he slept with many), the missed work, his slow-to-pay-bills attitude, nothing bad stuck. He was "Radar Gene," and as long as he lived in St. Jude—short of committing a double homicide (and even then some would give him the benefit of the doubt)—that was all Lane needed to be.

Collins did not look up from his clipboard until the thundering herd of sixty boys, all clad in blue shorts and reversible blue and white mesh tank tops, stood silent.

"Take a seat, boys," he said. "It'll be your last chance for awhile."

Gudy, P.K., Jimmy, Cheyo, and Jack sat together at the rear of the crowd while Jenkins and Connolly pushed their way front and center.

"I want to thank you all for coming out today," Collins said as he handed the clipboard to Scooter and paced in front of the boys, head down, hands clasped behind his back like a professor delivering a lecture.

"It's great to see so much interest in the basketball team. I wish you all could play. I really do. Unfortunately, we have fifteen spots on varsity, twelve for junior varsity, some which will be filled by varsity players not getting playing time, and twelve for the freshman team. That means quite a few of you will be going home in a couple of weeks. And I'm sorry for that. But you're all in high school now, and in high school only the best make the team and only the best of the best play. Just the way it is. Obviously you all believe you have the ability to play on one of the squads or else you wouldn't be here. And that's good. Nothing wrong with self-confidence. You may think you'll make the team because you're tall, quick, a good shooter, or have a lot of hustle. Maybe you made the team last year, or you played great in intramurals last year and think you're ready for varsity. You all have your reasons.

"Now, because so many are trying out, and because we want to be fair, we're going to have two cuts in the next two weeks. The first one is Friday. The second the following Friday. In the mornings we are going to run you like you've never been run before. In the afternoon, we'll do ball handling, shooting, rebounding, and defensive drills. The purpose of the dual workouts is to not only see who has the skills to play this game, but who has the desire. Neither one, by itself, will be enough to make this team.

"So here's what it comes down to." Collins stopped pacing and squared himself to the group. "Fifteen of you are going to play varsity. And that fifteen may not be the tallest, quickest, strongest or most talented. It'll be the fifteen that Coach Havlik, Coach Lane, and I think will give us the best opportunity to win. The fifteen who will make the best team. Because that is what we are about—building a winning team. You aren't going to make this team because you tried hard. And we're not going to hand out varsity letters for effort. They will be earned based on your accomplishments on the court and behavior off the court. It's that simple. Any questions?"

Jack looked at Gudy who raised his eyebrows, and for the first time Jack felt doubt about making the team. Not because of his ability, but whether he, or any of the Rams, fit into Collins's plan. They were seniors—no JV or freshman spots for them. The Rams made varsity or went home. Perhaps Collins had decided Jack's punishment would be the humiliation of being cut.

Scooter blasted the whistle and for the next hour and a half, Jack gave no more thought to success or failure. He ran until he puked into the nearest green bucket, P.K. right ahead of him.

Put Your Back Into Your Business

The next two weeks were a blur of blowing whistles and blowing chow.

Morning practices started with five minutes of jogging and ten minutes of stretching. Then the boys broke into three smaller groups and for ninety minutes did defensive conditioning drills, sprinted from baseline to baseline, and ran the bleachers. They responded to the SCREECH of the coaches whistles like sheep dogs trained to herd the flock home, Converse All-Star sneakers squeaking like a band of crazed kazoos. Jack scrambled to keep up.

SCREECH

Legs bent, one hand high, one at the waist, feet shoulder width apart, slide-squeak-slide-squeak-slide-squeak to the right

Jack's thigh muscles ached.

SCREECH

Smack the floor with both hands and slide-squeak-slide-squeak to the left

SCREECH-SCREECH

Drop for a pushup

"Jeezus," Jack mumbled.

SCREECH

Slide-squeak-slide-squeak, right

SCREECH

Slide-squeak-slide-squeak, left

Jack bumped into guys on either side of him. Lane called a break—to do sit-ups.

SCREECH-SCREECH-SCREECH

"Line 'em up, boys. On the baseline," Scooter said.

SCREECH

Jack high-stepped with the rest down the court, back arched, arms churning, like a bunch of goose-stepping Nazis on speed.

SCREECH

They touched the far baseline and high stepped back.

SCREECH

"Again!"

SCREECH

"Again!"

SCREECH

"What's the matter Jenkins?" hollered Scooter. "Forget how to run? Henderson, wipe that smirk off your face. Five more, thanks to Jenkins and Henderson. You two should get married. Let's go, boys."

SCREECH-SCREECH-SCREECH

"Give me twenty-five sit-ups and hit the bleachers," Collins now. "Five straight up and down, then five crossover steps. Hit it."

SCREECH-SCREECH-SCREECH

"Take ten. Get some water," Lane now. "Stretch. Then line up for washboards. Henderson, have you scheduled conjugal visits with that trashcan or do you like sniffing puke? Suck it up, Jack, half hour to go."

Jack puked again.

SCREECH-SCREECH-SCREECH

"Washboards," Scooter again.

The boys lined up on the baseline, sprinted to the near free throw line, then back to the baseline, up to half court, back to the baseline, to far free throw line, back to the baseline, and sprinted the entire length of court.

"Had enough, Henderson?" Lane hollered.

Chest heaving, Jack lurched back up the court.

SCREECH-SCREECH-SCREECH

"Again."

SCREECH-SCREECH-SCREECH

"Again."

SCREECH-SCREECH-SCREECH

Along with half the boys, Jack dropped to his knees.

"Alright, boys," said Collins, closing practice. "Hit the showers."

Then they would do it all again in the afternoon. Except the boys saw and touched a basketball, dribbling, passing, running fast breaks without the ball hitting the floor, passing all the way, finishing with a layup. But no dunking.

One day, when Jack thought the coaches were not watching, he jammed two-handed behind the head. Lane noticed, smirked, and turned away. Collins heard woofing, figured what Jack did, and made him run bleachers for fifteen minutes to the steady beat of Scooter's disapproving screech.

Come bedtime Jack saw his coaches when he closed his eyes. Scooter prowling around a green garbage can blowing his whistle. Collins silent, watchful. Radar Gene giving him a nod. One stud recognizing another, Jack liked to think. Then again, he may have been suppressing a belch, Lane always a few hours from a brew.

SCREECH!!!

Scooter's ever present whistle blasted through Jack's mind as he lay prone, body jumping from a pre-REM sleep tremor, the stocky, supercharged coach stalking across his brain shouting: "Time to call it a day, Henderson. Slumber time, Jack, slumber time. Let's go, Hendo. Lights out. Lights out. Little sleep, baby, little sleep. Good night, Irene, you know what I mean?"

SCREECH!!!

And Jack would roll over and sleep, deep and hard, the clattering alarm rattling him awake at five to do it all again.

SCREECH!!!

Street Fighting Man

Exhaustion left Jack no time to worry about Mary Lou, a respite he accepted, relieved to be absorbed by something beside her illness. Despite Jack's pleas, the doctors recommended a longer stay, "a change in strategy," Sam said, in hopes she might stabilize.

As for basketball and Coach Collins's boot camp training sessions, Jack and all the Rams survived the first cut, and by the second week the puking and pain ended. In part because Jack's seventeen-year-old body had adapted to the routine. In part because Collins now needed to determine who could play. Having cut those without the desire by means of the previous week's brutality, he used more of the morning practice for ball handling, passing, shooting, and defensive drills. In the afternoon practices they played three-on-three half-court games and ten-man full-court scrimmages, the coaches introducing basic principles of Collins's motion offense and man-to-man defense.

Toward the end of Thursday afternoon's practice in the second week, Jack was paired with Gudy and Brewster against Connolly, Cheyo, and Jenkins for a half-court three-on-three drill. Collins had started separating the boys into smaller groups the second week, and the fact that he mixed Cheyo, Gudy, and Jack with varsity returnees boded well. Jack worried about P.K and Jimmy, who often played with juniors and sophomores with no previous varsity experience. But Collins gave no hints, face as blank as a sponged blackboard.

On that day, Gudy, Brewster, and Jack played defense. Jack covered Jenkins as he tossed it in to Cheyo at the free-throw line with Gudy on him. Cheyo faked to Jenkins, who cut right then pivoted to face up to the hoop. Connolly posted underneath, faked right and cut left to set a pick on Jack as Jenkins drifted toward the basket.

"Pick left!" Brewster shouted.

Jack hopped back a step, allowing Jenkins to separate, then fought through the screen. Jenkins cut under the hoop and Cheyo zipped a two-hand overhead pass through Gudy's hands hitting Jenkins in stride.

As Jenkins rose to bank the ball with his left hand Jack planted his right foot and leapt. Jenkins released his shot as Jack's hand swept past the rim, fingertips grazing the ball. It bounced off the backboard and down, glancing off Jenkins's knee and out of bounds.

"Goaltending," Jenkins said. "You blocked it after it hit the glass."

"Bullshit. I hit ball, ball hit glass, then you. Our ball out."

"No freaking way, Jack," Jenkins said, snatching the ball off the hardwood, dribbling to the top of the key. "Goaltending all the way. Right Brewsty?"

"I gotta say, it looked like a clean block to me, man."

"You gotta be kiddin'. No way. Our ball out."

Brewster shrugged.

"Next time," Jack said to Jenkins, "go up strong, not like a chick playing H-O-R-S-E in the back forty, and maybe I can't block the shot or you draw the foul. That block was clean. Our ball out."

Jack turned toward Gudy and—BAM!—the ball slammed off his right ear, knocking him to one knee.

Stunned, vision blurred, he cupped his ear.

"Sorry, Jack," Jenkins said, grin splitting his beet-red face. "Thought you called ball out."

"Sonuvabitch." Jack rose and charged Jenkins, Scooter's whistle screeching in his throbbing ear. Jenkins, confirming all theories about basketball players' boxing ability, threw a punch that began in Missouri and landed in the lakes of Minnesota, missing Jack's lowered head by a foot. Although Jack never played tackle football, he tagged Jenkins with a textbook, shoulder-to-gut tackle, driving him backward and down onto the wood floor, the wind whooshing from the other boy's chest.

As Jack raised his right hand to drill Jenkins, the thunder of half-a-dozen shoes rumbled and tumbled upon him.

"Knock it off, knock it off," Scooter yelled. "What the heck? I walk away for a second and this stuff happens. What the heck?"

"Jack!" Gudy shouted as he yanked him away, pinning Jack's arms to his sides with a bear hug.

"Sonuvabitch, cheap-shottin' sonuvabitch," Jack yelled, feet kicking into the air, as Gudy lifted him off the ground and turned him away from Jenkins.

"Jackie... Jackie, that's enough now man. This ain't like you. You ain't no fighter. C'mon man. C'mon." Gudy's words brought him back from the brink. He stopped squirming. Gudy was right. Except for fights with Becky as toddlers, which Mary Lou broke up with a trip to the kitchen corner, he had never hit anyone in his life. A vision of his mother strapped down behind the steel screens of the mental ward flashed across his mind. He went limp under Gudy's grip.

"Let me go," he said, chin dropping to his chest.

"You cool man?"

"I'm cool. Let me go."

Gudy let go and tousled Jack's hair.

"It was a cheap shot," Cheyo said to the approaching Collins. "Jenkins hit Jack with the ball when Jack turned his head. It was a cheap shot, coach."

"Yes it was," said Coach Collins, who strolled from across the gym like a man out for a Sunday afternoon of bird-watching, voice steady, brown eyes evaluating the writhing Jenkins. Scooter cooed at the gasping boy, pulling the elastic waistband away from his heaving stomach.

"Relax, Randy," Scooter said. "Just got the wind knocked out of you. You'll be OK."

"But," Collins continued, not taking his eyes off Jenkins and sounding more like a philosopher on a hill than a coach in a gym, "Jack didn't have to retaliate. If this were a game, and Jenkins our opponent, they'd both be ejected even though Jenkins was in the wrong. Jack losing his temper didn't resolve anything. Just cost us a player. Hurt the whole team. You boys have to learn to control your emotions regardless of the provocation. Play with intensity, not anger. In control. Always in control."

Collins turned to Jack.

"In case you care," Jack said, shrugging, "I'm OK, too."

"Glad to hear it," said Collins, ignoring the challenge in Jack's tone. "As soon as Jenkins gets his breath you two boys go run bleachers until the end of practice. Scooter, make sure they keep up a good pace."

"You got it, coach," said Scooter as he took Jenkins' hand and pulled him to a sitting position. "Let's go Randy, break time's over."

Within a few minutes Jenkins and Jack raced side by side, up and down the bleachers. Before they could collapse, Collins called everyone together at center court.

"Good practice," he said. "And no practice tomorrow morning."

The boys whooped and hollered.

"OK, OK, settle down. The bad part is this practice will be the last for many of you. Names of those who made varsity, JV, and freshman team will be posted outside my office tomorrow morning by 7:30 a.m. Those who made the teams, meet here tomorrow at 3:30 p.m. to pick up your uniforms and get individual and team photos.

"For the rest, I'm available to talk with any of you individually as to why you didn't make it. But I won't change my mind. The decision is final. I want to thank all you boys for your effort the last two weeks. I know it hasn't been easy. And you've made Coach Havlik, Coach Lane, and my job difficult. We've got tough calls to make tonight. But know this. We're proud of all of you, and you should be proud of yourselves, whether you make the team or not."

Jack glanced at P.K., who shook his head sideways, certain he was an *or not*.

Hello, I Love You

Cheyo topped off the Ram's clear plastic cups from the Old Style keg, one of four scattered around the half-block-long, partier-packed, Fiji Frat house basement. The Rolling Stones roared from JBL speakers perched in the corners.

"Man, Collins would crap a cow if he saw us now," P.K. said.

"Boys," said Jimmy, sticking one hand inside his shirt like Napoleon and giving his best Coach Collins the leader look, "I am unable to crap a cow. I'm from Chicago... However, I think it is appropriate, based on what I see here tonight, to reiterate that there will be no rules regarding drinking on this team. No pledge cards to sign or oaths to take. I am not your mother or your father or your kindergarten teacher. That doesn't mean there will be no repercussions..."

"Does that mean the shit will hit the fan, Coach?" Cheyo said.

"Yes, Jackson." Jimmy shook his head in mock frustration. "The shit will certainly hit the fan. Remind me to get you a dictionary, son.... Now as I was saying, know this, it is illegal for people under nineteen to drink. Should you drink, and should you get caught, you will be held accountable by the law, the school, your fellow teammates, and your own conscience. The extracurricular policy will be enforced by the administration. Strike one, you miss twenty-five percent of the season. Strike two, season over for you. Strike three, you're done with extracurricular activities for the rest of high school. Think about that the next time you are tempted to have a beer. Think about the impact that behavior will have on everyone around you and your own future. Just as Cain slew Abel, there will be consequences...."

"Uh, coach, I'm not sure…" Cheyo said.

"The shit will hit the fan, Jackson. Anything else, boys?"

"So we're on our honor, Coach?" Jack said.

"Yes, Henderson," Jimmy said, his face stone-cold-sober Collins. "Anything else?"

"Yeah, one more question," Gudy said.

"'Yes, son,'" Jimmy said, his wooden gestures freeze-framed in the dance-floor strobe light.

"Are you out of your mind?"

"I knew it was a mistake to put you Rams on varsity!" Jimmy said, giggling. "'Scooter? Whistle? Lane? Oh, Lane, for God sakes, at least be sober when I'm talking to the boys about drinking. My God, my God, why hast thou forsaken me?"

"To the Rams," yelled P.K. hoisting his beer.

"Shadoobie," Jimmy shouted.

All bona fide varsity basketball players as of 7:30 that morning and now on their honor, the five boys and Luke tapped cups, slammed their brews, and refilled them.

Feeling a serious buzz engulf him, Jack sipped the cold beer and stepped away from the keg. At seventeen, he was an experienced drinker and knew when to ratchet it down a notch. Some kids like P.K. drank until they puked. But Jack hated to lose control. Unlike P.K., he could not crash at Luke's pad. He had a curfew, and Sam, whether smashed or sober himself, would be waiting up.

"Takes one to know one," Jack spat at a glassy-eyed Sam one night, staggering in after splitting a case with Gudy and Cheyo at the drive-in, while Sam drank scotch alone at home.

"Son," Sam said, voice husky yet soft, "you can learn as much from my faults as my virtues."

Shoving thoughts of his psychotic mother and drunk father to the side for the moment, Jack wrapped himself in a cocoon of feel-good-fuzzy-warmth, sinking into a retreat he could find no place else.

Lost in the groove, Jack did not notice the tall blonde splitting the crowd like Bo Derek at Studio54. Gliding through the swarm, blue eyes locked on Jack, Ms. Linda Stevens expected guys to slide out of her way, ogling her ass as she passed. She was accustomed to the way girls wrinkled their noses, jerking their boyfriends close, knowing that with a glance she could bring them to heel like dogs on a leash.

"Hello, Jack," she said, handing a cup to Cheyo without a word, knowing Cheyo would fill it to the brim while thanking her for the privilege. "Why am I not surprised to see you here?"

"Uh, hi, Ms. Stevens." Jack lowered his beer and tucked in his shirttails.

Rocking to the beat, Linda sucked the frost off the beer.

"Wow, that first sip always tastes so good."

Jack ducked his head and drank.

"Ms. Stevens, I'm Jeff Gudman," Gudy said, eavesdropping from the keg, slapping Jack's arm and flashing a 'get your shit together' glance. He shook hands with Linda like a Frat president welcoming a parent. "Jack and I have been friends since we were kids. I sure appreciate your standing up for him. Dunham's always looking for a chance to nail Jack. Says Jack's a rabble rouser. Who the hell calls anybody that anymore? The guy is out of it. Thinks Eisenhower is president. Anyway, thanks. Right, Jack?"

Jack nodded.

"Thanks," Linda said wresting her hand from Gudy's, "I think. How'd you guys get in here? The Frats usually have someone working the door. The university is supposedly cracking down on underage drinking."

"Underage? Us?" said Gudy. "Only in America. In Germany we'd be well into our second decade of beer drinking. Milk is for babies, the German's say. Men drink beer. Vee are men."

Linda stared Gudy down.

"Jawohl, fraulein," Gudy said, clicked his heels together and flashed a Sergeant Schultz, heil Hitler salute straight from *Hogan's Heroes* reruns. "I know nothing. Noooothing. I shall banish myself to the Eastern Front."

He spun on his heels and goose stepped towards Cheyo and P.K. who sang along to AC/DC's "Dirty Deeds."

"Someone is sure full of himself," Linda said.

"Our friend, Luke, is being rushed by the Frat."

"Come again?"

"You asked how we got in."

"Right, I did. So what's the occasion? Why are you guys out? Or is this a typical Friday night?"

"Well, for us I guess this is kinda typical. But it's also an occasion. Five of us made the varsity basketball team this morning."

"Don't jocks have rules about drinking, smoking, that stuff. Especially during the season?"

"Reggie Collins, our coach, you met him at school, he doesn't believe in pledge cards," Jack said, neglecting to mention Collins did not condone underage drinking either and put the boys on their honor.

"I know who Reggie Collins is and not because he was at our meeting. When I was in junior high Reggie Collins was a God here. All-everything. Good looking.

Great student, member of Athletes in Action, president of the only black frat on campus. Everybody loved Reggie Collins. Because he didn't try to fit in. He was who he was. And because of that, he fit in everywhere. Interesting dynamic, don't you think?"

"I suppose," Jack said feeling like a student. "I don't know the guy that well. Seems like a hardass to me."

"Reggie Collins, a hardass?" Linda laughed. "I never thought of him that way. I just thought he was cool."

"People change when they get older, I guess."

"For the better, hopefully."

"Well, you can hope," Jack said between gulps of beer.

"Kind of a pessimistic view from a senior in high school. You need to mellow."

"Thought I was," Jack said lifting his cup.

"Mellow, Jack, not drunk."

"You mean get high?"

"Not often. Not when I'm forty with kids. But, yeah, right here, right now, yeah. It beats waking up with a hangover. You ever smoked a doobie, Jack?"

"Nope."

"You should try it."

"Sorry. Not interested in becoming a Head."

Linda laughed and touched his forearm. Color rushed to his cheeks.

"Oh, please," Linda said, waving her hand. "You think because you drink beer you're going to end up a wino? We're not talking about snorting coke or shooting heroin. Just a doobie."

"Not every drunk's a skid row wino," Jack said, eyes meeting Linda's.

Linda's smirk vanished as she turned away from Jack's gaze. AC/DC blasted from the amps, uniting the cellar as everyone chanted along.

Jack and Linda stood still.

Without a word, Linda took Jack's beer and set both cups on a table. Grasping his hand, she led him across the room, past the scattered cliques Jack saw at every party. The scruffy TheretoGetDrunkBoys jammed around the dining hall tables. Three day beards, t-shirts and long johns covered by unbuttoned flannel shirts hanging over faded blue jeans or white painter's pants; they slammed shots and played quarters.

Jack nodded to a couple he knew.

"Check out that fox," he heard from a small group of sharp-dressed guys, wearing cotton golf shirts, designer jeans, or long sleeved, big collared polyester shirts, cuff peeking out from the sleeve of "Members Only" jackets. Behind them, tweed clothed AcademicTypes raised their pipes in salute and continued arguing about Nietzsche.

BusinessGuys, Fiji's and Fiji friends who graduated a few years earlier, nodded at Jack, while girls, who had not noticed him earlier now checked him out, wondering what they missed, as he and Linda ascended the steps, leaving the beer, bullshit, and booming bass of the basement behind.

Comfortably Numb

As they walked through the living room on the first floor Jack spotted Jimmy and Sandy McCarty, close together on a couch. Sandy and her crowd must have just arrived, Jack thought, he would have remembered had she been below. Sandy's arrival would have caused as much a stir among the boys as Linda's, two belles of the ball if there ever were. But with Linda squeezing his hand, Jack was not about to stop and visit. He trailed her up to the second floor, where the sound of Pink Floyd's "The Dark Side of the Moon" slipped through a closed door along with the aroma of pot.

Linda knocked and the door opened a few inches. After a short pause she pulled Jack through, sliding sideways in order to slip through the narrow gap, the entrance blocked by a pale, red-headed, red-eyed Fiji in a Hawaiian shirt enthroned on a bamboo barstool, a doped sentinel of sorts.

"He's cool, Freddy," Linda said, nodding to Jack.

"You robbin' the cradle, Linda," Freddy said, bloodshot eyes floating above a droopy red Fu Manchu, measuring Jack's potential as a narc with a quick up and down. "Big for his age."

"Be nice, Freddy. It's Jack's first time."

"It's cool. Just blowin' you shit, Jack. You're too big to screw with. C'mon in, man."

Freddy closed the door.

"You bring your own Linda, or you looking to buy?"

"I got a couple of joints. Should be plenty for us, thanks anyway."

"Cool. Enjoy."

The room had a pool table at one end, a Ping-Pong table folded next to a pop machine at the other, and in the middle a TV where three stringy-haired, skinny white guys lounged on cushioned chairs, taking hits from a bong and watching "Roadrunner" cartoons with the sound off. Candles flickered under a faded poster of Richard Nixon pointing at a map of Cambodia and saying, "The devil made me do it." Although the night was crisp, several windows stood open, a box fan perched on a sill in a vain attempt to clear the air.

In the middle of the room about a dozen guys and girls gathered, smoking joints, hitting bongs, one couple lay together whispering like a husband and wife might before drifting off to sleep, another made-out, groping between hits. Linda led Jack to the edge of the group, pulling him down onto throw pillows.

"OK," Linda said, "have you ever smoked a cigarette?"

"Of course," Jack said, waving his hand.

"Don't take offense. You're a jock, I figured you didn't smoke. Silly me, what was I thinking."

Linda slipped a hand down her T-shirt, fished out two joints and pulled a Bic lighter from her jeans.

"Anyway, this is basically the same, except you take a longer drag and hold it for as long as you can before you blow it out. Best to take a good hit so you don't waste any. We don't set these in an ashtray and let them smolder."

"I've seen people take hits," Jack said, rolling his eyes.

"You must be a real pain to teach and coach," Linda said as she fired up, took a hit, and held the joint out to Jack.

Jack hesitated.

Linda released a stream of smoke above his head.

"You don't have to, Jack. But take a hit, or I will. This stuff isn't cheap on grad ass pay."

Jack took the joint between his thumb and forefinger, trying to be Peter Fonda in *Easy Rider*. The slender tip pursed between his lips, he took a long deep hit, holding the smoke in until his lungs burned before releasing, coughing, more like Jack Nicholson, now, the drunk taking his first hit, glancing through watery eyes to see if anyone noticed.

"That's OK. Everybody hacks on their first one. It's not exactly like a cigarette. It's cool."

They smoked the rest of the joint in silence, letting the high and the music soak in, Jack enjoying Linda's presence and the encroaching numbness.

Linda took the last hit, then got up, put coins in the pop machine, and returned with a 7-Up.

"Can't stand that pot taste in my mouth for long. Want some?"

Jack took a sip and lay down, propping pillows under his head. He felt as if he were floating on a raft down a lonesome country creek. He heard the rippling water, felt the breeze from shore, enjoying the rolling sensation as he fluttered downstream, hushed conversations swirling about like the rustle of fall leaves.

Linda tugged his hand. "You OK, Jack?"

"Yeah, I'm cool."

"Want some more?"

"Absolutely."

Jack pulled himself to a sitting position as Linda lit the second joint. The river floated beneath, Tricky Dick gloated from the wall, and the music and smoke drifted above. Within a few minutes they finished the second joint and Linda stretched out next to him, holding his hand, staring at the ceiling. Supertramp spun on the turntable, a full-length version of "Take the Long Way Home" filled the room. Amazed at how his mind could be adrift yet active, Jack felt his body go numb. Time froze, his place in space fluid, the music a revelation from above that opened his soul, revealing everything, while resolving nothing. He lay motionless until the song ended and the rumble of real, not recorded, human voices broke the spell in an argument over what album to play next. Jack sat up, rolled his head from side to side, shrugged his shoulders and mind, and tossed off the so-called great thoughts like a damp, winter coat.

"Damn," he said to himself as he lay back down and closed his eyes. "You're high as a kite."

As if in confirmation, he saw a dancing Dick Van Dyke, dressed like the Good Humor ice cream man in white pants and a rainbow-striped sport coat in his mind. A beribboned and rosy cheeked Julie Andrews skipped along by his side, the two of them holding hands with his mother and sisters singing—"Let's go fly a kite, up to the highest heights, let's go fly a kite, and send it soaring...."—then vanished. He laughed out loud.

"Now you're mellow," Linda said rolling onto her side. "See the difference?"

Jack turned to face her, their eyes finding one another in the dim room. Linda brushed wisps of rebellious hair away from his forehead, fingertips dancing and drifting down his cheekbone, lingering, caressing, gentle, the warmth of her touch and the effect of the pot soothing him in a way he had not felt since he was a small boy. Those sub-zero winter nights when the reassuring steam from the cast iron radiator had lulled him into deep sleep. He lay his hand on Linda's, enveloping it, the cold, flatness of his palm melding with and giving way to her heat.

"You have the saddest eyes I've ever seen," Linda said. "Like you're worn out. Like you're an old soul. I saw it that day in the library. It made me feel sorry for you, thinkin' like, wow, what's been done to this kid, make him so old, so alone. What has been done to you Jack? What's wrong?"

Was it that easy to see? He pressed Linda's hand to his face, savoring her calming touch. He had taken pride in keeping his mother's problems and his feelings to himself. "It's nobody's business," Sam said. "It would only embarrass your mother. Fewer people who know the better."

Teachers like Dunham figured him for a screwed-up, what-you-got-to-rebel-against teenager, not a kid with any serious problems. Just a smart-ass. People could keep their sympathy. It was no business of theirs that his mother was crazy, his father a drunk. Petty people with their small-minded judgment, their lazy gossip. Sam was right. It was nobody's business. Screw 'em. Screw 'em all.

And yet, this girl, to whom he had not spoken more than a few words, who knew nothing of him or his family, had sensed something from the moment they met.

How could that be? How could a secret be revealed by a look, a touch, the holding of a hand?

Linda's hand slid out from under his. Tears streamed down his cheeks, soft sobs erupting from his chest.

"I'm sorry Jack," Linda said, cupping his face. "I didn't mean to upset you. I shouldn't've brought you up here. Jesus. I'm twenty-four, you're seventeen. I got you smoking pot. Then I say something like that to you. I'm sorry, Jack. I'm really sorry."

"It's not your fault." He pushed her hands away and wiped his eyes. "There's just some stuff with my mom."

Despite himself, the tears continued. He cursed his weakness, cursed the pot. Should never have let his guard down, let the shit float to the surface. Now it would repel Linda, like it repelled anyone who learned the truth about his family.

But she was hugging him, pulling him into her, his chin on her thin shoulder. He melted into her, sobs shaking him, sinking down beneath the music from the turntable.

Shattered

"Jack, Jack Henderson? Is Jack Henderson in here?"

The ceiling lights flashed on.

"What the hell?" one of the Roadrunner watchers yelled. "Turn the lights off, man. That ain't cool. Freddie, where you at? You're supposed to be watchin' the door."

But the red-eyed Freddie did not respond. Mouth full of Cheetos, he sat propped up against the pop machine.

"Screw you, pal," said a voice Jack recognized as Gudy's. "Jack, you here?"

The lights went off.

"Sonuvabitch," said Gudy, "I'm gonna kick your grass-smokin' ass. I'm just tryin' to find—"

Jack rolled away from Linda and rubbed his eyes.

"Gudy, I'm here, man. Where's the fire?"

"Jack?" Gudy said to the darkness, uncertain what direction to turn his voice. "Hey man, Luke's goin' ballistic downstairs. Ready to go to war over Sandy McCarty. I'm not sure what the hell's happenin'."

"Must be jocks or Fijis," one of the cartoon guys said. "They're the only ones fight over chicks. Like there ain't enough to go around. Assholes."

"I bet that's what you prefer, you—"

"Gudy, shut up, man," Jack shouted. "I'm comin'."

Jack and Linda sat up.

"I gotta go," he said, lowering his voice.

"Sure sounds like it."

"Hey, listen, about all this…the crying. I mean, thanks, I appreciate what you did…but, you know…well, I sure hope you won't say anything about…"

Linda brushed tears from his cheek.

"It stays here, Jack. Tell the guys you were about to score. Who knows? Maybe in a few years…"

"Few years?" Jack winced.

"'Fraid so. I had no business bringing you up here. I'm sorry."

"Just friends then, huh?"

"That's not a bad thing, Jack. From what I see you don't have any friends who look as good as me."

Jack laughed.

"Jackie, for chrissakes, you comin' or what?"Gudy shouted, sounding to Jack as if he was closing in on the stoned cartoon guys.

"He probably was before your dumb ass showed up," one of the stoners yelled.

"Listen you weasely …"

Linda gave him a hug like a mother sending a child off to school. "Go, before you have two fights to break up."

Jack stared at her for a moment then jumped to his feet.

"Let's go, Gudy."

"Beep-beep, assholes," the cartoon guy said as Jack grabbed Gudy by the arm and shoved him through the door.

"Hey, Jack, I'm sorry, man," Gudy said as they walked down the hall to the stairs. "Was that guy right? We're you about to nail that babe? Man, I'm sorry. But I didn't know what to do. When Luke gets like this you're the only one who can settle him down. I'm sorry, man."

"Don't worry about it. She informed me that we are 'just friends.'"

"That's always a kick in the balls."

Shouts rose from the living room, and they raced downstairs, leaping the last few steps and landing with a thud on the hardwood floor. Luke and Jimmy were face-to-face a few feet in front of them.

"I'm tired of your shit," Luke said.

Luke crouched in his wrestling pose, beer in one hand, thick index finger pointing at Jimmy ten feet away, a trembling P.K. caught in the middle, arms out like a referee separating fighters before the bell rings. Behind Jimmy, Cheyo whispered in his ear, tugging at his arm, trying to turn him away.

"C'mon, fellas," P.K. said. "Just stop it. The chick ain't worth it."

"Tired of my shit?" Jimmy said, ignoring all the efforts at détente. "What the hell, Sarge? I was the one talkin' to her first—doin' just fine, I might add—until your dumb white ass shows up with your racial rant. Now your gonna stand there and tell me your tired of *my* shit? What the hell? Why you tryin' to make time with a chick you see me makin' time with?"

"Because you got no business makin' time with Sandy," Luke shouted, the veins in his neck bulging as he set his beer on the coffee table in front of the couch and took two steps toward Jimmy, stopping short of P.K.

Jack had to do something. The guys expected him to take control. But this was not the basketball court, not a controlled environment with defined rules, a place where through the force of physical abilities he could impose his will. Too much stimulation bombarded him. High, beer-buzzed, trembling from the encounter with Linda, exhausted from the unearthing of emotions long buried, his heart thumped, the adrenalin flowed, but like a car with a damaged transmission Jack could not shift into gear.

"Hey Sarge," Gudy said, flashing a pissed look into Jack's bloodshot eyes. "We all know you're sweet on Sandy, but, man, you've had a couple years to make a move, and you never have. Everybody supposed to wait on you forever?"

"Naaah," Jimmy said, shaking his fist. "Just me. The Neeeegro."

"That's it. That's the shit I'm talkin' about. You sonuvabitch…" Luke shouted.

He burst past P.K., knocking his brother down like a wobbly bowling pin, hit Jimmy in the gut with a shoulder and wrapped his arms around his waist. As Jimmy rained punches down on Luke's head, the blows as ineffective as hail on a steel roof, Luke arched his back, twisted, and slammed Jimmy onto the floor with a chandelier rattling smack.

"Holy shit," Cheyo said and rushed to pull Luke off Jimmy.

But before any of them could separate the two, the room overflowed with Fijis there to break up the fight. As the frat boys stepped in, Jimmy and Luke turned their anger on them. Luke pulling a couple of Fijis off Jimmy as together they fought their way out the door. The rest of the Rams backed out of the house behind them like outlaws exiting a saloon.

"Assholes need to mind their own business." Luke said draping a heavy arm over Jimmy's shoulders.

"Damn straight."

"It was my fault, man."

"No, man. This one's on me."

"Nah, you're right, I need to cool the racial shit."

"We both do," Jimmy said.

"We cool?"

"We cool."

They piled into P.K.'s beat-up '63 Chevy, Jimmy, Gudy, and Luke in the back, whooping it up and high-fiving—"Guess I'm not rushin' the Fijis anymore!"—laughing as Cheyo jammed the Stones "Some Girls" eight-track into the stereo.

"Take me home first." Jack rolled down the window and stared at the passing houses, the cold air slapping his face.

He stopped as he walked up the sidewalk to the side door where P.K. dropped him. Inside, framed by the family room window, the painted white wood chipped and pealing, he saw Sam passed out in the brown leather recliner. No longer the strong soldier of his youth he was trying to hold down the fort, awaiting the cavalry, the return of his wife. A half-empty Scotch bottle sat on the table, a Lucky smoldering in the ashtray Jack had made in grade school. On TV, Johnny Carson, Ed McMahon, Bill Cosby, and Freddy Prinze sat laughing together on a *Tonight Show* rerun.

Jack froze at the sight of Prinze. Not long ago, the twenty-two-year-old Chicano comedian had taken a pistol and splattered his brains onto a wall after telling a friend, "I need to find peace."

"Shattered, shattered," Cheyo chanted, as P.K. pulled away.

Locomotion

Monday morning, basketball practice started in earnest, and Mary Lou came home.

The season opened in three weeks when four local teams faced off for the Thanksgiving weekend round-robin tournament. With three returning players, Brewster, Jenkins, and Connolly, plus three juniors who hadn't played varsity, Alex Pitman, Jake McElroy, and Tommy Tompkins, plus the five Rams and four other boys who split time between varsity and junior varsity, the coaches had little time to teach the motion offense and man-to-man defense. Jack braced himself for intense practices.

The grunting and whistles of wrestling practice echoed around the Wreck, while scattered around the basketball courts were orange cones, chairs and duct taped X's. "Since we have so many new players this season," Collins began, "we're going to conduct a crash course in the motion offense for the next three weeks. That may seem like plenty of time. But while the principles are simple—maintain your spacing, cut and screen with a purpose, constant movement—the execution is not. It takes time to learn and requires every player to be able to handle the ball. There's no place to hide in the motion. Everybody has to pass, shoot, and dribble.

"It also requires…" Collins paused to look at each boy. "That we play as a single unit. Everyone on the same page. No room for selfishness, for laziness, for a *me first* attitude. You will all be expected to set hard screens. You will all be expected to pass, to be patient, to look not for any shot but the best shot, and to play as a team.

"Coach Lane here," Collins said nodding toward Radar Gene, "was one of the greatest individual high school players I ever saw. Unbelievable shooter. Great anticipation on defense. Still holds the school record for steals and scoring. But coach, why did you guys not win state?"

"We got beat by a better team. Proviso held me below my average, and nobody else stepped up. We lost."

Collins shrugged.

"One of the greatest players this state will ever produce, and he couldn't get it done alone. And let's be clear. I'm not trying to hurt anyone's feelings here, you're a fine group of high school basketball players, but there is no Gene Lane among you. If we are going to win, it will have to be as a team. There isn't one of you who can carry us to a championship. And the championship is our goal. Nothing else."

Collins stopped and faced the boys down.

Lane looked at them as well. No aw-shucks false modesty or cocky grin, just sipping his coffee, checking if any of them were brash enough to make a face or roll wide eyes. Next to him, Scooter shifted from side to side, ready to blow his whistle and get practice underway.

"And don't think because I started with the offense," Collins paced in front of them, "that defense takes a back seat. Defense, which you can also learn from Coach Lane's experience, is what wins championships. We play an aggressive man-to-man. We don't play zone. We will never play zone. Again, no place for anyone to hide. You will be expected to move your feet, fight through screens, take the charge. We will coach you. We will teach you. But in my mind, defense is about effort. It's about conditioning. But it's mainly about heart. You have it or you don't. And if you don't, I don't care if you are the second coming of Jesus Christ, you will be sitting on the bench next to me. Any questions?"

The boys sat still.

"Bring it in," Collins said, extending his hand. Lane and Scooter stepped up and stacked their hands on top, and the boys followed, forming a circle around Collins.

"Who are we?" Scooter asked.

"Hilltoppers," said some of the boys.

"*Who* are we?" Scooter said, raising his voice.

"Hilltoppers," all the boys said.

"*Who are we?*" Scooter shouted.

"HILLTOPPERS!"

"That's more like it," Scooter said, chomping a stick of gum and clapping his hands. "Let's go now, boys. Little hustle."

"Henderson, Jenkins, Davis," Lane said, motioning them toward two folding chairs facing away from a basket on opposite ends of the free throw line, a basketball on the seat of the chair to the right.

"Finally, a shooting drill," P.K. mumbled to Jack.

"Show 'em how it's done," Lane said to Jenkins, who lined up to the outside of the left chair.

SCREECH went Lane's whistle.

Jenkins raced to the far side of the chair on the right, crouched low, snatched the ball and fired a shot, following it to the hoop. The ball hit nothing but net. Jenkins retrieved it, dribbled to the chair on the left and dropped the ball into the seat. He ran to the far side of the right chair, then back to the left, grabbed the ball and shot again, repeating the sequence.

"Stay low, Jenkins," Lane shouted, "triple-threat position."

Lane crouched as he spoke, long fingers gripping an imaginary ball in the shooting position, tucked tight to the right side of his body, ready to shoot, dribble or pass.

"Always triple-threat," he said, looking at Jack. "No one-handed, ball waving, playground stuff."

Jenkins raced between the chairs and the basket.

SCREECH

"OK, Jack. You're up," Lane said.

Jack sprinted at the sound of the whistle; knees bent low as he secured the ball and squared to shoot in triple-threat position. Like Jenkins he swished the first shot. After a half-dozen back and forths, he was panting and his shots clanged off the front of the rim.

"Bend those legs, Jack. Explode on the jumper. Triple-threat, triple-threat," Lane said.

SCREECH

P.K. took his turn, then Jenkins, then Jack, running the drill for another ten minutes.

SCREECH

"Rotate," Scooter hollered, waving at Jack, P.K. and Jenkins.

"Leave it to these guys to take the fun out of shooting," Jack gasped to P.K. as they ran to Scooter.

"OK, guys," Scooter hollered, from the top of the key, "you know this one. Quick feet, shot, stop and drop. On the baseline."

The boys lined up, Jack to the left of the lane, Jenkins in the middle, P.K. to the right.

SCREECH

They raced to the free throw line.

"Quick feet, quick feet," Scooter said, as the boys pitter-pattered in place in front of him.

"Shot," he hollered, right arm shooting up.

The boys jumped, their arms straight in the air.

"Quick feet, quick feet – left."

The boys scooted left, shoes drumming the floor.

"Right... shot."

The boys leapt.

P.K. grunted.

"Left. Quick feet, P.K. Quick feet."

"Take the charge. Take the charge."

The drumming stopped. The boys froze then fell on their butts and slid back on the waxed floor as if an opposing player had run them over.

"Up, up. Don't assume the call. Up. Up."

Jack's shirt was soaked.

Scooter ran them for another five minutes.

SCREECH

They raced to Collins station as did Cheyo, Brewster, and Gudy.

"Three-on-three boys," Collins said, bouncing a ball. "Offense completes ten passes in a row. No steals, kick-aways, double-dribbles, traveling. Ten in a row. No turnovers. Do that, keep the ball. Turn it over, defense gets the ball. Nobody shoots. Not trying to score. Let's go."

Collins tossed the ball to P.K. who dribbled to the top of the key. Jack and Jenkins drifted to opposite wings, Brewster on Jack, Gudy on Jenkins.

SCREECH

Jack broke to the basket, then back to the wing, executing a sharp V-cut and breaking free from Brewster. P.K. tossed the ball to Jack. He faked Cheyo with a jabbing step to the left and broke right where Jenkins set a solid screen.

"Pick," Gudy hollered.

Cheyo fought through it, but not in time to stop P.K. from receiving the return pass from Jack.

"Nice screen, Randy," Collins said.

The ball zipped between the three boys for eight more passes, Connolly, Gudy, and Brewster chasing.

SCREECH

"Ten. Good job, offense. Your ball out. Defense, you have to talk. Move your feet, wave your arms. Let's go."

SCREECH

P.K., Jenkins, and Jack played keep away again. Jack caught the third pass on the left wing, palmed the ball in his right hand, extending his arm behind him.

"Stop the showboating, Jack," Collins said. "Triple-threat, triple-threat."

As Jack lowered the ball to tuck it in, Brewster knocked it loose.

SCREECH

"Ball out, defense," Collins said. "Nice play, Brew. This isn't the playground, Jack. That stuff isn't going to fly. Be strong with the ball. Triple-threat. Pass and move."

"Wow, you can palm the ball," Jenkins said. "Knock that shit off before I knock you on your ass."

The two boys edged toward each other.

SCREECH

"Enough," Collins said. "Ball out. Let's go."

Cheyo, Gudy and Brewster kept the ball for two turns, before Jack stole a pass. After exchanging possession three more times, Collins halted play.

SCREECH SCREECH SCREECH

Play stopped at all baskets and the boys took a water break.

The last twenty minutes of practice they played a five-on-five scrimmage. Those not playing shot sets of ten free throws, reporting how many they made to team manager Whitey Hauser, a pale, skinny sophomore. The coaches mixed and matched lineups, yelling at the free throw shooters to substitute. Scooter and Lane refereed, while Collins paced up and down the court with the offenses, talking to the boys as they played but not interrupting the flow.

"Patience, P.K. You're the point. You control the pace... spacing... Triple threat, Jack, come off that pick in triple threat... Don't fight the defensive pressure, Gudy, work off it, back cut... Beautiful... Good shot, better pass. You have Jenkins to thank for that basket, Brewster... Sharp cuts, boys, sharp cuts... Fight through that screen, P.K.... C'mon boys, hustle, always hustle."

Halfway through the scrimmage, tired of the constant passing, the screens, the V- cuts, the work-work-work Collins required before they could shoot, Jack took the first pass from Jenkins as they crossed half-court and shake-and-baked against gangly Tommy Tompkins, a slow-footed junior. Rat-a-tat-tatting his dribble and stutter stepping, Jack faked the junior to his knees, cut past him, and lifted off, stretching over a lagging Brewster and finger-rolling the ball into the net.

For a moment Jack forgot he was at practice, the quick offensive burst a reminder of what he loved about the game, the flow, the challenge of the one-on-one confrontation, floating free above everyone and everything. Jack smiled and raced up the court to play defense.

SCREECH

"Henderson, save it for the highlight film," Scooter shouted. "We said three passes. I saw one. Hit the bleachers for ten up-and-downs. Jackson, take "Dr. J's" spot. Move it."

Jack shook his head.

"You heard Scooter," Collins said. "We say three passes, we mean three passes. Hit the bleachers."

Jack glared at Collins, who turned to talk to Jenkins.

"OK, let's go boys," Collins said, pivoting back to see Jack still there. "Something I can do for you, Henderson?"

"I made the shot. Three passes. Ten passes. That's bullshit, man. Why not just play the game? Take what it gives? Go with the flow."

"What if you missed, Jack? Anyone around to rebound besides Tompkins? Which team has the ball then, Jack? Where are you? Oh, that's right, at the far end of the court, out of bounds."

"I made the shot," Jack yelled.

"It's not smart basketball, Jack," Collins said, squaring up to Jack. "Not team basketball. It's one-on-one, streetball. And that's not the game winning *teams* play. I want to win, not see how many pretty plays you can make. The drill is three passes before a shot. Three passes. We're not looking for any shot. We're looking for the best."

Hands on hips, Jack thought of offering Collins the same middle finger salute he gave Dunham. Collins did not blink. The other boys and coaches stood silent. The sideline free throw shooting stopped. Even wrestling practice halted.

"Life's all about choices, Jack," Collins said. "You know our deal. What's it going to be?"

Gudy, standing behind Collins, jerked his head toward the bleachers.

"Goddamn points," Jack mumbled and trotted to the bleachers, hitting the first step with a bolt rattling thump.

Paint it Black

"Really a classic case, she is...uh—"

"Mary Lou, Doc..."

Sam and Mary Lou were sitting in Dr. Thaddeus Musselman's office two years earlier when the beefy, red faced psychiatrist diagnosed her paranoid schizophrenic.

"Yes, of course, Mary Lou," Musselman said from a cushioned leather chair perched behind a polished oak desk, "quite fascinating, from a clinical point-of-view, if you know what I mean."

"Sure, we get it, but can you help?" Sam said, sucking a Lucky.

"Well, there are drugs, like Haldol, the one we have her on now, and individual therapy sessions..."

"You're going to drug her, then talk to her? That works?"

"Well, Mr. Henderson, not exactly like that. It's more complicated. Cognitive behavioral therapy...uh, uh... than drugging and talking, as you put it...you see..."

Sam and Mary Lou stared across the shiny divide, in straight back hardwood chairs. Sam, legs crossed, squinting through the smoke, nodding. Mary Lou, hands in gray skirted lap, knees together, eyes darting from Sam to the doctor. Not speaking. Feeling like people who described near death experiences, soul hovering above, seeing all, but unable to engage in the human activity below as Dr. Musselman explained the progression of the "disease."

Mary Lou recalled the intent look on Sam's face as he tried to follow the doctor's lead, to get what he believed to be the best treatment. She empathized with Sam's struggle to reconcile the rational to the emotional, to accept her missing-in-action status, to not "take the illness, personally, Sam," as Dr. Musselman put it.

"I'm not taking the illness personally, Doc," Sam said, leaning forward, eyes meeting Musselman's. "No more than I did Kraut bullets. But the holes they tore into my buddies, I took that personal. I don't blame the illness, Doc. But I sure as hell blame it for what it's doin' to my wife, to our marriage, to our family. I damn sure take that personal. Let's cut the *clinical point of view* crap, Doc. Can you help *Mary Lou* or not?"

Musselman, face pale, nodded. "Yeah, Mr. Henderson, I think I can."

"Here's your tea, dear."

Grandma Henderson touched Mary Lou's shoulder.

Mary Lou flinched and the oak rocker creaked to a halt.

She had been home a week and began every morning with a hot cup of tea laced with honey and cream, settling into the padded rocker in front of the crackling fireplace, hair in a bun, face bereft of makeup.

"Thank you, Etta," she said, taking the steaming cup in trembling hands.

Mary Lou gazed out the front window where a November blanket of snow and ice made the dormant grass crunch under foot, the entire land frigid, the temperature never edging above freezing. A pang of guilt struck her at the sight of the lumps and bumps of dead flowers in her garden. She had neglected it the last few years, doing less and less each spring and summer until the wildflowers and weeds overwhelmed the colorful carpet of perennials, the sole nursery plants left, three bare rose bushes, their stakes like crucifixes.

"Farmer's Almanac says we're in for a long, cold winter," Etta said, tucking in the quilt that covered Mary Lou's legs.

Muted by the Haldol, but mind clearer than it had been in weeks, Mary Lou snuggled deep into the quilt, alternately drumming her fingers and sipping the tea, her emotions as flat as the Midwestern landscape.

Mary Lou stared into the flames, thinking of her father, Wally. There was a man who built a good fire. Always kept one going in the pot belly stove of his general store.

"Tell me about Wally. Wally Weller, right?" Musselman had said at a session, yellow legal pad propped in his lap.

"Yes…what do you want to know?" Mary Lou said, stretched out on a cushy leather couch, Musselman within her peripheral vision.

"Let's start with how you remember him? What's he look like in your mind?"

"Well, I guess when I think of him it's as a younger man. Black hair, clean shaven, cigarette dangling from his lip."

"What was he like?"

"Busy. Daddy was always busy. Always at the store. Owned a general mercantile a few blocks from our home. Seemed like he lived there. *Have to girls. Not really selllin' merchandise as much as I'm sellin' myself. No Wally, no sales.*"

"Hard worker, then?"

"I suppose."

Musselman shifted in his seat.

"A religious man?"

"Daddy?" Mary Lou said with a laugh. "Not any you'd recognize. He did believe in God, but more for practical reasons than from any kind of faith. *Sure as hell can't hurt*, he'd crack."

"Any one memory stand out?"

"I remember I always hugged *him*," Mary Lou said, folding and unfolding her hands. "I don't remember him ever hugging me or Momma or Sara. We always had to hug him."

Musselman's pen scratched the pad.

"Anything else? Any specific memories."

"Gosh, I don't know. It's been so many years."

"Try."

"Well, I guess the spring concert my senior year of high school. I was featured on piano. I remember stepping into the spotlight. The house lights were down, so I could not make anyone out, just heard the applause. I played exceptionally well. A Mozart waltz. When I finished and stood to take a bow, the lights came up. There, in the front row, clapping like crazy were Momma, Sara and my Aunt Thelma, Momma's sister. But no Daddy. He didn't make it."

"Why?"

"At the store. *No Wally, no sales.*"

Musselman cleared his throat.

"Any other memories?"

"I remember when he was dying," Mary Lou said, squirming on the couch. "He wasn't old, fifty-five. Just at the end of the war. I thought it odd, someone as busy as Daddy, dying just as the world was experiencing a rebirth. It was the cigarettes. Emphysema. The lack of oxygen affected his memory."

"Did you talk before he died?"

"Not really. I know he worried about me. Momma told me. He never understood my need to play music. Didn't understand what purpose it served. He only let me go to college because I received a scholarship. He wouldn't have paid for it...saw no reason."

"Anything else?"

"Yes," Mary Lou said, wiping a tear. "I remember one of the last times I saw him. He was sitting with Momma. I gave him a hug and a kiss and scampered away, off somewhere... But I remember as I reached the door hearing him say to Momma: *Who is that girl?*"

"How old were you when your father died?"

"Nineteen. Momma died six years later. Polio. Shriveled away in an iron lung."

"Mary Lou, it's noon. Why don't you have lunch in here with me?" Etta called from the kitchen.

The two women sat facing each other across the forest green table, Etta posture perfect, Mary Lou slumped. They ate grilled cheese sandwiches, tomato soup with Saltines and drank cold milk in silence. The *Paul Harvey Show* crackled from the AM radio on top of the fridge. The commodities report followed with that day's prices of corn and beans.

"Bumper crop," Etta said. "Low prices. What's a farmer to do?"

"Not farm," Mary Lou said.

Etta laughed. Mary Lou straightened up and loosed a weak grin.

"Amen, to that, Mary Lou. Amen, to that."

Finished, Etta cleared the table and Mary Lou, exhausted, retreated to the rocker and fell asleep.

A whoosh of cold air, the slam-bam of the back door, and the high-pitched voices of Becky and Maggie, home from school, rang through the house. The seven hours of their school day had slipped by like a single breath. The girls' cheeks were rosy and chilled as they kissed her. Their fresh auburn hair, their skin soothing to the touch, their inexplicable, naïve, and infectious happiness pulled Mary Lou out of the chair and into the kitchen.

"C'mon, Mom, let's bake with Grandma."

Maggie scaled the side of a long-legged stool and took charge.

"Chocolate chip, Mom. That's what I was thinking of all day in school. Warm, chocolate chip cookies right out of the oven."

"Hmph," Becky said. "That explains why you spend so much time in the corner of Mrs. Harper's room. Thinkin' 'bout cookies instead of your work."

"Tattletale. Miss Becky the goody-two-shoes of Washington Street School. You—"

"Maggie," Mary Lou said, "you've never been in trouble at school. Goodness gracious, what's gotten into you?"

Maggie bent her head to the floor, wringing her hands as Becky gaped at Mary Lou then Etta.

Etta knelt, opened a cupboard door, and hauled out two mixing bowls.

"Maggie, you and your mother can discuss your behavior when your Dad comes home. Becky, you take care of yourself and let your parents take care of Maggie."

"But they're not. They're not taking care of any—"

"That's enough now, Becky," Etta said, eyes lowered as she lifted an electric mixer from a cabinet. "Let's bake cookies."

Becky stomped on the floor, walked to the avocado green refrigerator, and got eggs, milk, and butter. Her sister's back turned, Maggie put her thumbs in her ears, waggled her fingers, and stuck out her tongue .

"Maggie," Etta said, "get down off your throne and get the wooden spoons out of the drawer."

Mary Lou wheeled around on the white linoleum, lost in her own kitchen.

"Here, dear," Etta said as she touched Mary Lou's elbow, handed over a bag of chocolate chips, and guided her to the counter. "You make these better than I do. I'll preheat the oven. If you don't mind, I think I'll have a cup of coffee and let you and the girls make cookies. Is that OK?"

"I'm not sure I remember…"

"You will, Mary Lou. All the batches of chocolate chip cookies you've baked? You could do it in your sleep."

"I feel as if I am. I don't know…"

"C'mon, Mom," Maggie said and tugged her away from Etta, who twisted a black knob on the oven to 350 degrees, poured a cup of coffee, and sat at the kitchen table with a *Good Housekeeping* magazine.

Butter, eggs, vanilla, flour, salt, brown sugar, sugar, and baking powder were arrayed on the tiled countertop. Mary Lou stared at the assortment, hands trembling as she reached for the stick of butter, picking at the edges of the wrapper, struggling to loosen the corners.

"Let me crack the eggs," Maggie said, scooting the stool up to the edge of the counter, balancing on skinny knees next to Mary Lou, tiny freckled hands steady, as she snatched an egg from the cardboard carton and rapped it on the beveled edge of the mixing bowl.

Mary Lou twitched at the sharp click.

"Look, Mom, clean break," Maggie said, eyes shining.

"Yes," Mary Lou said, forcing a smile, letting Maggie crack another egg while she added butter, brown sugar, white sugar and vanilla, then beat the mixture with a wooden spoon, gauging the increments more from instinct than memory. She looked across the counter where Becky poured the flour, salt, and baking powder, measuring before dumping them in a smaller bowl, sifting them together.

"Can I use the electric beaters to mix everything, Mom?" Becky asked.

"No, me, me!" Maggie shouted.

Mary Lou beat the eggs, butter, and vanilla, trying to remember how she had determined the portions a moment before, then, seeing the sugar and flour, her mind returned to her father's store and the shelves with kitchen staples. Wally used a long wooden stick with a short hook to retrieve items from the top—"Can a corn"—he hollered, five pound bags of flour and sugar toppling into his big, soft hands like a pop fly in baseball settling into an infielder's glove.

"Mom?" Becky said.

Mary Lou kept mixing.

"Maggie, you cracked the eggs," Etta said as she rose from the table and walked to the counter. "Let Becky mix, you can dump in the chocolate chips."

Mary Lou felt her father's touch on her elbow.

"See, you remember. I knew you would."

"Yes, of course, I remember," she said, pleased because her father never touched her. She turned to smile and welcome his approval, but Etta stood by her, not Wally. Mary Lou stopped mixing and gazed down at the bowl, lips pursed, eyes vacant.

"I think I'd like to go back… to the fire," she said.

"OK, Mommy," Maggie said. Still crouched on her knees, Maggie hugged Mary Lou about the neck and kissed her cheek, then busied herself with opening the chocolate chip bag. "We'll bring you cookies when they're baked."

Becky shook her head, seized the bowl from Mary Lou, dumped the contents into her own, plugged in the electric mixer and punched the button. "Yeah, thanks Mom," she shouted, beaters whirring.

Mary Lou averted Becky's gaze, stumbled back a step, and wiped her hands on a towel.

"Just for awhile, girls, just for awhile…I'll be back," Mary Lou said, then turned and scurried to the rocker, swirled the quilt over her shoulders, hands and legs shaking as she drummed her fingers on its solid oak arms, the twilight shadows of November creeping across the snow-covered lawn, the fire popping and snapping, thoughts once again drifting to the past, to her father—

"Hi, Mom."

Mary Lou jerked up to see Jack.

"Looks like your fire needs help." He snatched a couple of logs from the wood bin and set them on the smoldering embers.

"Oh my. I drifted off. What time is it?"

"'Round six o'clock. I just got home from basketball practice."

"Is your father home?"

"In the kitchen. He said I could come in and wake you. It's almost supper time."

"Where are the girls? Have they finished the cookies?"

"Yep, I grabbed a couple when I came in. Don't tell them, but they're good. Grandma must've helped."

"Actually, I did," Mary Lou said, straightening up. "Don't spoil your supper."

"You must be feeling better. You sound like a mom again."

"Again? I didn't realize I had stopped being a mom, Jack."

Jack frowned as he turned his back to Mary Lou, grabbed an iron poker and jabbed at the logs, poking and prodding them until flames flickered along the base of the stack then leapt to the top. He grabbed a few smaller pieces of kindling and propped them on end across the bigger logs. The hearth glowed.

Mary Lou stared at her son kneeling on the red brick. Taller than Wally, just as lean, hair not black but brown and just as thick and unruly. The muscles in his straight, broad back undulated beneath a red and black flannel shirt as he stirred the embers, the heat in the room rising as the flames brightened.

"I'm sorry, Jack."

"It's not your fault," Jack said into the fire. "You can't apologize for something you can't control. It just pisses me off, you know...the way things are."

Jack rose, placed the poker in its holder and sat down on the floor to the right of Mary Lou, his legs bent, forearms resting on bony knees, long, lean fingers dangling.

"Not bad, if I say so myself," he said examining the fire. "Better, huh?"

Mary Lou reached out, hand no longer trembling, and stroked her son's hair. The giggling voices of Maggie and Becky floated down from upstairs. She could hear Sam and Etta talking, Sam telling a story that made his mother laugh.

"Much better. You build a good fire, Jack. You build a good fire."

All in the Game

At the end of practice on the Wednesday before Thanksgiving, Collins gathered the team. He waved a program with team photos of the Hilltoppers, Centennial Chargers, University High Eagles, and the Plainview Huskers.

"As you know," Collins said, pacing in front of the boys, "the Plainview-St. Jude Intercity Round Robin tournament starts Friday. We drew Centennial for our opener. You've heard the preseason hype. How we're one of the top AA teams in the state. How the smaller schools in Class A, like Plainview and Uni-High don't stand a chance against us, how even AA Centennial, a bigger school than us, is outmanned."

Collins stopped and looked at the team.

"Don't believe it for a moment. We haven't made a basket. Haven't won a game. Haven't played in front of a crowd of 8,000 like you're going to see at Conklin Fieldhouse. We'll only see crowds like that again if we go deep into the state tourney. And let me tell you, we're a long way from that. Don't get me wrong. I absolutely believe we have the *potential* to be a championship team. But *potential* and actually taking care of business *aren't* the same thing. Ignore the pre-season hype from friends, family, fans, and the press, positive or negative. Just go out and play our game. Everything flows from that."

But word was out about the Rams coming on board at St. Jude. The sports editor of the St. Jude Harbinger, Art Carmody, a balding, leisure-suit-wearing lump of middle-aged WASPness, knew of the Rams success in the summer Y league. Upon learning they were playing for St. Jude, he titled his column on the morning of the opener "Running Rams Take the Hill" and mentioned that Jack had finished second to Hassan Jones in the MVP voting. It didn't matter that Jack and Gudy were the only Rams starting. Brewster, Connolly, and Jenkins completed the first five, with Cheyo and Jimmy the first off the bench, and P.K. getting minimal playing time.

At the pep rally that day students waved posters of rams butting heads or rams standing on a mountaintop with *Rams Take the Hill* in big, block letters. As Coach Collins called each varsity player's name, Jack and the rest of the Rams stepped out from the line the team formed at half-court and gave the raucous crowd a wave. Connolly's and Jenkins's glares burned against the back of his neck, but Jack did not return them.

"We thank you for your support," Collins shouted into the microphone, raising his voice above the din. "And we promise, win or lose, to represent St. Jude in a manner you can point to with pride. Because WE ARE..."

"HILLTOPPERS!" the students roared along with the players.

"We can't hear you down here. Come again? WE ARE..."

"HILLTOPPERS!"

"One more time. WE ARE..."

"HILLTOPPERS!"

The pep band broke into the St. Jude fight song as the crowd screamed "WE ARE...HILLTOPPERS." Sandy McCarty and a half-dozen short-skirted cheerleaders, decked out in the navy blue wool sweaters with the white *SJ* embroidered on the front, cartwheeled and back-flipped between the team and the crowd. White panties flashing as they spun, the girls pumped fists and clapped hands when they landed, Sandy giving Jimmy a smile as she did the splits. The entire gym echoed and shook with the chant *WE ARE... HILLTOPPERS* until the band stopped and Principal Locke dismissed the students.

A few hours later, as they put on uniforms and warm-ups in the university locker room, Jenkins tossed Carmody's article on the graffiti-carved pinewood bench separating his row of lockers from Jack's.

"Nice of you Rams to ride in and save us, Henderson."

Brewster, a few feet down the row, massive frame teetering on the narrow bench as he wedged huge feet into high-topped leather sneakers, loosed a booming laugh.

"Man, Jenks, you are consistent," Brewster said, shaking his Afro'd head and grinning. "I gotta give you that. When I saw that article this mornin' I thought, my man Randy ain't gonna like this. No sir. And sure enough, here we go."

"We didn't write the article, man," Jack said, chuckling along with Brewster, trying to blow it off, as he stuffed his street shoes into a battered, gunmetal locker.

"Kinda puts a target on us. Good motivation for Centennial. I'd prefer to fly in under the radar."

"I'm not so sure," said Jenkins. "I kinda think y'all like bein' saviors. Liked the signs in crowd this afternoon. Isn't Carmody a friend of your old man's?"

"My dad knows a lot of people. He's the mayor," Jack said, turning to face Jenkins as he slipped on his navy blue game jersey with the number forty-four, same as Sam's when he played for St. Jude. "Whattaya want me to do about that? He knows Carmody, and they're friendly, but it isn't for political reasons. Besides, Carmody ain't a real reporter. He's a sportswriter. Nobody cares what he thinks."

"Well, it ain't right," Jenkins said. He looked at Brewster. "And you know it, Brew. These guys getting all the ink and haven't played a minute of high school ball. Ain't right and ain't fair to the rest of the team."

"Look, I wasn't thrilled with the article," Jack said, glancing first at Jenkins then Brewster as players gathered around. "I know the Rams haven't done shit as far as high school ball goes. And I'm sorry your buddies didn't get their name in the paper because they got slid to the end of the bench. But the fact is we did beat you guys in the Y-league and a few of us are gonna get playin' time this year. You knew that when we came on board. What's it matter if it's in the paper? Besides, he called you the best point guard in the twin cities. Said Brew was a top prospect for a Division I scholarship. Why don't you accept the compliment and drop this shit. I mean, what the hell? What's the problem?"

"The problem is," Jenkins said, jabbing a finger across the foot-wide bench, "that we've been playin' ball for three years, coming to practice, riding the bench, working our ass off for senior year, for the payoff, to see how good we can be, and along come the Running Rams, bunch a beer-drinkin' smartass college prep boys stealing our chance, our turn, and screwin' everything up with their streetballin', don't-give-a-shit-about-nothin' attitude. So, we're asking ourselves, What's the point? What've the last three years been about? I mean, this is it for us. We ain't goin' anywhere after this year. We're going to work, not to college. This is it, man. Senior year. And you stole it from us."

"Yeah, well, life's a bitch, then we die," Jack said, the T-shirt philosophy ringing more true than he liked. He snatched his warm-ups from the bench, slammed the locker shut, and stalked to the door to the hallway, where he would wait until Collins called the team together before warm-ups.

"Screw you too, Jack," Jenkins shouted. "Screw you and the horse you rode in on!"

Jack stopped and turned around, fists clenched. Cheyo, Gudy, P.K., and Jimmy, dressing down the aisle, heard Jenkins shout and circled around behind

Jack. Connolly and the varsity players from the previous year joined Jenkins. The narrow aisle now filled by the entire team, with Brewster stuck in the middle.

"Don't do it, Jack," Brewster said, face as hard as mahogany. He rose from the bench and twisted his head toward Jenkins who took a few steps forward, his buddies following. "You too, Randy. All y'all. Stop it. You dudes really care about this team, this shit stops now. You and your buddies want to fight, wait 'til the end of the season. Then feel free to kick the shit out of each other. Don't matter to me. But until then, chill. Or I'll take care all you skinny white boys. You too, Jimmy, Cheyo. We got our first game coming up in an hour. Set this shit aside."

Water dripped like a ticking grandfather clock in the showers. Jack swallowed hard and strode out the door, the Rams clearing a path.

Two hours later, the Hilltoppers found themselves seven points down in the third quarter to Centennial. Carmody's article fired up the Chargers as much as it divided the Toppers. A contingent of Centennial fans took up the lower seats behind the two benches, cheering their team and jeering the Toppers with shouts of "WE ARE...HILL FLOPPERS!"

After a basket by the Chargers put St. Jude nine points down, Jack caught the inbound pass from Gudy along the right sideline and dribbled across half court where two defenders leapt forward, arms waving, legs spread, feet sliding, trying to trap him in the corner between the half court line and the sidelines. Jack hammered his dribble on the court and shouldered through the double team before the boys could get set, leaving a lone defender in the lane, stationed inside the free throw line. Jenkins, the point guard, sprinted parallel to Jack in the middle of the court, Connolly even with them on the left sideline. They had a three-on-one advantage.

"Jack," Jenkins hollered motioning for the ball.

Jack knew he should release the ball to the center of the court to Jenkins, who could then attack the single defender, forcing him to commit to the ball, Connolly, or Jack. In the split second it would take for the player to decide, Jenkins could take the ball to the hole or dish left or right.

But Jack did not give up the ball. Instead he juked to his left, then drove hard to the right, determined to sky over the defender and lay the ball in the basket. But the senior center for Centennial, Billy McGuire, a six foot five, red-headed jumping jack, quick as any guard, did not take the bait to the left and went airborne with Jack. Ball palmed in his right hand, arm pointing to the sky like the torch on the Statue of Liberty, Jack soared to the basket, certain he could finish with a flourish and silence the Centennial crowd.

Instead, he heard a swift torrent of sounds: *SMACK* as McGuire slapped away the shot. *THUD* as the leather ball struck the glass backboard. Followed by, *YEAH BABY, TAKE THAT JACK!* from the Centennial bench as McGuire caught the ball and fired it the other way, catching the Toppers out of position, creating a three-on-one break with the point guard dumping to a trailer on his left. Brewster, caught alone, fouled the shooter as the ball rolled through the hoop, creating an opportunity for a three-point play.

The score keeper buzzed as the boys lined up for the free throw, and Cheyo came in for Jack.

Collins said nothing as Jack passed him on his way to the bench.

TAP, TAP, TAP. Scooter's clipboard was tapping Jack's knee as Scooter crouched in front of him on the bench, showing the coach's touch and breaking the spell of humiliation of the last thirty seconds. "Can't do it by yourself, Jack," Scooter said. "Ball goes to the guard in the middle on the break—even if it's Jenkins. You hear me, Jack?"

"Yeah, I hear you, coach," Jack said, making eye contact with Scooter, fog clearing. "It won't happen again."

"You ain't gonna out talent a guy like McGuire. Now, keep your head up and in the game. You won't be on the bench long."

"Here you go, Jack." From behind the bench, Whitey draped a blue towel across Jack's shoulders then handed him a white paper cup of water.

"Thanks, Whitey," Jack said, and the Centennial crowd roared as the made free throw completed the three-point play and put the Chargers up by twelve.

Collins called timeout.

The boys on the bench gave up their spots to the five playing and stood behind a crouching Collins, forming a semicircle.

"OK, boys," Collins said, "we've dug ourselves a hole, but let's not panic. We're halfway through the third quarter. We have plenty of time. Remember your fundamentals, play smart. Move the ball on offense, move your feet on defense. Be quick, but don't hurry. We can win this game, but we need to get back to basics. Have to play as a team."

"Hear that Henderson?" Jenkins said.

"Davis," Collins said not batting an eye. "You're in for Jenkins. Tompkins, you're in for Brew. He has three fouls. Need to save him for the fourth quarter. "

"Coach, what the—" Jenkins began.

"Jenkins, one of the fundamentals is for you to listen to me. You don't speak. You listen. Leave the coaching to us. Anyone else have anything to say?"

The boys standing behind Collins looked down at the hardwood; the players on the bench drank water and toweled themselves dry.

"OK," Collins said. "Move the ball on offense, move your feet on defense, keep your head in the game, play as a team and we'll win. Let's go."

The boys closed the circle, joined hands in the middle and shouted, "Toppers!"

Scooter paced in front of the bench, chomping his gum and clapping his hands, chatting to everyone and no one before plopping down in his seat. Lane talked to Collins, glancing at Jack and Jenkins.

"Nice fast break, Henderson," Jenkins said. "Can't give up your streetball ways, can you?"

"I thought I could take him."

"Spoken like a true streetballer. Well *you* couldn't, but *we* could have. Three-on-one break, and we come up with nothin' because *you* thought *you* could. They take the ball, get a third foul on Brew, convert a three-pointer, and now we're down by twelve. All because of your hotdoggin', streetballin' bullshit. Great, just great."

"Let it go, Randy," Brewster said, wedging his big body between the two boys. "McGuire made a helluva play."

Jack dipped his head. McGuire did make a good play. But Jenkins was right, he should have passed.

Jack looked across to the opposite sideline where Sam, Mary Lou, Katy, Becky, Maggie, Grandma Henderson, and Roger sat. Katy had taken Becky under her wing, acting as a basketball mentor. While everyone else watched the action on the floor, eyes darting with the movement of the ball, bodies shifting as play raced from basket to basket, leaping to their feet at close calls or good moves, Mary Lou clapped in rigid rhythm, eyes flat, out of sync with the surging and shaking crowd. Jack's eyes met his mother's, and he waved. She stared past him. But Katy waved, then pointed at her green eyes, Jack, and the court.

Images of Katy from the varsity girls first home game flashed in Jack's mind. A coach on the court, she directed the other players from her point guard position, dribbling the ball and calling out plays. On the bench, the subs on the floor, Katy shouted out encouragement. Always on task, her mind and eyes never wandering like Jack's. Taking his cue from Katy, Jack returned his attention to the game.

With Jenkins, Brewster, and Jack on the bench, Centennial opened up a fifteen-point gap by the end of the third quarter. Collins put the three back in the game in the fourth and the Toppers made a run. Brewster and Jack scored six points apiece, Gudy and Jenkins adding four each and, along with Connolly, the Toppers played stifling defense, holding the Chargers to eight and whittling the lead to three. Then, with forty-five seconds to play, Jack drove the lane, tried to dish to a wide-open Gudy on the baseline, and threw the ball out of bounds. After that, all they could do was foul the Chargers and hope for missed free throws. But the Centennial players, focused on upsetting St. Jude, did not choke at the line, converting all their one-and-one opportunities. Final score: Centennial 56, St. Jude 53.

"**Toppers Knocked Off Hill**" screamed Carmody's headline the next day. Collins made copies and posted them on each player's locker. They responded by beating University High that night, Jack and Brewster combining for thirty-one points and twenty-one rebounds against the outmanned Eagles. Then they lost to Plainview the following evening. The Hilltoppers, the team that reporters like Carmody and other sportswriters had predicted might go undefeated during the regular season and make the Elite Eight come tournament time, were off to a 1 – 2 start.

Straight From the Heart

The Toppers next game was the Saturday following Thanksgiving weekend, and Collins's response to the two losses was predictable. The two-a-day practices that had ended with the beginning of the season started again, the boys at the Wreck by 5:30 a.m., then back after school. The emphasis on offense, passing and shooting, and Scooter's defensive drills, made for a less tiring week than a week of solid sprints, but they did not neglect conditioning. Collins ended practice with washboards and handed out bleacher runs to every player who missed a free throw, threw a bad pass, loafed on defense, or failed to follow orders.

The hard work paid off as the Toppers won three of four games before Christmas break. Defeating McKinney, Allen, Longboro, and losing by two to Valley View, bumping their record up to 4-3 and earning release from two-a-days after the second win. While the team played well, Jack was not the dominant force predicted. The intensity of play, chest-bumping defenses, floor-burning dives for loose balls, and sprints to fill the lanes on fast breaks, made for a sharp contrast to playground or Y ball. The game moved quicker than Jack could respond. He rushed shots, felt smothered by double teams or match-up zones or full court presses, things he never encountered in streetball. Although averaging fourteen points, six rebounds, and three assists per game, Jack shot less than forty percent from the field and turned the ball over a couple times as well. Calls for illegal picks, blocking, and basket interference were mental lapses as much as physical errors. Mechanical and stilted on offense, his mind labored to read the defense and execute the screening, back cutting, and passing that kept the motion offense in sync. Jack did not recognize and react, negating the subconscious stream to muscles and nerves which converted thought to action, the free flowing form that defined him at the Y or on the open-air asphalt courts of the street. But he rebounded well, played good defense, shutting down his man and picking a couple of steals each game. With no thought but to stay with his man, Jack's natural athleticism emerged on defense as he prowled the half court like a caged cougar, quick to counter any moves with sudden leaps and bounds, blocking shots, taking charges, disrupting opponents' offensive rhythm. His defense kept him in the starting lineup.

As for offense, everyone from Sam to coaches to teammates to Whitey to a freshman girl in PE class offered advice:

"Drive to the hole… shoot from the perimeter… pass first… shoot first… let the game come to you… call for the ball more… be more aggressive…don't press…" on and on until he had so many thoughts they paralyzed his body.

On Christmas morning Jack sat reading the sports page at the kitchen table while Mary Lou cleaned the breakfast dishes. Thanks to the twice-a-week therapy sessions with Dr. Musselman and the gradual reduction of the Haldol, Mary Lou no longer drooled or sat for hours in front of the fire. Grandma Henderson did not "visit" every day. Mary Lou was once again washing, cooking, cleaning house, helping the girls with homework, and playing the piano. When she skipped a beat, brown eyes blank in the midst of a conversation, she recovered in a downbeat with a "Now I remember…" But home was not the only place Jack saw a difference. When he took a breather on the bench during games, Jack noticed Mary Lou involved in the action, firing on all cylinders.

Jack liked the whole-note pace of Christmas day, as if one minute equaled two. The house overflowed with a smorgasbord of aromas, a basting turkey, baked apple and pumpkin pies, percolating coffee, the lingering scent of a breakfast of scrambled eggs, bacon, and butter-soaked biscuits. The mixture of fragrances floating in the warm home, while outside, snow skittered across the ground, blown by a raw, northern wind under a weak December sun. Jack settled into a padded chair and spread the paper in front of him, sipping hot tea, content to be.

"See your name in the paper again?" Mary Lou teased as she sat down across from him. "Enjoy being famous, do we?"

"Infamous, actually," Jack said, looking up. "The sportswriters use kid gloves with high school jocks, but if you read between the lines, they let people know we're not playing as well as we could. And they know it's because I'm not livin' up to my rep. Not scoring like I should. My own teammates are giving me a hard time. Fans, too. I heard a guy sitting behind the bench say I was overrated, 'big time.' Makes me wonder how many people are sayin' the same thing. Especially after I miss a shot or commit a turnover. Seems like I can't get into the flow of the game, relax, and just play, 'cause I'm worried about screwin' up, worried about what people are sayin'. Heck, the paper isn't even picking us to get to the finals at the Rail Splitter Tournament at Murpheesboro this week. And we were preseason picks to go to state…"

"Is Art Carmody saying you're overrated?"

"How'd you know?"

"Art's always been better watching from the sidelines than playing. I remember him from high school. Nice boy, but he was no great athlete. Certainly not as good as you or your father."

Jack grinned and folded the paper closed.

"Take it easy, Mom," Jack said, eyes dancing as they met his mother's, pleased she rose to his defense, but more so Sam's. "No need to go to war. He isn't naming names. Just making references to our inability to score like the preseason buzz said we would. 'Team and some players not living up to expectations.' That type of stuff. Nothin' personal."

"If you can read between the lines, so can everyone else. Artsy Fartsy. What does he know?"

"Mother, what did you call him?"

"Artsy Fartsy?" Mary Lou smiled and waved her hand. "I shouldn't have said that. Don't repeat it. That's what we used to call Art in high school when he got annoying. Art had the ability to annoy. Looks like he hasn't lost it. Anyway, it's early in the season. You'll play better. The team will play better. Give it time."

"We don't have time, though. That's the problem. We're a quarter of the way through and we're one game above five hundred. Lot of people thought we'd go undefeated and we've lost three games. That we'd be one of the top teams in the state. We're nowhere close. And a lot of it is my fault. I'm not playing as well I should be. Or maybe I'm not as good as I thought."

"Well, I don't know a lot about basketball," Mary Lou said, holding a warm mug, "but I think you're playing just fine for your first year of varsity."

"'First year of varsity,' Mom?"

"Well, honey, oh, I don't know, it seems to me… Oh, never mind. What do I know about basketball? That's your father's area of expertise."

"No, Mom," Jack said, semi-serious, semi-patronizing, not wanting to upset her, yet thinking how bad he must be playing if she noticed. Mary Lou came to life when her son touched the ball, but was more attuned to the pep band playing the school fight song, Chicago's "25 or 6 to 4," or "Sweet Georgia Brown" during timeouts.

"It's OK, Mom, say what you got to say. God knows everybody else is."

Mary Lou traced the rim of the cup with her fingertips.

"Well, let me put it this way. I remember, at Smith, me, a small town girl from the Midwest, the daughter of a secondhand-store owner, feeling like a secondhand girl in the midst of these bright, beautiful, wealthy girls from prominent families. I felt out of place, not worthy, I guess, and it made me nervous, out of kilter. No matter how hard I tried...it's hard for me to explain..."

"No, go ahead, Mom," Jack said, leaning forward. "I know where you're coming from."

"Anyway, as a music major, I had to give several recitals as a freshman. Performance was a big part of the program. But I didn't do well. I knew the music. Played well in practice, let the music flow, but then I'd start thinking about the performance, sorority sisters, professors, the audience of prominent families, my parents—even though they weren't present I wanted to do my best for them— trying so hard to get it right that by the time I stepped on stage I was a nervous wreck. Couldn't bring myself to relax and play. It was horrible. I was angry and embarrassed and frustrated, which, of course, made things worse. It got to the point where I thought of quitting, talked to my parents about it when I came home at Christmas. It was so humiliating."

Mary Lou shook her head at the memory.

"But you didn't. Why not? What happened?"

"Your father. Your father happened."

"What do you mean? You dated Dad in high school, right? Didn't he join the service when you went to college?"

"He did, but he wasn't scheduled for induction until the spring. And he knew from my letters and from Christmas that I was struggling, not doing well at my recitals, having trouble fitting in. So he hitchhiked out to see me before he went into the service. Pick up my spirits. Hitchhiked all the way from St. Jude, money in his shoes, change of clothes rolled up in his canvas Boy Scout backpack.

"He was a sight when he arrived at my house on campus," Mary Lou said, smiling. "Looked like a hobo—a fresh-faced hobo but a hobo nonetheless— clothes wrinkled, muddy boots dripping on the carpet, red hair a mess. I can see him standing in the foyer as I came to the top of the long stair case. He looked like a boy who'd run away from home. I felt sorry for him and, God forgive me, embarrassed, worrying what the girls would think of such a mess of a boy calling on me, but also thrilled that he'd come all the way from St. Jude. I knew he had hardly any money. Knew what a sacrifice it was to travel such a long way to see me, yet I was so concerned about what those girls thought, how they'd judge him as a hayseed, like me…

"Oh well, let's say it wasn't my best moment. But before I could go down-stairs and shoo him away to a boarding house to get cleaned up, some girls and our housemother, Wilhelmina Schneider, came into the foyer. You could see their noses rise when they spotted him, the girls scrunching together, Mrs. Schneider stopping at the sight of your father then approaching imperiously. And all I could think was, 'I'm through.'"

"What happened?" Jack said, trying to picture his father at eighteen, dirty and broke, being approached by a pack of snooty preps. "Dad put 'em in their place? Tell 'em they weren't any better than him and he had a right to be there? Or did they get the best of him, too, like they did you?"

"No, no, neither. Your father was not defensive or aggressive. He was himself. His Midwestern, small town, Eagle Scout, polite, confident self. Sam walked right up to Mrs. Schneider and that gaggle of girls, introduced himself, said he wanted to see me, told them I 'was his girl,' complimented them on what a beautiful house and what an attractive group of women resided in it. Then he said how he admired anyone who attended college, and those fine people, like Mrs. Schneider, who looked after other folks children like they were their own, and what a fine thing that was, and, boy, if this was what he was going off to war to fight for, well, by golly, that was alright by him because young girls and a fine woman like Mrs. Schneider and this wonderful college were worth fighting for. 'Yes ma'am,' he told Mrs. Schneider. 'It's my honor. It certainly is.'"

"You're kidding?" Jack said as they laughed. "I didn't realize Dad could lay it on that thick when he was my age."

"He's always had the gift of gab. But not insincere. Your father really does like people and it comes across, even when he's laying it on thick. So, of course, they fell for him like he was Frank Sinatra. Talking and giggling, offering food, something to drink, and Mrs. Schneider ordered one of the girls to come get me— I'd started walking down the steps at that point—and she called out, 'Mary Lou, why didn't you ever tell us what a fine young man you're seeing? Come along, dear, don't keep Sam waiting.' And your father turned and walked to the bottom of the staircase to meet me, taking my hand at the last step, giving me an oh-so-respectable peck on the cheek, and he whispered, 'Now you see how to do it, Mary Lou? You just got to play the game. We're as good as any of 'em, Mary Lou. Any of 'em. Just play the game. Play the game.'"

"And then I linked his dirty shirt-sleeved arm with mine, and by the time we walked the half-dozen steps to Mrs. Schneider and the girls, things changed. I could see it in their eyes. They saw me differently than they had a few minutes before. Your father made them see a value in me they'd refused to recognize before. And he'd showed me it did no good to be a meek, mild, self-conscious wallflower apologizing for doing nothing more than being. For worrying about everything. Because I, Mary Lou Weller, was as good as any of them."

"And so your next recital…"

"That night, your father in the front row, spiffed up, escorting Mrs. Schneider with a slew of sorority girls surrounding him… And I played as well as I've ever played. Went on stage not thinking about anything but the music—and your father, of course."

"So, because Dad made you popular, you played well? How does that apply to me playing better basketball?"

"No, Jack, no," Mary Lou said, warm hands on his. "Your father didn't make me the most popular girl on campus. I still had problems with different girls from time to time. But he made me realize it wasn't because of me, that nothing was wrong with me. I was letting people convince me there was and accepting it as if it were true. Living up to their expectations instead of my own. Allowing them to categorize me, label me. Of course it affected my ability to play. Like what Carmody, your teammates, and the fans are doing to you right now. You're so worried about pleasing everyone, living up to expectations that you're not able to relax and just play. It isn't about being popular, Jack, or perfect. It's about being true to you. Your Dad didn't restore my standing among stuck-up college girls. He didn't make me a better musician. He helped me restore my faith in me. And once that happened, I was able to allow my true self to emerge. To play and sing from my soul, to be in the moment like, well… Like Elvis, if that helps. Or Julius Erving."

"Elvis? Dr. J? I didn't realize you were a fan."

"Oh, don't be a smart alec; you know Elvis is not one of my favorites and I've only seen Julius Erving on the six o'clock sports. But I do appreciate one thing about both. Their ability to be in the moment. 'Aesthetic perception as a mode of transcendence' Schopenhauer called it. Best achieved through music, he thought, but attainable in other ways, I think."

"Say what, say who?"

"It's from a philosophy class I took in college. Schopenhauer was a nineteenth century philosopher who thought the ability to live in the moment, achieve transcendence from our self-consciousness, was best achieved through the arts—writing, painting, sculpture, music. But we can only do it for short periods of time. Some folks not at all, although they can experience it through others—say, listening to Beethoven and immersing yourself in the music to the exclusion of the outside world. Time stands still. You're in the moment and have 'achieved transcendence through aesthetic perception.' At least that's how I remember Schopenhauer. Make sense?"

"Yeah, kind of. The way folks lose themselves in a song, I get that. Sure."

"Makes sense to me, too. But I think there's a physical means of achieving transcendence, not just intellectual. I think athletes do it all the time. Not for entire games, but at certain moments. Like Julius Erving when he dunks a basketball. I doubt there's a trace of self-consciousness in his mind. He's in the moment. Transcendent."

"That's deep stuff, Mom."

"Jack, what do you think separates Elvis? I mean there's hundreds of professional singers with voices as good if not better? So why's he special? What makes him connect with people?"

"I don't know... the Colonel, the hip shaking, a white guy singing black songs, stuff like that."

"In part, but what I think separates the true artist from skilled practitioner, Elvis from the typical professional singer, is the ability to sing from the heart. To be in the moment. To set aside worries about hitting the note and sing. Just sing. Elvis just sang."

"I suppose the drugs and the booze didn't hurt," Jack said with a laugh. "Loosened him up. Like they did for Judy Garland, Jim Morrison, Jimi Hendrix—"

"That's not funny," Mary Lou snapped, squeezing his hands. "Drugs and booze smother the soul. People succeed in spite of them, not because. But even they weren't talented enough to overcome the drugs in the long run. The drugs destroyed them."

They looked at one another.

"Mom...is that why you stop taking the drugs Dr. Musselman prescribes...'cause you think they're smothering you?"

"Maybe," Mary Lou said, ducking her head, withdrawing her hands and cupping them around the mug. "I don't know why I do what I do..."

"Well," Jack said, regretting the question, worried he had rattled her fragile psyche, "I'm glad it worked out for you at college. I dig what you're sayin' 'bout Elvis, Dr. J. But how'm I gonna get there? Who's gonna restore my faith in my game so I can just play... I mean play in a high school game like I do in a streetball game? Hit the note, the shot, without thinking. Who's gonna do that?"

"You are, Jack," Mary Lou said, perking up, "with help from Coach Collins."

"Collins?" Jack laughed and pushed his chair back. "Mom, I've been with you all the way up 'till now. But you don't know Coach Collins. I don't think he's sold on me right now."

"Really? Then you need to think harder, Jack. You do understand that a lot of people think the reason you didn't get expelled was because of your father being mayor and pressuring Mr. Locke?"

Jack bit his lower lip.

"But they don't know your father. Don't know he'd never do that. That he holds you accountable for your behavior, good or bad. Those people weren't sitting in that room when Coach Collins said he'd let you stay in school if you'd play ball… Follow the rules… play the game, Jack. Seems to me Coach Collins took a big risk for a boy he didn't know all that well. And from what I've heard about Coach Collins, I don't think he did it solely because you're a great basketball player, but because he saw basketball as a way out for you. Like it might've been for him. I think he did it because he saw an opportunity to help, to give somebody faith in themselves that they didn't have or weren't getting from…"

Mary Lou dabbed her eyes.

"Look at me," she said, standing up, wiping her hands in the white apron Becky sewed for her in Home Economics, "I Love Mom" emblazoned in pink across the chest. "Turning our talk into a lecture. Taking a conversation about you and turning it into one about myself. Isn't that like me these days? With a mother like me, John Walter Henderson, I know there's a place in heaven for you. For goodness sakes."

Jack looked at his mother, thinking he should correct her, hug her, let her know the talk had been good, had not been all about her, had helped, but instead he slouched in the chair, averting his eyes, embarrassed by his mother's embarrassment.

A laughing Sam bounded into the kitchen, a Barbie doll toting Maggie on his shoulders. Upon seeing Jack and Mary Lou, Sam's smile slipped away.

"I'm sorry…didn't mean to interrupt. Everything OK?"

"Yeah, Dad," Jack said sitting up straight. "Actually, yeah…I think so. Mom gave me a little advice about basketball. I think she might've helped me with a few things."

"Really? Well… that's good," Sam said, Maggie squirming on his shoulders.

"Yeah, she told me to remember I was as good as anyone else and to just 'play the game.'"

Mary Lou smiled at Sam, the sheepish college girl he helped save from herself. If only he could do so now, Jack thought.

"Sounds like a helluva good piece of advice," Sam said with a wink at Mary Lou as he tickled Maggie. "What do you think, Mags?"

"I think every day should be Christmas."

Moon Dance

The week between Christmas and New Year's the arctic air that had enveloped the Midwest since Thanksgiving broke for a few days. The warm weather melted the snow and ice, tricked the brown, dormant grass into a light shade of green. The winter sun shone in the cloudless blue sky, drying roofs, driveways, and streets. People backed grimy cars out of garages, attached rubber hoses to outdoor spigots, filled plastic buckets with soap and water, and washed away a month's worth of salt and stains. Kids broke out Christmas gift bicycles, balls, Frisbees, roller skates, skateboards, and ran rampant across the neighborhood, mothers thanking God for placing the cabin-fever-breaking-respite in the middle of the two-week Christmas vacation. Sam, Jack, Becky and Katy took advantage of the false spring to play eighteen muddy holes of golf at the public course, slipping and sliding with each swing, cleaning clay-caked metal spikes on the shoe brushes at the tee boxes, splattering sweatshirts and jeans with muck. Jack and Becky giggling when Mary Lou stopped them at the back door, making them strip to t-shirts and shorts, Sam included, before shooing them off to the showers.

New Year's Eve night arrived clear and bright, a silver moon surrounded by sapphire stars shining down upon Plainview-St. Jude. Mary Lou and Sam were off to the country club for dinner and dancing, Sam trim and slim in a charcoal-and-gray-checked blazer, white shirt, burnt gold tie, and black slacks, Mary Lou in a burgundy dress and heels, pearls dangling from slim, pale neck, hair soft on her shoulders, brown eyes shimmering as she descended the staircase, pausing for a moment on the last step, Sam, Etta, and the kids awaiting her entrance as if she were a queen.

"Hubba, hubba," Sam said as Becky and Maggie rushed forward to hug Mary Lou.

"I'm constantly amazed she married your father," Etta said, standing with an arm around Jack.

"Why Mother," Sam said, spinning and flinging his arms wide, "you don't think I'm dashing and handsome?"

Everyone laughed.

"Dashing, perhaps," Etta said. "But Robert Redford is handsome. Jack is handsome."

"True enough, Mom, true enough," Sam said with a wink and a grin Jack's way. "It must've been my gift of gab that wooed Mary Lou. Now, if the peanut gallery doesn't mind, and in spite of some opinions as to my worthiness, I'd like to take my wife out for an evening of dinner, drinks, and a tripping of the light fantastic."

"Oh Gawd, Dad," Becky said.

"I think it's nice," Maggie said.

"Madame," Sam said with a slight bow, "may I have the honor?"

Sam strode forward and extended a hand to Mary Lou, still standing on the steps. The girls, clinging to their mother, turned and looked up at Sam.

"What do you think, girls? Is he worthy of my company?"

"YEEAAAAAHHHHH."

"Very well then, sir, you may be my escort," Mary Lou said, grasping Sam's hand.

"YEAAAAAAAAAHH," the girls screamed again as Etta and Jack clapped.

"Jack," Sam said as he draped a mink stole around Mary Lou's shoulders. "What's your plan for tonight?"

"P.K. and I are goin' to Cheyo's. Hang out with the Rams. Cheyo's parents just got cable and a VCR. Gonna watch *Dirty Harry*, I think."

"You guys take it easy and be home by 1:00. Don't worry your grandmother. We should be right behind you."

"Happy New Year," Mary Lou said as she gave the girls a hug and Jack and Etta a peck on the cheek. "We'll see you in the morning."

"Speak of the devil," Sam said as he opened the door to find P.K. preparing to enter, his hand on the outer doorknob.

"Hi, Mr. Henderson, Mrs. Henderson."

"Come on in P.K.," Sam said as he and Mary Lou slipped past. "Jack, you guys take it easy now."

"Got it, Dad. Happy New Year, already. C'mon in P.K. I'll be ready in a sec."

Etta and the girls retreated to the TV room as Jack grabbed a jacket and slipped into a pair of low cut black Converse tennis shoes.

"Man, Jack. How old is your mom?"

"P.K., man, cool it. For Chrissakes. She's in her fifties. Been married for thirty years. You're givin' me the creeps."

"I'm just sayin'..."

"Well don't. Jeezus, we gotta get you a girl."

"Look who's talkin'. When's the last time you had a date?"

"Point taken," Jack said, rising and laughing. "Between practice, games and school we're livin' like monks. Maybe that's part of Collins's punishment."

"What about Kate?" P.K. said, poking Jack in the ribs. "As much as you hang with her, it's like you're datin' already."

"Katy? We're just friends."

"So you say."

"P.K., man," Jack said, color rising. "Give it a rest. Date my mom, already. But stop the matchmaking. C'mon, let's drink some beer."

The boys plunged into the night, cutting across the unfenced backyards of the subdivision, zigzagging towards Cheyo's a few blocks away. They approached the two-story brick house from the rear and saw people moving about in the kitchen and heard Bob Seeger's "Night Moves" blasting from the stereo. They knocked on the door and opened it in one motion, like the small town kids they were, the notion of walking into anything unexpected or not for public viewing never occurring to them. They expected to see the Rams settled around the TV, sipping brews.

Instead, a blitzed Cheyo, two-day beard blackening his coffee-colored face, greeted them. Behind him, stood a halfway gone Billy McGuire, the Centennial player who blocked Jack's shot during the Twin City tourney opener. Thirty-odd kids milled around the kitchen and spilled into the den, dining room, and living room. Jack paused when he spotted Katy. She was with girlfriends and they were dressed for a night out. It was the first time Jack remembered seeing Katy in anything other than jeans or workout clothes. Wearing light makeup and a form fitting black dress with heels, this was not the girl he played golf with earlier.

Katy returned Jack's stare with a smile.

"Holy crap," P.K. said, slapping Jack on the back, not noticing Katy. "Looks like word's out Cheyo's parents are in the Caribbean."

"Cheyo probably cranked a few brews and started calling people," Jack said, turning away from Katy. "You know how he gets. Party hearty. Hope the neighbors are out partying themselves, though."

"Jack Henderson, my man," the lanky McGuire shouted from across the kitchen where he and Cheyo poured beer from a keg. "You and P.K. staying or leaving? You want a cold one or not?"

Jack and P.K. exchanged a knowing glance, both thinking about Sam telling them to take it easy.

"What the hell," P.K. said to Jack, "we can always run home if the cops show."

"Is that a trick question?" Jack shouted at McGuire. "Get us a beer, you drunken Irishman."

Jack and P.K. high-fived a few guys from St. Jude, back-slapped a couple of Billy's friends, who they knew from playing pickup games at the Y, and slipped through the crowd to the keg. Jack, Billy, Cheyo, and P.K. exchanged soul shakes and smiles.

"Billy," Jack said after they all had a brew in hand, "how'd you south side Irish Catholics sneak into a respectable Protestant neighborhood? They only let my Catholic ass settle here 'cause my dad's the mayor. What's the deal? Plainview cops get tired of your green piss on the sidewalks and run you out?"

"That they did, Jack me boy," Billy said affecting a drunken brogue, "'tis a sad state of affairs indeed, considerin' one of 'ems me uncle."

The boys exchanged laughs and high fives.

Seeger sang, and Cheyo and P.K. bolted to the den to crank up the stereo, leaving Jack alone with Billy.

"My man, Jack Henderson," Billy said, white foam fizzing on his upper lip. "Jeezus, you played a helluva game against Blooming Grove. Go-Go Jones looked like he was gonna shoot you after you hit that buzzer-beater. Holy Moses. Way to go. I can't stand that Blooming Grove bro. Can't stand 'im. I mean what the hell kinda name is 'Ass-on.' No wonder he wants everyone to call him Go-Go."

Billy was talking about the Rail Splitter Classic Tournament that St. Jude, Centennial and fourteen schools from across the state had played in the week after Christmas. St. Jude surprised everyone, and themselves, by winning the title. Jack played his best ball of the season. Taking Mary Lou's words to heart he tuned out the fans in the stands, the critics in the papers, the well-meaning advice givers, listened to the coaches, and let the game come to him, trusting his instincts, taking the shot when he had it, passing off when he did not, and hustling his ass off on defense. Sixteen of his seventy-two points over the four games came off steals converted to lay-ups or dunks and he ended up being named to the all-tourney team along with Brewster. But as well as Jack played, Hassan "Go-Go" Jones was the best player hands down. And despite St. Jude upsetting Blooming Grove, Jones was tournament MVP.

When Jack sat on the bench and Go-Go ran the floor, Jack watched him. Jones' skin stretched thin and taut over sleek, sinewy muscles, blue veins pulsing, head topped by a wild and high-right-Jimi-Hendrix-in-'69 Afro. Jones could play center, skying to out-rebound any seven-footer; forward, taking it to the hole and dunking with either hand; or guard, with more assists per game than most point guards. He scored from anywhere on the court and loved to pose for a split-second after draining a long range jumper, right arm extended at a forty-five degree angle from his shoulder, hand limp after the follow-through like a swan dipping its head, bouncing on the balls of his feet as he nodded a goateed chin to the hoop like a believer bowing to the altar, a "never any doubt" look on his lean face. Go-Go Jones was the best player in the state and Jack knew he pissed him off by sinking that shot, placing a giant target on Jack that Jones would zero in on if the two teams met again.

"Yeah, I'm not too sure what Go-Go thinks of me. But I gotta tell you, Billy, Blooming Grove bro or no, the guy's the best damn ballplayer I ever played against. The dude can flat out play."

"Arrogant punk, if you ask me. Posing like a statue after hitting a jumper. What the hell is that?"

"Well, like my old man says, it ain't braggin' if you can do it."

"Well, hell, if we were nineteen like Go-Go and playing against sixteen year-olds, we could do it too."

"It don't hurt, that's for sure. But man, Go-Go's been playing varsity since his sophomore year, so he'd a been sixteen goin' against seniors, and he was All-State then. You gotta give credit where credit is due, Billy."

"Not to a criminal I don't. You know he spent weekends in jail last summer for a burglary rap, don't you?"

"I've heard a lot of things about Go-Go. Heard he got a girl knocked up and she moved to Detroit to have the baby. Heard he was Bob Marley-lovin' pot head. Heard all sorts of shit. But that don't make any of it true. Hell, I played against him last summer down at the Y in Blooming Grove *on a Saturday*. How'd he manage that if he was in the county jail?"

"All I know is what I know," Billy said, voice rising, before he chugged his beer, smacked his lips and poured one more. The phrase made Jack think of Mary Lou's conspiracy theories. "And what I see. You remember the name of his Y-team. Black Man in America. Picture of that Black Muslim, white-hatin' Elijah Mohammed on the front. I'm tellin' ya, the guy's gotta chip on his shoulder the size of Mount Rushmore. Heard they threatened to kick him off the team 'cause he said he wasn't gonna stand for the national anthem before games. I mean, c'mon Jack, what is that shit?"

"I don't know, Billy, I don't know," Jack said, lowering his voice in hopes of Billy lowering his, looking for an escape from a conversation that had taken a turn he did not anticipate. A couple of black kids from St. Jude stood in the doorway between the kitchen and the den, and their heads jerked around at the mention of Elijah Mohammed. Jack did not know them, only that they were underclassman, so he did not expect any trouble, but Billy was loud, and booze flowed.

"Well, *I* know," Billy said. "Shoulda kicked the black bastard off the team just for makin' the threat. Go back to Africa, or East St. Louis, if you don't like it. That's what I say. Hey, Jack. You know what the definition of confusion is, don't you? Father's Day in East St. Louis." Billy's laugh boomed. He slammed his beer and refilled the cup. Jack watched the black kids talking and staring at Billy.

"Yeah, I've heard that one," Jack said not smiling. "But be cool. I know you're kiddin' around. But not everybody here knows that."

Billy glanced at the black kids.

"Sorry bros," Billy said lifting his beer and smiling. "Let me buy you one."

One of the black kids waved a hand, shook his head, and they walked into the den.

"Man, try to be nice to some people," Billy said.

"Hey, Big Mac, you can fill me up," one of Billy's buddies hollered. As Billy turned, Jack slipped away.

Peering into the living room, Jack saw Sandy McCarty clinging to Jimmy, while her running buddy Cindy Wilson, a brown-haired, brown-eyed girl with a raucous laugh and a taste for beer equal to the guys, chatted with Luke, the two scrunched together on a cooler. Gudy was the only Ram missing, forced to babysit his little sister. Katy was not in the room.

"Hey Jack," Jimmy shouted. "What's shakin', man?"

Jack slid past the two black kids from St. Jude, thinking he should say something but not knowing what. He felt their accusing eyes as he soul-shaked with Jimmy.

What the hell, Jack thought, as Jimmy started to ramble on about seeing *Blazing Saddles* the night before. He was not Billy McGuire's keeper or the world's conscience. Those black kids have a problem with Billy they can take it up with him. Same goes for Go-Go Jones. Jack did not have any issues with the guy, McGuire did. Now, if Jimmy had been standing there, Jack would have said something. Or if McGuire had said shit about Jimmy. But that was different. Jimmy was one of Jack's best friends. Still, he couldn't shake the look in the black kids' eyes.

Family Tradition

Jack and P.K. strained to hit the last high note of another Hank Williams, Jr. song. Kids applauded, booed, and hollered for different music.

"Sorry, my redneck friends," Jimmy said. "The people have spoken. You guys'll need to go outside if you want to sing any more country. It's almost midnight. Time to crank up the Earth, Wind and Fire for the chicks."

"Hey, man, who put you in charge," P.K. said. "Where's Cheyo?"

"Last I heard, passed out in his bedroom. And since I'm the ranking minority in the house, I'm now the unofficial host. Enough with the redneck review."

"Man," Jack said, "just when I thought we'd whitened you up a shade. C'mon, Jimmy, you can admit it. We won't tell the brothers. You dig Hank Jr., Johnny Cash, Waylon and Willie. You know you do."

Jimmy laughed as he slapped a cassette into the player.

"Jack," Jimmy said. "Why don't you and P.K. join Cheyo? After that performance, ain't no girl here gonna kiss your drunk ass at midnight anyways."

Jack looked around the room. Jimmy had a point. The good-looking girls were taken, and he wasn't drunk enough to kiss any of the rest. "P.K.," he said. "Time to hit the roof."

"Cool," P.K. raised his cup. "Perfect night for it."

They flipped the lid on Luke's cooler, grabbed more beers and walked into the foyer.

Katy stood at the front door as she and her girlfriends prepared to leave.

"Hey, Katy," Jack said, as P.K. raced up stairs. "Where you been? Haven't seen you since I walked in."

"In the den," Katy said, breaking away from the group. "Watching Dick Clark and Times Square. Heard you singing, thought you might take a break and wander in."

Katy flashed a weak grin, wrapping herself in a shawl.

"I'm sorry," Jack said, sidling over to her. "Got into my beer."

"*News flash,*" Katy said, fingers forming invisible quotation marks.

Jack draped an arm over Katy's shoulders.

"You sure look nice, Katy."

"You sure are buzzed, Jack."

"Ah, Kate, gimme a break."

"Happy New Year, Jack," Katy said, sliding out from under his arm and retreating toward the girls.

"What, no midnight kiss, Katy?" Jack said, smiling, arms open wide.

Katy's green eyes sparked and her jaw tightened.

"Let's go, Katy," one of the girls said. "He's drunk."

Katy stared at Jack, then stepped into his arms, wrapping her hands around his neck and gave him a long, slow kiss. Jack, beer in one hand, rested the other on her hip.

"Woohooo… yeah… right on Katy," the girls hollered.

Katy pulled away first, but lingered, balancing in three-inch heels, forehead resting against Jack's.

"Happy New Year, Jack," she whispered and turned away, high-fiving her girlfriends as they walked out, slamming the door behind them.

Jack stood alone in the foyer.

"Hey, Jack," P.K. shouted from the second floor. "What're you doin'? We got beer to drink."

Jack touched his lips.

"Alright, alright, already," he said and smiled.

He vaulted upstairs and joined P.K. in Cheyo's room.

"What?" Cheyo said, sitting up, as P.K. raised a creaking window. "Who? Where'd you guys come from? What's goin' on?"

"Chill, Cheyo," P.K. said, "just hittin' the roof."

"How many people are still here?" Cheyo said standing.

"'Bout the same as before you passed out," Jack said. "I think you been out a couple hours. You feelin' OK?"

"Not really, but I didn't puke or nothin'. I better go downstairs and see what's happenin'. Hair of the dog might help."

"Yeah, good idea," P.K. said. "That's what you need, more beer."

"Look who's talkin'," Cheyo said as he tucked his shirt in. "I been at a few parties where you caught a second wind after a short nap, P.K. Ain't no biggie. I'll be fine."

Cheyo stopped at the door.

"Don't be singing your silly ass country songs and get the cats howlin'."

"We're cool," said P.K.

Jack and P.K. plopped down on the roof on opposite sides of Cheyo's bedroom window and reclined against the red brick wall. The unopened beer cans laid flat between them, tops pointed toward the house to keep them from rolling down the pitched shingle roof. They sipped beers in unison, smacking lips, exhaling, and laughing, finishing the others sentence as they replayed the evening: Jack's uncomfortable conversation with Billy, the country songs. Jack did not mention Katy's kiss.

Cheyo's two-story house faced several ranch style homes that backed up against an empty cornfield, giving the boys an unobstructed view of the flat Midwestern landscape framed between two tall evergreens growing in front of the house. Sparkling stars accented the darkness like pearls against black velvet. It was clear, the night temperature had not dropped to freezing, the warm front determined to hang on through year's end, helped by a steady breeze from the south.

"Can't remember a week like this for awhile," Jack said. "Be nice if it'd stay this way."

"Well, if it did, it wouldn't be special and we'd find something else to bitch about. You know what Mark Twain said: Everybody complains about the weather, but nobody does anything about it."

"I'm not talkin' strictly 'bout the weather."

"Neither was Twain, I reckon," P.K. said.

Jack laughed, extended his palm and P.K. slapped it.

"Hey, Jack, about your mom…"

"Yeah?"

"I am sorry, man."

"Hey, she's a nice looking lady. That's no secret. Forget about it."

"No, that's not what I meant. I mean, I know we've talked about what's goin' on with your mom before. And I know you don't want to talk about it, but I'm sorry 'bout what's happened. That's what I meant. And I hope things stay good. I hope she gets better. She's a nice lady. She doesn't deserve this. Or you and your family. I'm just sorry, man. All the Rams are."

Jack took a swig of beer, afraid to speak, fearful his voice might crack. Instead he pointed at the night sky.

Low on the horizon a white light exploded, followed by a red, a blue, another white and then a flurry of all three, rising, then popping and falling into the country club lake where the boys swam during summer. In the clubhouse Sam and Mary Lou would be toasting the New Year and sing "Auld Lang Syne." From downstairs, horns, whistles, and Earth, Wind, and Fire blasted through the closed windows as drunken teenagers, imitating images of sloshed parents, screamed and screeched, kissed and hugged.

Jack slapped P.K. on the shoulder. They raised beers, sucked them dry, and popped the tops on the last two, watching the fireworks rise, burst into brief, bright color, then dim, fading to black as they fell to the chilled dark water of the lake.

Cherry Tops

The first cop car cruised down the street, no siren, no cherries and then hung a U-turn and pulled up in front of Cheyo's house. Two more cruisers whipped up, and the cars emptied, with one cop staying behind by the radio, two cops walking toward the front and three slipping around the back.

P.K. began to stand, but Jack yanked him down.

"But..." P.K. said.

"Shh. We can't get down in time and there's no way out. Lie down and be quiet. They ain't gonna think about anybody bein' on the roof in the middle of the winter."

Jack and P.K. crushed the empty beer cans and set them on the shingles. As the cops walked beneath the overhang, the boys lay on their bellies, right hands holding half-full beers, and crawled to the guttered edge of the roof. They trembled at sharp raps on the front door below and froze when they heard the music stop, the door open, and shouts of—"Cops, cherry tops!"—and the rumble and ruckus of thirty-plus kids trying to scramble out of the house.

The cop in the car, seeing and hearing the commotion, flipped on all his lights and cut loose the wailing siren. Lights popped on in the houses around and in front of Cheyo's. Neighbors stepped onto porches and driveways in bathrobes and slippers. Nobody looked up to where Jack and P.K. lay.

"We gotta get up against the house and under the eaves," Jack said. "If the cops come upstairs and look out a window, we're screwed."

They slid up the slanted roof and stretched out against the brick wall. They held their breath when light from Cheyo's room leaked out onto the roof. And all but shit a brick of their own when they heard a voice from inside.

"Pattillo," someone shouted, "anybody upstairs?"

"All clear," Pattillo answered as he turned off Cheyo's bedroom light.

P.K. and Jack scooted to the front of the roof behind an evergreen and watched for a half hour as the cops questioned groups of kids on the front lawn. They took names and phone numbers, cutting a few kids loose, like the black underclassmen from St. Jude, with the promise parents would receive a phone call the next day. They gave sobriety tests to guys like Billy McGuire, who fell on his ass when the cops asked him to close his eyes and touch his nose. They escorted the drunks into the house to call parents to pick them up. Some kids slipped away undetected, Luke and Cindy being two, Luke pulling Cindy around to the side yard when the cops confronted Billy. If the neighbors noticed any escapes they did not bother to shout out, content the party was broken up, the street cleared of cars, and peace and quiet restored.

Two of the last to leave were Jimmy and Sandy. The cop named Pattillo stood under a streetlight writing out tickets while the couple huddled at the curb holding hands until a white Ford F-150 pickup, with "McCarty Plumbing and Heating" stenciled in black on the drivers-side door, approached. A red Datsun compact followed close behind. Sandy dropped Jimmy's hand and took a step away as the pickup screeched to a stop. Her dad, a rangy, blond-haired guy, dressed in a white T-shirt, carpenter jeans and steel-toed boots, stepped down from the cab, while Jimmy's dad, Professor Keino, maneuvered his long, lean body out of the Datsun, white Adidas running shoes shining bright against slick black sweats. Neither greeted the other or their children.

Officer Pattillo turned and talked to Mr. McCarty, who rocked from side to side in the steel-toed boots, clenching and unclenching his fists as he listened. Professor Keino stood motionless, hands in sweat-suit pockets, eyes focused on the officer despite Pattillo acting as if the professor was invisible. Pattillo finished and handed each man a ticket, acknowledging Professor Keino for the first time with a "if there's something you don't understand, call the city attorney. He can simplify the process for you."

Mr. McCarty shooed Sandy toward the truck with a jerk of his thumb. He stared down Jimmy, who ducked his head, then turned his glare on Professor Keino, who met it with a steady gaze. The cop took notice and let his hand rest on the barrel of the foot-long flashlight in his belt. McCarty gave him a glance then climbed into his truck, slammed the door, and sped away. Professor Keino said a few words to his son and walked him to the car, his arm across Jimmy's slender shoulders.

By 1:00 a.m., Cheyo's grandparents arrived and the cops left. Jack and P.K. slipped through Cheyo's window and down the steps. As they opened the front door they heard a beer-buzzed Cheyo in the kitchen, making his case:

"Jeez, Grandma, you don't need to call Mom and Dad in the Caribbean. It's not a big deal. The cops gave me a ticket to appear. It'll be a $100 fine, tops. And it shouldn't even be that. I mean, what the heck, I'm eighteen, so are a lot of my friends. Old enough to vote, to die for my country, to live on my own, to smoke cigarettes. You'd think I could have a party without St. Jude's finest busting down the doors. Jeez, what's the big deal…"

Jack squeezed the door shut behind them, and he and P.K. raced to their houses, dreading the dawn of New Year's Day.

Sunday Morning Coming Down

"C'mon Jack," Sam said as he snapped the bedroom shades up, sunlight splashing across Jack's bed. "Let's get this over with."

Jack rolled over and looked at the alarm clock. 9:15 a.m. Damn it. Sam already knew. Jack rubbed his eyes and sat up in bed.

Sam leaned against the edge of Jack's oak desk, posters of Jim Morrison and Farrah Fawcett over either shoulder. "OK, Jack, no bullshit, now. Were you and P.K. at Cheyo's last night when the party got broken up?"

"Yep."

"How'd you manage to avoid the police?"

"We were sittin' up on the porch roof when the cops pulled up. Between the darkness and the evergreen trees, they couldn't see us. And I guess they weren't expectin' anybody to be on the roof in the middle of winter. So we lay down flat until they left, then hustled home."

"Pretty cool-headed."

Jack shrugged.

"Coach Collins called this morning," Sam said.

"Coach Collins? I figured you found out about this from Chief Royal."

"Nope, haven't heard from the Chief. He doesn't know you were there and probably doesn't care at this point. The party got broken up, all the kids got home safe, parents notified. They'll hand out fines, leave the rest to the parents, and that'll be that. Isn't the first time this has happened in the history of Man. Collins doesn't know you were there, either."

"You gonna tell him, Dad?"

Sam stuck his hands deep into the pockets of his brown corduroy pants and stared at the floor.

"Not my coach. Not my teammates. Not my call."

"Meanin' it's mine, and I should tell Collins myself and get suspended for a quarter of the season just when we're playin' well, just because I was drinkin'? Somethin' I figure Coach Collins knew we might be doin'. Somethin' you knew we might be doin', and didn't stop me from doin' because you were doin' the same thing when you were my age? Does that make sense to you, Dad? 'Cause I got to tell you, it seems hypocritical to me. On all sides."

"Now you hold on a goddamn minute," Sam said yanking his hands from his pockets and pointing his finger at Jack as he approached the bed. "Yeah, I figured you and your buddies might be drinkin' beer. But no, I didn't figure Cheyo was having a huge party. And I didn't figure you'd hang around if he did. I figured you'd be smart enough to try to talk Cheyo into sending everyone home so he wouldn't get in trouble, and if he didn't you'd have the horse sense to get on out. What the hell, Jack? Party that big, cars out on the street, bunch a kids walking in and out of the Jacksons' house, music blasting It didn't cross your mind that one of the neighbors might call the cops?"

Jack thought about how he and P.K. joked about just that when Billy McGuire offered them the first beer.

"Yeah, that's what I thought." Sam sat on the edge of the bed and sighed. "When I was eighteen—"

"I know, Dad. You were in the Army, and by God you had to be a man back then—"

"Don't interrupt me," Sam said, his eyes locking on Jack's. "Quit acting like you know everything about me and your mother because you don't. You don't know half what you think you know. And you're wrong about the rest."

Jack blushed.

"Now, what I was going to say was, I was eighteen when I finished basic training in South Carolina. Got my stripe as a private first class and a weekend pass. Me, Ollie, Kenny Carlson, and some of the guys went into town to whoop it up. Our drill sergeant, big strappin' Southern sonuvabitch named Barkley gave us the standard warning about repercussions, even went a step further and told us what bars and neighborhoods to avoid. Did everything he could to save us from ourselves. Of course, we ignored him. Well, long story short, we got liquored up, got into a fight with some civilians didn't like us talking to their local girls, and me and Ollie ended up in the town jail. Carlson let Barkley know where we were or we'd a been considered AWOL, and he came down, checked if we needed any medical attention, then talked to the police chief and got us released."

"So, he got you off the hook?"

"Not exactly," Sam said and chuckled. "When Ollie and I got back to base, Barkley tore off our stripes, busted to buck privates, threw us in the hole for twenty-four hours, then made us peel potatoes and clean the latrine for a week. We never said anything to Barkley. Me and Ollie never talked much about it. But we both knew he'd done right by us. Could've been a lot worse if the local's got their hands on us. And I'll tell you this, next time we got a weekend pass, we took Barkley's advice."

Sam smiled, shaking his head, while Jack looked at his father trying to imagine him at eighteen, in jail, nursing a hangover.

"The thing is, Jack," Sam said, squinting through bifocals at the sunny blue sky, "you're going to be eighteen in April. Graduating a few weeks after that. By law, free to do what you want. In some states, free to drink. In any event, not a kid anymore. Now, whatever mistakes your mother and I might've made raising you, whatever problems we may have—and I know it hasn't been great around here the last few years—we did teach you right from wrong. That doesn't mean you won't screw up from time to time. We all do. The question is, are you going to stand up and be a man when you do? Accept the consequences? Be a leader? A high school basketball team isn't an Army platoon, this isn't a life or death deal, but even if Coach Collins never finds out you were at that party, all the boys on the team know you were there. How are they going to feel about a guy who sits silent when his buddies get punished? How good you think your team's going to be then?"

Jack flopped onto his back and stared at the ceiling.

"Collins is going to kill me. I'll be runnin' washboards and bleachers for three weeks. And wait 'til Carmody's next column. Christ almighty."

"Well, you play you pay, Jack," Sam said and gave him a tap on the knee before rising to leave. "Let Carmody have his say. Let everyone. Good for the soul to get ripped a new one occasionally. Keeps us humble. Running sprints at the Wreck in January beats the hell out of shovelin' shit in South Carolina in June. Team meeting's at eleven. We go from here."

Jack groaned. *We go from here...You play you pay...Keeps us humble...Onward and upward...Do the right thing.* The old man had a saying for any occasion. But they were true. Jack heard himself speaking them when a situation arose, a reminder of what his father would have him do, and they often made the difference between the right decision and the wrong one. And when he did screw up, *it's not the end of the world...keep your dobber up...live and learn...we go from here.*

Jack, P.K., Cheyo, and Gudy drove to the Wreck in P.K.'s Chevy, eight-track off, talk limited to greetings and conjecture about how bad Collins would come down on them, with the exception of the babysitting Gudy.

"You guys won't catch flack from me," Gudy said, always the class act. *"But for the grace of God,* as they say. Never thought I'd be glad I stayed home with my little sister on New Year's Eve."

They pulled in next to Coach Lane as he unfolded his lean frame from a '69 cherry red Corvette. Pale and unshaven, outfitted in black sunglasses and a weathered, brown leather bomber jacket, faded blue jeans and tan Tony Llama boots, Lane had pried himself from a redhead in a warm bed because of them. He did not say hello to the boys but walked with them into the gym, not removing the shades.

Brewster, Jenkins, Connolly, and the rest sprawled across the pine bleachers at the far end of the court chatting about what a bitch it was to be at school on New Year's Day, the one day, except Sundays and Christmas, that Collins held no practice. Jimmy sat alone in the second row, fingers interlocked, elbows resting on knees. In the middle of the Hilltopper logo at center court, stood Collins, clean-shaven and calm. He made notes on a white clipboard as Scooter, who had just finished a workout, nodded his crew-cut head under the hood of a blue St. Jude sweatshirt. Lane joined them, boots clomping on the hardwood floor, eyes blinking and squinting as he slid the sunglasses up, pushing bed-head blond hair away from his forehead. None of the coaches acknowledged the four Rams, who were greeted with silence from their teammates. They sat surrounding Jimmy under the unrelenting glare of Brewster and Jenkins.

"OK boys," Scooter said, blasting his silver whistle and clapping as the three men approached, "look alive."

All the boys sat up straight, feet flat on the bleachers while Scooter's eyes darted from boy to boy. He and the yawning Lane, thumbs tucked into front belt loops, stood behind Collins.

"I'd say I'm sorry," Collin said, "to drag you into the gym on New Year's Day, but it wasn't me who caused this meeting. As I'm certain you now all know, there was a party at the Jackson home last night. I have spoken to Cheyo, and he has admitted to drinking as has Jimmy. Per the three-strikes-and-you're-out extracurricular policy passed by the school board last spring this means they are automatically ineligible for twenty-five percent of the season, in this case, the next seven games.

"Consider yourself fortunate," Collins said looking at the two boys, "because if it were up to a lot of people around here, you'd be off the team. End of story."

"As far as basketball and this team goes, you two will be here at the Wreck every morning at 5:30 a.m. to run under the eye of Coach Havlik. You will also participate in afternoon practice, and you will attend all games in a coat and tie. Any additional violation will result in your dismissal from the team and your ineligibility for extracurricular activities for the rest of the school year. And, as a reminder for you freshman, sophomores, and juniors, a third strike means you're done with extracurricular for the remainder of high school. The death penalty, so to speak. I hope it never comes to that, but if it does, you're done. No questions asked."

Collins paused and let the words sink in.

"As for the rest of you," he continued at his professorial pace, head down, "this situation poses a challenge. While Cheyo and Jimmy aren't starters, they are two of the first boys off the bench and are big contributors, so it's not going to be easy to replace them. But our starting lineup is intact and you reserves will—"

"Coach," Jack said raising his hand as he glanced at P.K.

"Yes, Henderson."

"Well, uh," Jack said, standing, P.K. rising with him, "I'm…well…P.K. and I were at the party last night too…and drinking. We just didn't get caught."

"Sheeeit," Jenkins blurted, "wouldn't you know it!"

"That's enough, Randy," Collins said as he stopped pacing and locked eyes with Jenkins.

"But Coach…"

Collins glared at him, and Jenkins shut his mouth. Chin sinking into his chest, Collins paced, jaw muscles churning, face darkening. He took a deep breath and planted himself in front of Jack and P.K.

"I appreciate your honesty. You're both suspended for the next seven games. Join Coach Havlik in the a.m."

"Now," Collins said taking a few steps backward and spreading his arms like a preacher at Sunday service, "before I go any further, was anyone else at the party? Anybody else do anything self-centered and stupid over Christmas break?"

He let the questions float for a few seconds.

"Well, thank the Lord for small favors. OK, everything I said a moment ago continues to apply. The rest of you are going to have to step up. Play and practice like these four don't exist. Which they don't for the next seven games, thanks to putting partying ahead of the team. I'll see you all at afternoon practice tomorrow. Any questions?"

The boys sat quiet.

"OK, that's it boys," Scooter shouted. "Head for home."

Lane slid his sunglasses down and bolted. Collins and Scooter walked toward the coaches' offices.

P.K. turned to Jack as the boys stepped down onto the hardwood. "Could've been worse, I guess."

"Could've been better," Jenkins said. "You assholes could've been kicked off the team."

"Nobody's talkin' to you Randy," Jack said, turning to face him. "Mind your own business."

"Mind my own business?" Jenkins said, voice cracking, a sarcastic smile splitting his face as he slipped on his letter jacket and jogged down the bleachers, Brewster and Connolly right behind. "Mind my own business? Is that what you said to me? Mind my own business? Who the hell's business do you think this is, Jack?"

"Hey, we screwed up. What do you want from us? We screwed up, and we're sorry. We ain't perfect All-American jocks like you, Randy, wearin' our letter jacket in July. We don't live and die for basketball. We like to have fun once in a while. What the hell, you think NBA players drink Ovaltine and go to bed at 9:00? College players? We had a few beers. If we were couple years older, nobody'd say a goddam word."

"Yeah, sure, if we we're a few years older," Jenkins said hopping down to face Jack. "And you call *me* dumb. I don't know if you've noticed, but you're not a few years older. You're part of this team, and you knew what would happen if you got caught doin' this shit. We're just startin' to play well. We're seven weeks from the start of the state tournament, and now you guys are out for seven games. And you're tellin' me to mind my own business? Coach is right. You Rams are a bunch of self-centered jerks."

"Hey, like I said, I'm sorry. Maybe we are jerks. Or maybe we don't live and die for high school basketball like holier-than-thou-high-school jocks like you."

"Bullshit," Jenkins said edging to within a foot of Jack. "That's the excuse you're using, Jack, for not havin' the guts to lay it on the line. It's easier to be a playground legend than a real high school ball player puttin' it on the line in front of God and a full gym on Friday night. Ain't it, Jack? Can't fail if you're not really tryin', right? It's your way of runnin' away, ain't it? Wonder where you learned that?"

Jack lunged toward Jenkins, but P.K. got to Randy first, taking him to the floor with a thud. Connolly jumped on top of P.K. and Jack pounced on Connolly. Tommy Tompkins stepped in to break it up, yanking Jack by the shoulder, and

Gudy, thinking Tompkins was taking sides, popped Tommy in the face with a short, sharp right. Bodies flew as the Rams fought the varsity players.

Jimmy and Brewster faced off, waiting for the other to throw a punch, but neither boy twitched.

"C'mon, man," Brewster sighed, "help me save these honkies from themselves."

Together they turned toward the knotted pile of white boys and pulled them apart, Brewster going after his friends, Jimmy after the Rams.

The SHREEK-SHREEK-SHREEK- SHREEK-SHREEK- SHREEK of Scooter's whistle pierced the air, and Lane came alongside Brewster and Jimmy, his big hands pulling boys out of the pile and tossing them aside.

"Enough!" Collins shouted.

The boys stumbled away from each other, Jenkins bending over at the waist, Tompkins rubbing the cheek Gudy slugged, Jack nursing his shoulder.

"Let me guess," Collins said. "Henderson and Jenkins." He eyed each boy whether he looked his way or not.

The players hung their heads, waiting for the chew-out, then jerked when Collins began to shout:

"Now this is the Law of the Jungle...as old and as true as the sky;
        And the Wolf that shall keep it may prosper, but the Wolf that shall break it must die.
        As the creeper that girdles the tree-trunk, the Law runneth forward and back—
        For the strength of the Pack is the Wolf...and the strength of the Wolf is the Pack."

Collins stopped, brown eyes bright, staring again at each boy until they returned his look. Then he wheeled and walked out the gym.

Scooter's whistle wailed. "Practice at 6:00 a.m. tomorrow! For *everybody*," he shouted. "Happy New Year's, boys! Happy New Year's!"

Riding the Storm Out

Out of Bounds
Art Carmody, *St. Jude Harbinger* Sports Editor

Rams Run off Team

The Harbinger has learned that four members of the surging St. Jude Hilltoppers basketball team were suspended from the team for the next seven games. Suspended were forwards Jack Henderson and Cheyo Jackson, and guard P.K. Davis and guard/forward Jimmy "Kip" Keino.

Head Coach Reggie Collins stated the four were punished for "violation of team rules" but would not elaborate. It is a matter of public record, however, that Jackson and Keino, both 18, were ticketed early New Year's morning by the St. Jude police for illegal consumption of alcohol by a minor and ordered to appear in court next month.

Also ticketed for illegal consumption was Centennial forward Billy McGuire. Centennial coach Joe "Butch" Donegal said McGuire would miss the next three games per team rules.

The Hilltoppers, picked by this reporter as contenders for the state title, struggled early in the season as newcomers Henderson, Jackson, Davis, Keino, and starting forward Jeff Gudman—the self-titled "Running

Rams"—struggled to adapt their game to Collins's disciplined motion offense and aggressive man-to-man defense. But last week they surprised everyone by winning the Rail Splitter Classic, upsetting Blooming Grove and preseason Mr. Basketball Hassan "Go-Go" Jones in the finals. Henderson, who averaged 18 points and 10 rebounds a game during the Toppers 4-game run, hit the game winning shot with a stop and pop 20-foot jumper at the buzzer over Jones and was named to the all-tourney team along with Brewster.

Every high school team automatically qualifies for the state tournament, which begins in late February. And barring any additional problems the four boys will be eligible to play. But the missed games could be detrimental to a team incorporating so many new players into the rotation—Henderson, a starter, Jackson and Keino, the first players off the bench, Davis the backup point guard. All are in their first year of varsity ball.

It is anybody's guess how they will perform in the pressure cooker of the state tournament with 20 plus varsity games under their belt. But based on their behavior off the court, this reporter has to wonder if they have the commitment to be taken seriously as championship contenders. It seems some of the Rams have priorities besides basketball. That's too bad for such a talented group. But it's worse for their teammates and the loyal St. Jude fans that have been waiting since the heyday of assistant coach "Radar" Gene Lane for a team to take them back to the Sweet Sixteen.

As a reporter I am not allowed to root for or against any player or team, but I do root for everyone to play their best, to play to their potential. Let's hope the Rams, and Billy McGuire, realize that can only happen by spending time on the basketball court, not in a court of law.

They should ask themselves if years from now they want to be remembered for their record on the basketball court during March Madness, or their criminal record for mad acts on New Year's Eve?

Here's to hoping they make the right choice. For all concerned.

"Shit," Jack said, folding the paper as he sat on their front porch step.

He had hurried home from afternoon practice to read the evening edition of the *St. Jude Harbinger,* hoping against hope that Carmody would not write a column about the suspensions. But he knew better. This was the stuff columnists live for.

"Guess I don't have to ask."

Jack looked up to see a rosy cheeked Katy approaching. He scooted over.

"Like my old man says, *you play, you pay*," Jack said, setting the paper aside.

"Glad the girls and I left when we did," Katy said. *"Rather be lucky than good."*

Jack laughed.

"You girls drinking, too?"

"Few of the girls. Not me. I drove."

"So, when we kissed, you..."

Katy bowed her head, blushing.

Jack propped a finger under her chin.

"Me too," he said, and they kissed.

"Well," Katy said, snuggling close, "what now? We going to do this?"

Jack pulled her in close. "Think we have been."

They sat in contented silence until the winter sun set.

In the larger world, all hell was breaking loose: Inflation roared, unemployment and mortgage rates soared—*stagflation,* the pointy-headed economists called it. But this was St. Jude, and it was winter, and that meant basketball reigned supreme. With the glow of the holidays fading, with Christmas bills coming due, and nothing but short, dark days on the horizon until March, the success or failure of the local teams provided an avenue of escape people were glad to travel.

And the combination of basketball and underage, boozed up kids, stirred up fans and non-fans alike. Chatter scattered like buckshot across diners, barber shops, bowling alleys, and bars. From truck drivers to CEO's, short-order cooks to country club elites, ministers to strippers, everyone had an opinion and deluged the *Harbinger* with letters. For Jack, home became a sanctuary from the hue and cry.

"Man, Dad," Jack said at supper a few days after the story broke, "I didn't think this would be such a big deal."

"It's January in Illinois, Jack. People don't have a helluva lot else to do except talk basketball, drink, or both."

For the next week Jack sat at the kitchen table after practice and scanned the letters, reading portions out loud to Mary Lou as she cooked dinner.

"OK, Mom," he said one afternoon, hair wet from the locker room showers, "now, this guy, who refers to himself as a WWII vet says 'eighteen-year-old boys are old enough to fight and die for their country. They should be able to have a beer and play basketball. As a society we need to get over the hypocrisy of making laws and rules for the sake of making laws and rules. You can't legislate morality. You can't stop people from drinking, gambling, engaging in prostitution. We've tried to do all at various times in this country and we've never succeeded. I say let the boys play ball and have a beer. It's nobody's business but theirs and their parents. The school and the law need to butt out.'"

"Mmmm," Mary Lou said as she stacked stiff spaghetti into boiling water, bending the pasta into place as it softened.

"Here's one. This guy's not a supporter: 'The players knew when they made the team that certain rules would apply. If it were up to me they'd all be off the team. Their actions reflect a 'me-first' attitude that is all too prevalent among our young people today. I'm surprised that any coach who proclaims to be a disciplinarian has allowed this to occur without taking more decisive action. Perhaps it's not a change in players St. Jude needs but a change in coaches. And what about Mayor Henderson, who also happens to be town liquor commissioner, and whose son is in the middle of all this? Why have we not heard from him? Why was his son not ticketed? Perhaps a change in city leadership is needed as well...'"

"That's not fair to Coach Collins or Dad," Jack said, eyes on the paper. "Collins is following the rules that the school board wrote. He shouldn't have to take that flack. And how come this guy didn't call for Coach Donegal's resignation at Centennial? Billy's suspended for three games, not seven. Racist son of a—"

"Jack," Mary Lou said, stirring tomato sauce.

"You know it's true, Mom. I haven't seen one letter yet that's called for Donegal's resignation or questioned his decision making. Not one. And what about what this jerk is sayin' about Dad? That I didn't get busted at the party because I'm the mayor's son? I didn't get busted because the St. Jude cops didn't see me. Not because they let me go. None of this is Coach Collins or Dad's fault."

"No, it certainly isn't," Mary Lou said as she adjusted the knob on the burner, Jack aware of what was left unsaid.

He was getting used to people leaving things unsaid. The Rams never mentioned the suspension or the flack that he, as the star player and mayor's son, caught from the press and the fans. He told himself not to be paranoid, but the more times he walked up to a group of kids at school and the conversation stopped, the teenagers looking down or flashing fake smiles, then somebody saying—"Jack, hey man, didn't see you"—the more self-conscious he felt. At least Jenkins, Connolly, Brewster and the rest who were pissed with him did not add to that feeling, he thought with a grim smile. They paid him no attention at all, taking Collins's speech about the suspended boys' nonexistence literally. He didn't expect high-fives or help up from the floor at practice, but since the fight on New Year's Day, they did not even get angry.

As for the coaches, during afternoon practice Collins, Lane, and Scooter focused on the backups who would be playing in Jack, Jimmy, P.K. and Cheyo's place. In the mornings, Scooter was all business as he shouted out drills and blew the chrome whistle. "Hit the bleachers... Washboards now, let's go... Give me twenty-five sit-ups, twenty-five pushups... Let's go boys, let's go, little hustle," sending them off to the showers with a wave of his hand instead of a piercing SHREEK, as tired of the morning workouts as the boys were.

The first game of the suspensions was against Corn Belt Conference foe the Black Hills Miners, a Class A school a couple hours south in the middle of coal country which fielded no football team, focusing instead on basketball and baseball as the two main varsity sports. Their longtime coach was sixty-year old Stan "the General" Patton.

"The original hard-ass," Sam said.

The son of a coal miner, Patton, like Sam, numbered among the millions of WWII vets who attended college on the GI bill and landed jobs their fathers dreamed about. Knowing what the mines could do to a man, Patton worked as a teacher and a coach with fearful intensity and no desire to follow his father's footsteps.

A crew-cut fossil from 1950, the year he started coaching at Black Hills, Patton stalked the sidelines in a starched white, button-down shirt, black suit, and a skinny rep tie in the school's black and red. He imposed strict conduct codes—including a short hair rule—on his players, all of whom he demanded run year round: cross country in the fall and track in the spring, unless they played baseball, in which case Patton personally ran them in the morning. Raised in a secluded, coal-mining burg like Black Hills and playing for the same man who coached their fathers, uncles, brothers, and cousins, Patton's players did not complain. They took digs from opposing teams during warm ups about their haircuts and old school layup drills—"Hey, GI Joe, the girls coach teach you layups?"—then, after the opening tap, proceeded to apply a lock-down, whirling-dervish full-court press and fast-break offense that left opponents gasping and calling timeout three minutes into the first quarter.

Patton was one of dozens of small-town legends spread across the Midwest, loved by many, hated by a few, and respected by most. But all for one reason: He won. Unafraid to speak his mind, Patton made no bones about what would have happened to any boys on his team caught drinking. "It's like I tell my boys, there is no *I* in team," he told Art Carmody in a pregame interview. "You're either with us or against us. You may not agree with everything I say or do, but you have to trust I'm right and be smart enough to be dumb enough to go along with the program. If you do, things are going to work out. If you don't, you're gone. My way or the highway. But not everybody thinks the way I do. These new coaches have new ideas. But the Hilltoppers are a good team with or without the suspended boys. I'm just glad we got 'em coming to the Pit. Gives us a fighting chance."

The Miners' home court, The Pit, was built during the Depression and resembled an oversized, red brick silo. The hardwood floor sat below ground level surrounded closely by varnished oak bleachers, dark and smooth from forty years of fans sitting, standing, sliding, and stomping. From one end of the gym a faded red and white electronic scoreboard and clock looked down on the court, the players names stenciled on white poster board and slid into slots beside red lights that indicated when a player was on the court. Patton instructed his captains to take the basket facing the scoreboard for the second and fourth quarters if they won the pregame coin toss so the opposing team would have to turn to check the clock at halftime and the end of the game.

Students ringed the court in the lower-level seats, and the cheering and jeering was loud and constant. The pep band set up behind the visiting team's bench, blasting the school fight song at timeouts so opposing coaches had to shout their instructions over the din. Visiting fans were granted a small section of seats at the end of the gym farthest from their team's bench, their cheering obliterated by the band and the legions of red-and-black-shirted Miners fans that surrounded them. Welcoming opponents and their fans at the start of a game, the public address announcer cautioned the Black Hills faithful not to be "too tough on them" before introducing "YOUR Black Hills Miners" as The Pit erupted and the Miners burst through the locker room door and onto the court, circling the gym and slapping hands with the courtside students, the concussive noise bouncing off the walls and the steel girders of the low-pitched roof.

As the Hilltoppers took the court, Jack's skin tingled with goose bumps from the booming band and screaming fans. Dressed in matching navy blue blazers, white shirt, gold tie, and grey flannel trousers, Jack, Jimmy, Cheyo, and P.K. stood motionless by the bench, teammates warming up a few feet away as the din descended down from the rafters, and the short-haired Miners circled the court. Black Hills' star player, J.J. "Davy" Crockett, a skinny, pale, pimpled six-foot seven Appalachian forward, broke from the string of players, took a bounce pass from the team manager, drove to the hoop and jammed the ball with rim-rattling fury, the stringy muscles of his neck throbbing as he loosed a crimson-faced war whoop. The crowd roared and stomped as the pep band switched from the school fight song to Queen's "We Will Rock You," the students singing at the top of their lungs.

"Jeezus H, Christ," Jack shouted. "These people are pumped."

"And white," Jimmy yelled, features twisted, "nasty white."

Jack knew Jimmy and Sandy broke up at the insistence of Mr. McCarty. The idea of Sandy going against her father's demands, even when he could not have been more wrong, was too much to ask of a seventeen-year-old girl raised to obey her elders. But Jack had said nothing to Jimmy about it. The guys rarely talked girlfriends. But Jack knew it was more than that.

Although Jack did his best to view Jimmy the way he did the rest of his friends, he knew he did not always succeed. And he sensed Jimmy did not always see the Rams the same way they viewed one another. As close as they all were, there was a separation, a reservation in Jimmy that held him apart. Measured and shaded at times, like the bullshitting patter he engaged in with Luke. Other times raw and violent, like the fistfight at the Fiji house. But it was always there, under the radar.

Even in a relatively tolerant town like St. Jude, the blue-black Keino's hid in plain sight. The Professors Keino wore dashikis and beads on campus, speaking the King's English better than most Americans. But they were also churchgoing Christians who made mission trips every summer to Africa or Appalachia or Alabama, practicing what they preached. Still, for some in St. Jude none of it mattered: "I don't know, they're nice people and all, but I'm not comfortable with 'em." People might point to their too-perfect English, their east-coast academic egg-headedness, or their exotic clothes, but at seventeen Jack knew bullshit when he stepped in it. The real reason was as deep, dark, and superficial as the Keino's skin. And for people like Mr. McCarty, that was all that mattered.

Something bumped Jack's right foot and a cold spray splashed his pants. A shaken can of Schlitz beer, punctured in the side and tossed at the St. Jude bench. Three more slid across the hardwood, and Jack, Jimmy, Cheyo, and P.K. jumped to one side, the spray dousing the fans. Across the court a chubby kid with a Charlie Daniels "Long Haired Country Boy" T-shirt waved a poster with a mug of beer at the top and beneath it two handcuffed figures, one black and one brown, stood in St. Jude basketball uniforms, while beside them a white figure with blond hair said to a cop—"Arrest them, but let me go, my Daddy's the Mayor!"

"C'mon, c'mon!" the kid shouted. "C'mon and do somethin' about it, preppie!"

Jack froze as other kids joined with Long Haired Country Boy:

"Preppie 'fraid to fight!"

"What's the matter, Henderson? Gonna cry?"

"Where's your Daddy, now?"

"What about you Chico? Superfly? Gonna back your boy?"

"Ah, shit. Y'all is wimps!"

Before Jack could think what to do, a blue-suited black blur slid past.

"Jimmy..." Jack said, then stopped.

Coach Collins strode across the court to the Long Haired Country Boy and snatched the poster, tearing it in half, then in half again, before shoving it into the kid's gut. Long Haired Country Boy stepped back, head down, as Collins spoke. Collins then turned and marched to Coach Patton.

Jack could read Patton's "What-did-you-expect? You-should've-kicked-those-boys-off-the-team!" grinning lips as he stood by the bench, arms out and palms up.

Collins put his hands on his hips, took a step toward Patton, his black face inches away from the old white coach as he talked and gestured toward the kids with the sign. Patton's grin dropped, eyes turning hard. Collins did not back off. The crowd, aware of the commotion in front of the Miner's bench, quieted to a murmur, people pointing toward the two coaches as the band stopped playing and the warm-ups came to a halt. Scooter and Lane stood beside Collins while Patton's assistants lined up behind him. The two head coaches glared at one another.

"BZZZZZZZZZZZZZZ," boomed the scoreboard buzzer.

"Ladies and gentleman," the public-address announcer said, "please join the Black Hills Miners pep band and choir for the singing of our national anthem."

The crowd stood, but no one looked at the flag. The band did not play, and the players stayed where they were, everyone's eyes on the two coaches.

"Have it your way, then," Patton said as he motioned to a pair of police officers. Patton pointed at the Long Haired Country Boy and his buddies, and the cops escorted them from the gym, the boys jerking arms away from the officers as they left. Scattered applause mixed with boos rippled across the gym.

Collins wheeled around and called the Toppers to the bench, lined them up along the sideline, and they all put hands on hearts. Patton's team did likewise. The band played the anthem, but not a single soul, except the high school choir, sang along.

Two minutes into the game, Jenkins drove the lane and Crockett whacked him across the nose. The ref ignored the foul and called Jenkins for traveling. Jenkins clutched his face and writhed on the floor, blood squirting through his fingers. Neither Crockett nor any of the Miners offered to help him up or apologize. Jack, who had been assigned to help Whitey, grabbed a couple of white towels and rushed to Jenkins aid along with Scooter. Lane jawed with the ref, demanding a technical be called for the foul, while Collins called the four starters to the bench. A squat and stooped retired local doctor named Keck joined Jack, Whitey, and Scooter with Jenkins. They propped Jenkins up and the doctor patted the sides of the bloody nose with liver-spotted hands.

"That hurt, son?" Dr. Keck asked.

"Not really, no."

"Well it ain't broke. Let's get you to the bench. Stop the bleeding."

"Can I play?"

"I don't see why not," Dr. Keck said and laughed. "But I wouldn't drive the lane again. I think Crockett's a mite stirred up."

"Yeah, well, we'll see about that."

"Son," Keck said, "I know you want to win, but I'd be careful how you go about it. After what your colored coach did to Patton, these folks are pretty fired up. Best to play ball and get out of here in one piece."

"They keep this up," Scooter said, "they're gonna have to call a few fouls."

"I wouldn't count on it," Keck said, shaking his head and laughing. "One ref is Patton's nephew, the other is on the town council. I don't think you're going to get a lot of calls, if you know what I mean."

Jack heard a whistle blow and the crowd erupt as the pudgy, bald ref who called the travel on Jenkins, made a T with his hands and rang up Lane for a technical.

Keck, Scooter, and the three boys exchanged glances.

"Let's get him to the bench," Keck said. "Help him up boys. I don't want him walking on his own yet."

Jimmy and Cheyo, charting shots and keeping stats, set down the clipboards and patted Jenkins on the back as the boys cleared a space on the bench. Dr. Keck took bandages from his bag as Whitey applied ice to Jenkins' nose. A few fans applauded Jenkins toughness. Some booed as Lane and Collins jawed at the pudgy ref. The pep band cranked up "We Will Rock You," and the student body stomped its feet. Gudy, Brewster, Connolly, and Tompkins milled around on the floor as the benchwarmers stared into the stands, hopping up and down, eyes wide, heads shaking.

Jack took it all in and then put his fingers in his mouth and whistled several times, waving at the boys on the floor until they all gathered round.

"Hey, fellas," Jack shouted, "I know it's crazy in here. But we've got to suck it up and stick together. We can't let these redneck bastards intimidate us."

"Easy for you to say," Connolly said. "You're not gettin' your ass kicked."

"I know," Jack said and faced Connolly. "I know. I should be out there. This is one night we need everyone. And I'm sorry. I'm sorry for partyin' and screwin' up the team. I'm sorry for bein' a jerk and not thinking more than a day ahead. I'm sorry, man, I truly am. But we got to go forward. We can't let these bastards get away with this shit."

"You sayin' we should take out Crockett?" Brewster said.

Dr. Keck looked up from bandaging Jenkins.

"Nope," Jack said, "somethin' better. We beat 'em at their own game. Let's ask coach to press 'em. Run 'em. They're too pumped up right now. Runnin' on adrenalin. They keep this up they're gonna be gassed by the third quarter. Let's rope-a-dope 'em like Ali did to Foreman."

"Hey, man," Gudy said, "we're shorthanded. We might gas ourselves."

"Maybe," Jack said and laughed, "but what the hell. Nobody's pickin' us to win right now anyway. At least they'll know we were here."

"I don't see it," Connolly said.

He had a point, Jack knew. The book on Black Hills was get the lead, break the press at half court and, unless you had a lay-up, settle into your offense, using as much time as possible, slowing the game down and avoiding the run and gun, helter-skelter game the well-conditioned Miners preferred. It was suicidal to run with them, and Jack could tell the rest of the Hilltoppers agreed with Connolly.

"Jack's right," a voice yelled. Jenkins shoved Dr. Keck's hands away and stood up next to Jack.

The boys stared, Jack included.

"It'd be nice if the sonuvabitch could play," Jenkins said. "And Cheyo, Jimmy, and P.K. But they can't. And right now we ain't got shit to lose. These pricks are gonna beat the crap out of us regardless. So let's press 'em and run 'em, and see who drops first."

"Coach'll never go for it," Connolly said.

"I wouldn't be so sure," said a voice from outside the knot of boys.

The players parted and Collins stepped into the middle of the huddle, cracking a broad smile.

"UCLA two-two-one full court press. Gudy, you take Jack's slot, the rest of you as we practiced. Second team, be ready. We're going to need fresh bodies. Randy, can you go?"

"Yep."

"Doc?"

"Can't say I agree with your strategy," Dr. Keck said folding his bag closed, "but, yeah, the boy can play."

"OK, boys, let's bring it in," Collins said, taking Jack and Jenkins hands into his and holding them together in the center of the huddle. "Let's do this. On three—We are…"

"HILLTOPPERS!"

"We are…"

"HILLTOPPERS!"

"We are…"

"HILLTOPPERS!"

They broke the huddle and the five starters, including a bandaged Jenkins, took the floor while the rest sat and Crockett shot the technical. Scooter and Lane huddled with Collins.

"We're going to run with them," Collins told his assistants.

"Uh, Reggie," Scooter said, "I mean, uh, no disrespect, but was that your idea?"

"No. The boys. Henderson and Jenkins, actually."

"We're gonna lose," Lane said.

"Yeah. But we're going to lose as a team."

The three men smiled.

"Well, what the hell," Lane said. "I've always been a down-in-flames kinda guy. No need to change now."

With Black Hills ball out, the crowd buzzed as the Hilltoppers set up a full-court press. Patton glanced toward the St. Jude bench, but Collins ignored him as he took a seat next to Jack, patting Jack's knee with the rolled up program he carried with him during games, a wrinkled, yellow sheet of paper poking out its end. Around Collins's wrist glistened a slim gold chain, the cross dangling from the chain cupped in the palm of his hand. It was no mystery that Collins was a religious man. But what was on the yellow sheet of paper no one knew. Guesses included everything from a prayer to a Bible verse to a poem, but nobody thought it anything to do with basketball. Collins never referred to it during play, folding it when the game ended and slipping it into his tan wallet.

"Henderson," Collins said, tapping him again with the program and looking him in the eye, "there can only be one coach on this team. Don't ever take over the huddle again. Understood?"

"Yeah, sure Coach, understood."

"Unless," Collins said with a smile, "I'm as distracted as I've been tonight."

Jack laughed.

"Now," Collins said, "this was your bright idea, so you keep these guys on the bench in the game and help them out with their assignments. This isn't going to be easy. OK?"

"OK, coach." Jack nodded.

Collins stood and walked over to Scooter and Lane, abandoning his usual seat on the bench and his reserved "let the boys play" demeanor. With four regulars out the backups would need all the help they could get. Together the three Topper coaches shouted instructions as the ref tossed the ball to Crockett, who in-bounded to a teammate, and sprinted along the sidelines as the Miners broke the Hilltopper press. Crockett caught a pass from the point guard on the right wing, juked past Gudy, and cut to the hoop, like in warm-ups. But this time, with Brewster guarding the hoop, Crockett hesitated and attempted a layup instead of a dunk. Brewster smacked the shot off the backboard, the block so clean and certain that not even the hometown refs dared call a foul. Gudy retrieved the ball, fired a pass to Jenkins who took a couple of dribbles, and flicked the ball to a trailing Connolly who laid it in.

The Hilltoppers on the bench leapt to their feet as Collins, Lane, and Scooter yelled and pointed as the starters scrambled into position to reset the press. Coach Patton berated the refs and grabbed Crockett by the jersey as he passed.

"Be strong with the ball, goddammit," Patton screamed. "Don't let that boy do that to you on our court."

Jack, Cheyo, Jimmy and P.K. high-fived as Jenkins turned and pointed at Jack. "Never thought I'd see that," Jimmy said. "Looks like Jenkins might be a Runnin' Ram."

"Naw," Jack said, "We're Hilltoppers."

We Are Family

"Tompkins," Collins shouted the next day in practice, "you have to rotate when the ball swings to the far side of the court. You can't plant yourself on the wing. We're running a *motion* offense. Henderson, take Tompkins's spot for a few plays. Tommy, come here and watch Jack. OK, let's run it again. Jimmy, P.K., Cheyo, don't cut them any slack. Play hard D. Fight through the screens."

Scooter blew the whistle, and the boys flew into action as Collins coached Tompkins through the play.

As they thought they might, the Toppers lost to Black Hills. But not until pushing the Miners into overtime when a shorthanded St. Jude ran out of gas and lost by five.

"The Pit is a tough place to win. You know that going in," Collins told reporters after the game in response to questions about his confrontation with Patton. "I'm proud of my players and how they handled things tonight. We left the Pit stronger than when we entered."

"Proud of all 'em, Coach?" Art Carmody said. "Including the ineligible ones whose poor off-court behavior probably cost you a win?"

"All of them."

And Jack, P.K., Cheyo, and Jimmy knew it to be true. Knew it when Collins confronted Patton. On the bus ride to St. Jude, Jenkins sat next to Jack and talked strategy for the rest of the season. The next day at practice Connolly and Gudy lifted shirts and displayed bruises inflicted by the Miners.

"I'd show you mine," Brewster said with a laugh, "but blue blends into black."

Like an Irish clan that fights like cats and dogs among themselves but turns as one against outsiders, the Hilltoppers had found a common foe: everyone who questioned them as a team. Reporters like Carmody. Fans like the Long Haired Country Boy. Opposing players like Crockett. The wags at the diners and the letter-to-the-editor writers. Anyone who doubted their toughness, their ability as individuals and as a team, and who rooted for their failure. Collins, Lane, and Scooter all agreed, after the fight at the Wreck, the Black Hills experience was perfect timing.

Now they had to get through the next six games.

Ten games were on the schedule in January with six in the next two weeks on a Tuesday, Friday, Saturday rotation. Jack, P.K., Cheyo, and Jimmy would be eligible to play by the twenty-first with another ten games left before the Regional opener at the end of February. In the mean time, the juniors, Tompkins, McElroy, and Pitman would get playing time instead of bench time.

"Jeezus H. Christ, Coach," Jack heard Lane say to Collins after that first practice following the Black Hills game, a rare sober smile splitting Radar Gene's face, "if those three juniors keep playing like they did last night, we'll be eleven-deep come tournament time. We might make a run at the championship in spite of ourselves. Sonuvabitch. After all the bullshit we've been through, who'd've thought? Never can tell with kids, can you?"

The two men laughed and slapped hands.

"No you can't, man," Collins said. "No you can't."

Things changed around the school and St. Jude, too. A buzz filled the halls and streets. The Hilltoppers showed grit in the loss at Black Hills. Carmody's column reported the players-only meeting Jack called while the coaches argued the no-call on Crockett.

"In blue sport coat and grey slacks," Carmody wrote, "one might have thought Henderson a fourth coach. And based on the play after the impromptu huddle, he might make a good one some day. But as the end result showed, the Hilltoppers need Henderson on the court, not the sidelines. Here's hoping he and his teammates have learned their lesson and return from suspension ready to play as hard as their teammates did against Black Hills."

A few days later a construction worker in a buzz cut stopped to talk to Sam as he smoked a Lucky and sipped coffee at the counter of "B&W's Diner."

"You know, Mayor, I read Carmody's column, and your boy and the rest showed guts the way they handled that Black Hills bullshit. I like the way they took it to 'em."

"Thanks," Sam said, tipping his head to the man.

"It's like I told my wife, boys screw up. Know I did. But that don't mean they won't be good men. 'Sides, your son, Davis, the Mexican kid and that black boy, they may be screw-ups, but they're our screw-ups, by God. Who the hell does Patton think he is lettin' that crap go on? And don't tell me he didn't think somethin' like that might happen. He runs that school like a drill sergeant runs boot camp. I wouldn't a blamed Collins if he'd decked the arrogant sonuvabitch. Like those Black Hills boys don't drink beer. Hell, those miners come out of the womb drinkin' beer. Rather drink beer than suck their momma's tit. You tell Jack and the boys to hang in there. I gotta good goddamn feeling 'bout this team. A good goddamn feeling."

Tuesday night St. Jude faced the Hoffman Heights Warriors at home. The crowd at the Wreck exploded when the Hilltoppers took the court for warm-ups and didn't let up until midway through the third quarter, when St. Jude opened the lead so wide Collins yanked his starters to keep the score from getting out of hand and let his bench get some game time.

Prior to playing varsity Jack watched a basketball game like the average fan. He followed the ball, focusing on offense more than defense, reacting to fouls and infractions with home-team-rooting emotion as opposed to rational analysis of the validity of the call. He cheered and booed with the crowd. But in the couple of months he had spent under Collins, Lane, and Scooter's coaching, practicing with and playing against boys with more skill, discipline, and fundamentals than the streetballers and intramurals he used to dominate, he had developed a different view of the game. He saw things he'd never noticed before: court balance and rotation, weak-side help, coaches calling defensive and offensive sets, substitution patterns, playing zone out of an in-bounds pass then slipping into man-to-man once the ball was in play. Each possession had a purpose, every cause a corresponding effect.

Basketball, he realized, was an unscripted dance of ebbs and flows. A series of contradictions of offensive design versus free-form improvisation, thought versus reaction, and control versus freedom.

As if to make Jack's point, Gudy stole the ball in front of the Hilltopper bench. Jack cheered as Gudy streaked down the court, breaking away from the pack. Legs churning, dribble beating like a tom-tom, Gudy soared, separating from the other nine for a fleeting second and all eternity, before slamming the ball home. As he raced past Jack, Gudy's eyes glowed, transcendence achieved. He rejoined the other nine, who seemed adrift without him, and the intricate dance resumed.

Of course, like towards the end of the Hoffman Heights game with the scrubs from both teams on the floor, the jazz-like dance could disintegrate into a helter-skelter mosh pit. The powerful poetry of basketball turned into silly rhymes. It was at that point Jack's interest waned and he looked across the court at Katy and his family.

With Sam being loyal to the bitter end and Mary Lou never one to leave a performance early—"Poor manners"—they always saw a game through. Sam calling out encouragement to the boys after a bad play, cheering the good ones, he and Katy explaining strategy to Becky, who watched with the same intensity as her father, brows furrowing in unison at a bad call, clapping when St. Jude scored.

As for Mary Lou, she kept track of a pigtailed Maggie, who, at six could come and go from the stands, spending more time in the hall playing with friends or down in the cafeteria eating popcorn and drinking pop than watching the game. Having sat through Sam's games in high school and now Jack's, Mary Lou knew more about basketball than the family gave her credit for. If Jack did not play, however, her mind drifted from the game, and Jack would see her watching the pep band and the cheerleaders.

Jack knew his mother's indifference to the game, so it was no surprise to see her ignore the action. Later, however, when the pep band played "Sweet Georgia Brown" during a timeout, Jack looked up expecting to see Mary Lou clapping her hands and swaying to the song, one of her old favorites. Instead, she sat motionless, head turned toward the band, not reacting to the music or the dancing cheerleaders, brown eyes seldom blinking, hands folded on her lap.

He looked away from her and leaned toward the huddle as if listening to Collins, but kept glancing back at his mother. Next to Mary Lou, Becky and Sam rose and gestured toward the court, jabbering and joking as they discussed a previous play. The people surrounding them also stood, stretching, rocking to the music, a few grabbing coats and leaving. As everything around her expanded, the band roaring, the pom-pom girls kicking higher, people bustling about and shouting, Mary Lou shrank, sitting small, silent and isolated within the din.

Across the court Jack watched, all too familiar with the turmoil that followed such stillness. He tried to convince himself she was daydreaming, like normal people do. But if the last three years taught him anything it was that his mother's mind was no longer normal. He thought of waving at Sam and Becky. To sound the alarm and rescue Mary Lou from herself. But such a move could draw unwanted attention and upset her. So he continued to stare in the hope she might look his way, flash a sign of recognition, and reconnect with the world outside her thoughts.

The buzzer sounded, the band stopped, the pom-pom girls skipped away, and the fans sat. But Mary Lou did not move until Maggie bounced up the bleachers and tossed herself into her mother's lap. Eyes wide now and blushing, Mary Lou nodded at Jack and cracked a tight smile. She hugged Maggie, glancing to see if her son was watching.

Quickly Jack switched his gaze to the court, not wanting to embarrass her, following the ebb and flow, contemplating the contradictions.

At Seventeen

"So what were you thinking at the game?" Dr. Musselman asked at the next session.

"I was drifting."

"Your father?"

"I suppose."

Mary Lou stretched on the leather couch. Dr. Musselman shifted his bulky body in the wingback chair. It was time to push Mary Lou harder, Musselman thought, to stop dancing around the real issue. Not that it would heal her. Paranoid schizophrenics could not be cured, only helped to understand the reasons they feel the way they feel and cope with the voices. Above all they must take their medication. The curse of the paranoid schizophrenic was a mind, calmed by meds, which persuaded them they were OK and to toss the pills.

"Tell me again, Mary Lou, what is your earliest memory of your father?"

"Well, I think I've told you, but—and it goes against other memories of him—it was of him and mother fighting."

"And you were how old?"

"I must've been four because Sara hadn't been born."

"That's right, you're five years older than your sister. Was your mother pregnant with Sara at the time?"

"No," Mary Lou said crossing then uncrossing her ankles.

"And you said you remember your father left?"

"Yes, he left the room. That's all I remember."

"The room? Not the house?"

Mary Lou lay still.

"I'm thinking," Musselman whispered, "that he left the house. For longer than you remember. What do you think? I know you were young and it was a long time ago."

Mary Lou folded and unfolded her hands. She cried. Musselman handed her tissues.

"It's OK, Mary Lou. Take your time."

"When did you figure it out?"

"It doesn't matter. But tell me what happened. It's important you tell me. Important for you."

"He was leaving for another woman."

"That's what the fight was about?"

"Yes. Of course, I don't remember that part. I heard my mother and Aunt Thelma talking about it a few years later when they didn't think Sara or I were around."

"Who was the woman?"

"An old childhood sweetheart. His one true love who he'd not seen in years and given up on before marrying my mother."

"Did he marry your mother, in part, because she was pregnant with you?"

"No. I was legitimate, as they say. This woman had left town, and then Daddy met Momma. But years later she returned, and Daddy still had feelings for her."

"So strong that he left you and your mom?"

"Well, times were tough, the depth of the Depression. My parents and the woman were all young. Perhaps he felt overwhelmed and was looking for a way out."

Dr. Musselman pursed his lips and scribbled on a yellow legal pad.

"I'm curious, Mary Lou, do you believe there is any excuse for a husband and father to leave his wife and child? I don't mean a divorce with child support. I mean abandon."

"No, of course not, no."

"Then why do you make excuses for your father? 'It was the Depression. He was young, overwhelmed.'"

"I guess one person's excuses are another's reasons," Mary Lou said, twisting the tissue. "Regardless, he came back."

"Well, yes, but why? He'd already run off with the love of his life. Abandoned your mother, and you. What made him return? What changed?"

Mary Lou sat up on the couch, feet flat on the floor as she snatched tissues from the box.

"You know why," she sobbed.

"So, he ran away when it was your mother and you but came back..."

"Yes, yes, goddamn him, yes!" Mary Lou shouted, tears streaming. "He came back because he found out Momma was pregnant with Sara. He came back because of Sara. Not because of me. That's why I always stopped by the store. That's why I waited for him at the end of the day. And what did it get me? He still missed my concerts. Before he died he couldn't even remember my name. He abandoned me. Again and again. Is that what you wanted to hear? All that psychobabble? My father abandoned me. My father abandoned me. Have we made a *breakthrough*? Goddamn men. You're all alike. Deaf and dumb. No wonder I run away..." Mary Lou stopped and stared at Musselman. "Oh, Jesus, surely you don't think..."

They sat silent for a minute, Musselman giving Mary Lou space to think before speaking.

"It's a piece of the puzzle, Mary Lou. You need to accept that your father abandoned you. Not your mother. Not your sister, not Sam, not your children. Your father. No one else is running from you. You don't need to beat them to the punch. Think about that the next time the voices tell you to run. And fight them, Mary Lou. Fight the voices."

"But what if I can't?"

"You've got a lot of people who'll stand and fight with you."

"And look how I've treated them. I'm no different than my father." She moaned and sobbed into her hands.

Take It to the Limit

"BULLSHIT, BULLSHIT, BULLSHIT!" the Hilltopper's student section chanted.

"No way that was a charge, Jack," Jenkins shouted as he jerked Jack up from the floor. "Keep takin' it to the hole."

"BULLSHIT, BULLSHIT, BULLSHIT!" the students yelled as the referee signaled four and four with his hands, Jack's uniform number, to the scorer's table.

It was the rematch against the Black Hills Miners, midway through the fourth quarter of the suspended boys' first game back, and Jack's dunk over J.J. "Davy" Crockett would have given St. Jude its first lead of the game. Instead they remained a point down, and Jack picked up his fourth foul.

"BULLSHIT, BULLSHIT, BULLSHIT!"

The St. Jude crowd, stinging from the treatment at Black Hills, had been rowdy at the start, screaming like banshees during a tight first half. They hushed when Black Hills opened up a thirteen-point lead in the third, but revved up when St. Jude closed the gap in the fourth. Coach Collins took full advantage of the experienced gained by Tompkins, McElroy, and Pitman during the suspension, and rotated eleven players in and out of the game. Like a prizefighter saving a reserve of energy for the final round, when the fourth quarter rolled around Collins unleashed his rested starters along with the two-two-one full-court press. Not as deep as St. Jude, the Miners felt the squeeze, turning the ball over and letting the Hilltoppers back into the game.

As he ran up court after the foul, Jack glanced to the sidelines and saw Black Hill's coach Stan "The General" Patton striding in front of the visitors bench, forever in his white shirt and black and red striped tie, hands clapping, grinning face a contorted scarlet, violet neck veins bulging. Patton was thrilled with the call, Jack thought, hopeful it might stem the Topper tide.

"Let 'em holler, Crockett," Patton shouted. "That was a helluva play, boy. Way to sacrifice yourself. Good hustle, good goddamn hustle. Now let's get two."

Jack passed the half court line and the scorer's table and looked to the Hilltoppers bench, expecting to see Collins shouting similar encouragement. Instead, Collins stood with his hands on his hips, staring into the howling student section, while Scooter shouted at the ref.

"You owe us one," Scooter yelled, hoping to plant a seed for the next close call. "No way Crockett had position. No way."

"BULLSHIT, BULLSHIT, BULLSHIT!" echoed through the Wreck.

Collins turned and marched to the scorer's table and snatched the PA announcer's microphone. "Not here, not here," he said into the mic, looking toward the student section.

The bullshit chant slowed, but did not stop.

"I said, not here!" Collins shouted and pointed at the students. "Not at St. Jude. We're better than that."

The chant faded then died, leaving a muffled murmur that rolled like an ocean swell around the gym. Collins handed the mic to the announcer, signaled for timeout and strode toward the bench.

As he did so the subdued swell transformed into a growing wave of cheers and a building crescendo of applause. The students began a different chant.

"We are HILLTOPPERS...We are HILLTOPPERS...We ARE HILLTOPPERS...WE ARE HILLTOPPERS!" The noise ricocheting off the concrete block walls as the entire crowd joined in.

Patton stared at Collins like a father caught in a lie by his son. The blood drained from his face, grin turning to a glare, as he stopped marching and called his players to the bench.

"What the hell does he mean 'we're better?'" Patton yelled at the Miner's team physician, Dr. Keck. "Uppity—"

"C'mon, Stan," Keck said, grabbing Patton by the arm and turning him to the bench.

Collins did not hear Patton or chose to ignore him. He unbuttoned the top button of his blue Brooks Brothers suit jacket and knelt on one knee in front of the St. Jude bench, head down. The five starters sat facing him, drinking water and wiping sweat off with white cotton towels.

Collins waved away the clipboard Scooter offered.

"You want to sub for Jack?" Lane asked. "That was his fourth, and we've got three-plus minutes to play."

"Nope, we'll keep him in," Collins said, lifting his head. "Need his offense."

Collins's brown eyes roved from Jenkins to Gudy to Brewster to Connolly to Jack. He pointed to his head then thumped his chest with his fist. "That's what it comes down to!" he shouted. "Keep up the full court pressure. Run the offense. Trust yourself and your teammates. Remember the 'Law of the Jungle.' Now let's win this thing. I'm sick and tired of losing to Patton and the damn Miners."

Collins stood and extended a steady right hand forward. Scooter, Lane, and the five starters covered it. The boys standing behind Collins closed in tight.

"We are," the team shouted in unison with the surging crowd, "HILLTOPPERS...WE ARE HILLTOPPERS... WE ARE HILLTOPPERS!"

Because of the foul the Miners had to take the ball the length of the court, allowing the Toppers to set up their press. To make it more difficult, the Black Hills basket was on the side of the court away from their bench, making it impossible for his players to hear Patton.

"Jack, Gudy, Brew," Collins shouted as the huddle broke, "because of Jack's fouls he's going to play safety on the press. Brew you take Gudy's spot at right middle. Gudy you go to left middle. All right, let's go!"

"This ain't the NBA," Patton shouted in the huddle. "No shot clock. So be patient. Get a good shot or make 'em foul. We have a one-point lead. We're in the bonus. Foul puts you at the line. Remember, as long as we have the lead, the pressure's on them to get the ball and score."

Crockett inbounded the ball to the Miners point guard, a five-foot seven, one-hundred thirty pound watermelon-seed-slick kid named Freddy "Mercury" Morrissey. Jack did not know if the nickname paid homage to Queen's smooth-sounding lead singer or the Miami Dolphins running back, Mercury Morris. Or if Mercury was what every fast kid was called by his buddies or by ground-down veteran sportswriters tired of trying to dub jocks with fresh handles. Regardless, the soot-freckled Mercury Morrissey gave opposing teams fits.

The full-court press on, Jenkins and Connolly, tried to trap Mercury in the corner, but he squirted free and hit Crockett in full stride with a looping pass at the top of the key. Gudy and Brewster tried to close, but neither possessed Jack's athleticism and Crockett crossed half court, avoiding a ten count.

Jack hung back in Brewster's safety position, knowing he might have picked the pass off. It was on such a play he drew his fourth foul. He leapt high, snatched the ball and drove to the hole. But Crockett, as swift as Jack, slipped in front of him and picked up the charge, forcing Collins to adjust the boys' places in the press to protect Jack. But Jack reminded himself to not be too aggressive. He was the safety now, the last line of defense. With Gudy trailing the ball, Jack kept Crockett and the Miner's center, Kurt Svenson, in front of him as the rest of the Toppers raced to pick up their man. Crockett waited for Morrissey than passed him the ball.

Then the cat and mouse game began.

Crockett and the three other Miners ran to the separate corners of the half court, leaving the point guard inside the half-court circle with Jenkins guarding him.

"Four-corners," Collins shouted. "They're running the four-corners offense. Stay with your man. Deny the ball. Force the five-second call. Don't foul unless I tell you to. Jack, stay with Svenson. Gudy take Crockett. Brew pick up the other forward."

The four-corners offense was designed to protect leads at the end of games and score, to move the ball within the square, the players in the corner cutting across the middle to free a man for an easy path to the basket or a backdoor pass for a lay up. It ate up clock, wore down the defense, and resulted in easy baskets or fatigue fouls and trips to the line. It required a strong point guard like Morrissey who could make free throws, but his teammates needed to be good ball-handlers and shooters as well. Morrissey could not dribble the ball for three-plus minutes.

The St. Jude crowd, recognizing the four-corners, booed.

"Play ball, Patton," the students yelled. "You gutless wonder!"

But Jack knew Patton made the right call. The Toppers had momentum, closing the Miners thirteen point lead to one. Out of timeouts, the only way Patton could hope to get a measure of control was to slow the game down. On his haunches at the far end of the Black Hills bench, leathery palms cupped around his mouth, shouting instructions his players could not hear, Patton knew the issue could not be forced, this game one the Miners must survive, not go out and win. Patton reveled in the catcalls, as the fans grew restless watching the Toppers chase Morrissey and the Miners around. Better to hear boos than cheers when the Toppers stole the ball off the press and Jack or Gudy slammed home dunks.

The old warhorse knew how to win a basketball game.

It surprised Jack, however, that Patton would keep Svenson in the game, the lumbering Swede easy for Jack to guard and avoid a fifth foul. At six foot nine, two hundred and fifty pounds Svenson was a man among boys. Clogging the lane with his bulk, he forced high-fliers like Jack and Gudy to adjust their drives, while his shoving and leaning took a toll on Brewster. But he could not dribble, shoot the ball, or rebound reliably. Svenson was a *basketball player* only because Patton said he was.

At first, the four-corners worked to perfection. Morrissey zipped in and out, dribbling, cutting, faking drives to the hole and then reversing, a gasping Jenkins focused on keeping the slippery guard from slithering past for an easy layup. After fifteen to twenty seconds, Morrissey gave up the ball to Crockett, or any teammate besides Svenson, who passed or dribbled for five to ten seconds before returning the ball to Morrissey. A minute fell off the game clock like a raindrop from heaven, and the frenzied St. Jude fans howled in frustration.

"Deny the pass," Collins shouted at Gudy, Brewster, and Lane the next time Morrissey had the ball in the middle. "Jack, Jenkins. Trap the ball. Trap the ball!"

Patton, hearing Collins, jumped up and whistled and waved like a traffic cop, desperate to signal his players. But Morrissey, back to the Black Hills bench, could not see Patton, and the coach's whistling was lost in the hooting and hollering of the Toppers fans. Morrissey dribbled hard to the hoop on the right side of the court where Jack stood keeping his body between Svenson and the ball. Jenkins denied Morrissey a path to the basket, the little man stopped short of the baseline, spun to his right and shifted the ball to his left, expecting to see Jack with Svenson and squirt between them and Jenkins toward the half court line.

But as Morrissey spun, Jack abandoned Svenson, planted his right foot on the base line and spread his left leg wide. Jenkins closed fast also and within a split second they bottled the slick Mercury on the baseline.

"One...two... three..." the ref counted, right hand holding a silver whistle in pursed lips, ready to blow, left arm marking the count with hatchet-like chops. If he reached five, the Toppers took possession. Morrissey's eyes searched for an open cutter between Jack and Jenkins's arms and elbows, but Gudy, Connolly, and Brewster stayed on their men, cutting off all hope.

In the corner stood the statue-like, blond-haired Svenson, arms extended, eyes wide, hands trembling.

"Mercury, Mercury, Mercury," he dry-mouthed, not wanting the ball but compelled by a sense of duty to call for it.

"Four..." the ref roared, left arm slashing.

Morrissey kept his pivot foot in place, ball faked toward half court then jab stepped to the baseline extending his short arms toward the crowd behind the basket and wrapped a short bounce pass around Jack's right leg to Svenson. The big man bent low, caught the ball and held it above his head looking, like Morrissey had, for an open man. But Gudy, Connolly, and Brewster had their men covered, Jenkins stayed with Morrissey, and Jack turned and closed fast on Svenson. Jack planted his left leg on the baseline, keeping his body between the center and the basket. Svenson would have to find an open player or dribble the ball up the sideline toward center court, a perilous trip even for an expert dribbler.

"One...two..." the ref began again.

Jack thrust his arms to the sky and edged as close to Svenson as he dared without fouling. The Swede's blue eyes bulged, sweat rolled down his flushed face. No man open, no timeouts left. The massive Miner had one path to freedom.

"Three..." the ref yelled.

Svenson pivoted away from Jack, brought the ball to his waist and laid it with a solid *THUMP* against the hardwood, shuffling up the sideline, white, size fourteen, Converse high tops skimming the floor, eyes on the ball, big body creeping like a man lost in the dark.

THUMP went the ball again, and Svenson slid down the line, Jack pressing him on every step.

The St. Jude fans screamed. The few Black Hills fans in attendance and the entire bench, including Patton, stood frozen, never having seen the senior center dribble more than a few times in succession during the course of his three-year varsity career.

THUMP, THUMP...Svenson dribbled twice in succession and took a full step forward, confidence growing.

"Sven!" a sprinting Morrissey shouted, freed from Jenkins by a pick from Crockett. Svenson, releasing the ball for another dribble, lifted his head and turned a few degrees to see Mercury streak by, arms waving, and as the big man's head rose, his huge foot followed. He dropped his hands to catch the ball and whip it to Mercury, but instead of one last reassuring *THUMP* against the hardwood there was a muffled *THUD* as the leather ball landed on the toe of the Swede's big sneaker and bounced out of bounds.

An ecstatic St. Jude student wearing dark glasses and a Blues Brothers fedora caught the ball as the ref shouted, "Toppers ball!" and pointed toward the St. Jude basket.

Svenson clutched his head as he ran down the court. Crockett patted him on the back. Patton kicked the floor, cursing not Svenson but himself for not pulling the big man during the timeout.

"Run the offense!" Collins pointed to Jenkins as he took the inbounds pass from Connolly.

Unlike a lot of coaches, Collins did not call timeout to set up a play at the end of a game. He believed this was where good coaching and practice paid dividends. No need to diagram a play and allow the rattled Miners to set up an inbounds defense. The Toppers either would execute the motion offense as taught or they would not. He could not play the game for them. "Practices are class, games are tests," he said many times. "And the end of a close game is like a final exam. Let's see how you do when the pressure's on." He could not play the game for them. He *would* not play the game for them.

Jenkins dribbled the ball toward center court, Mercury Morrissey picking him up at the half court line.

Jack and the boys waited for Connolly to join them, each player taking his position, readying themselves for the action to come, hearts revving like the Indy 500 field waiting for the green flag. Jenkins picked up his dribble at the top of the key and fired a pass to Jack on the right wing. Jack held it strong in triple-threat position, two hands on the ball in shooting position, ready to sink the jumper or pass or dribble penetrate. Crockett was in his face, bouncing, waving his arms, a bundle of nervous energy, determined to block Jack's shot from the wing or stop his drive to the hole.

"Make somebody else beat us," Patton hollered.

Jack jab-stepped and head faked, but Crockett did not bite and stayed on him like cling wrap. Brewster and Gudy flashed off screens, but neither could get open or in a good position to do anything with the ball but pass it back. The idea of slashing past the overeager Crockett passed through Jack's mind, his streetball, man-on-man instincts ready for the challenge. He glanced at the game clock. 1:20 left. Too soon. Jack saw the hulking Svenson lurking in the lane, threw a ball fake at Crockett and whipped the ball to Jenkins at the top of the key who fired it around the horn to Connolly on the opposite wing. Jack raced into the lane and set a pick for Gudy. Jenkins cut toward the hoop on the right as Brewster set a screen.

And with that, the Toppers cranked up the motion offense, the ball not touching the ground as the players flashed and dashed across and up and down the lane. Jack and Gudy popped out on the wings, Connolly and Jenkins rotated through and back up to the point. Brewster crisscrossed the court, setting picks, pivoting, back to the basket, the big man taking the occasional interior pass, looking for a cutter, throwing a fake at Svenson to keep him honest, set him up for the next play, then firing the ball to the wing or the key.

A low murmur of *ooohs* and *aaahs* spread across the bleachers, the standing crowd appreciative of the contradictory notion of the motion offense; its precision and free-flowing grace playing off each other, the ball be-bopping between the boys like pinball with a purpose. The mesmerized fans, like cool-cat-customers in a jazz club, let loose no prolonged cheers or screams. Everyone in the gym, including the Black Hills folks, was in the moment, marveling at the cuts, picks, passes and brief solos of the Toppers. Brewster's work in the lane, Jack's head and shoulder fakes on the wing, Jenkins taking two quick dribbles into the lane, then popping

out, testing, poking, prodding, looking for a crack in the Miners defense. And the
Miners countered, lunging, scrambling, Crockett face-up on Jack, Svenson leaning on Brewster, Morrissey scatting around Jenkins. Their defense flexed but did
not crack, as the crowd admired the simple beauty of a well-played game, the ten
boys dancing an unscripted basketball ballet, the finale approaching with every
tick of the scoreboard clock.

Patton paced and shouted.

Scooter chewed his nails and prayed the rosary.

Lane, decked out in a pearl shaded leisure suit and wide-collar blue shirt,
perched on the edge of the bench, fingertips tingling, ready to take the last shot.
Always the gunner, confident he would drain it, astonished whenever the ball
failed to fall but, with a true shooter's self-assurance, certain the next one would.

Elbows on his knees, game program in his left hand, gold cross stuck to his
sweating palm, brown eyes darting as the ball zoomed around the court, Collins
leaned forward on the bench, fighting the urge to shout, not wanting to interrupt
his players' rhythm, break their concentration.

"Let 'em play," he told himself. "Let 'em play."

As the clock ticked down below twenty-five seconds, Jack weaved his way
through the lane one more time, taking a pass from Connolly in the right corner.
Crockett fought through Brewster's screen, a step late getting to Jack, but managed to stay close enough to stop Jack from firing. Jack glanced at Crockett's eyes.

"He's gassed," Jack thought and nodded toward the far corner as he tossed the
ball to Connolly on the wing, faked Crockett to the left, and sprinted toward the
hoop, crossing out of bounds over the baseline as Brewster slid toward Jack from
the lower block and set a crushing screen on the trailing Crockett. As Crockett
sprawled on the floor, the slow-footed Svenson tried to reverse course and stay
with Jack.

In full stride, Jack peeled around Brewster, sweaty shoulders sliding white on
black, black on white, hopped back in bounds and raced toward the left corner,
free of all defenders. Connolly, who held the ball for a beat after Jack's nod, ball-
faked his man to buy Jack time, then cleared it with a blur to Jenkins at the top
of the key who zipped it to Gudy on the left wing who fired a fastball back to
the corner where Jack caught it with his right hand and jerked to a halt with the
shriek of rubber-on-wood. He did not hear the crowd or coaches, nor did he think
of his mother vanishing for days at a time, his father drinking himself to sleep, he
felt no worries about what people thought, had no cares about winning or losing
the game. The sound and fury of life, all the bullshit and the noise, floated like
flotsam and jetsam in his wake as Jack propelled forward on his singular, simple
mission, soul lost and found in the flash of an instant.

Pivoting toward the hoop on his left foot, he squared his shoulders to the basket; legs bent at the knees, his body strong from Collins's constant conditioning, and pulled the ball in, left hand resting on its side, right hand in shooting position. Although slow as an overloaded grain truck creeping uphill, the desperate Svenson took one last labored stride, shot his arms in the air and lunged toward a jumping Jack.

At the height of his leap, Jack felt the dimples of the leather ball as it rolled off his fingertips. He watched it arc toward the hoop, spinning like a satellite in the weightlessness of space, reaching its apex, then tumbling down toward the welcoming white net, landing with a cuuuuuush.

He knew it was good the moment the ball left his hand, knew it without thinking, knew it the way a loved baby knows his mother will comfort him when he cries, instinctual, unspoken, understood.

He struck the pose for a split-second, right arm extended, Svenson stumbling past him and collapsing in a mismatched heap of alabaster knees, chest, hands, and body, smacking the beige floor boards with a shuddering thump, while all eyes in the building watched the ball slide through the net.

The Wreck exploded. The St. Jude fans jumped and shouted, the Black Hills faithful groaned.

And with that, like an alarm awaking him from a deep sleep, Jack returned to the world. Conscious now of the crowd, the players, and the scoreboard clock ticking down, the game still on.

"Get the ball, get the ball," Patton shrieked.

"Set up the press," Jenkins yelled.

Morrissey snatched the ball as Svenson and Crockett scrambled to their feet.

The Toppers' scrambled to their defensive positions, no one slapping hands or smiling

Jack drifted to the left middle then remembered he was the safety as Crockett streaked down the opposite side of the court.

"Get back, Jack, get back!" Scooter shouted.

The game clock raced toward ten seconds as the ref started the five-count on the inbounds pass. Morrissey slid to the left side of the basket to keep his pass away from the backboard, set his stubby legs, and fired the ball over Connolly like a quarterback leading a wide receiver.

Crockett caught the ball over his right shoulder at the half court line and dribbled toward the left side of the hoop.

Jack, four steps behind and across the court, took an angle that would intercept Crockett in front of the hoop, if he could beat the fleet Miner to the spot.

But Crockett throttled down on his way to the basket, Svenson's turnover likely fresh in his mind, not wanting to take any chances with the ball careening out of bounds.

Jack sprinted, fast-closing footsteps now thundering above the din of the crowd, Crockett glanced back and saw him, dribbled faster, passed the foul line, and went airborne six feet from the basket, the ball in his left hand, left leg raised, rim between Jack and the ball.

Jack took one last bounding stride and leapt towards the hoop, right arm shooting to the sky. Crockett, who decided midflight to lay the ball off the glass, not certain he could dunk with his weaker left hand, released the ball below the rim with a flick of his wrist, floating it up toward the glass. Jack soared, right elbow even with the basket and tipped the ball before it brushed the board. The ball bounced off the glass, dinged the rim, and fell to the court. Gudy, following the play, grabbed it before it went out of bounds and dribbled, playing keep away from lunging Miners as the buzzer sounded.

Collins, Scooter, and Lane turned to each other and slapped hands. Jack, Gudy, and the rest of the starters hopped, hugged, and high-fived.

Crockett and Svenson shook Jack's and the rest of the Topper's hands, as did Dr. Keck with Collins. But Patton and his assistants turned and double-timed with the rest of the Miners to the locker room. The St. Jude students, vengeance theirs, poured onto the court.

As the student body bounced and skipped like children playing in the rain, Jack scanned the stands for his family, relieved to see Mary Lou clapping and cheering. He smiled, a wave of satisfaction washing over him with exhilaration, surprise, and calm. Katy popped out from the throng and Jack swept her up in a hug. They turned and waved at his family then whooped and dove into the mob of screaming kids.

Old Days

On the last Saturday of February, Jack sat on the couch in the living room leafing through the scrapbook Mary Lou kept to chronicle the Topper's season. Kneeling in front of him, Sam threw five T-bone steaks on an iron grill made to fit into the fireplace. The red, two-inch-thick steaks sizzled above the white-hot bed of charcoal beneath. Behind them Mary Lou played Gershwin on the piano, while the girls squeals escaped from the TV room where they watched a *Brady Bunch* rerun.

"I'll flip those in about ten minutes," Sam said to Jack as he sat in an easy chair angled toward the couch and the fireplace. "Should be ready to eat in twenty."

Sam took a sip from his scotch and water and fired up a Lucky.

"Nice of your mom to keep that scrapbook for you, huh?"

"Yeah, this is great. Like the one Grandma did for you."

Jack turned a page and came to the article on the game against the Miners in which Art Carmody wrote "this win might be the turning point in the Topper's season." Carmody's words had proven prophetic. The team went a respectable 4-3 during the suspended boys' absence, losing to Black Hills, blowing out Hoffman Heights, Uni-High, and Plainview before dropping a close one to Mount Pullman, then bouncing back against Springtown and losing in overtime to the Centennial Chargers and Billy McGuire. Following the home win against the Miners, St. Jude had ripped off nine straight wins, riding a wave of momentum into Tuesday's Regional opener, the first round of the state tournament, with a regular season record of 18-6.

While Jack, Gudy, and Brewster took turns leading the team in scoring, and Jenkins and Connolly continued their steady play at guard, everyone else chipped in too, Lane's dream of eleven players making a contribution coming to fruition. Jack glanced at the article on the Helena game where Cheyo stole the ball in the fourth quarter and fired a crosscourt bounce pass to Jenkins for a layup that gave the Toppers a six-point lead with under a minute to play and sealed the deal. On the facing page was a photo of Jimmy driving to the hole after he'd come in for a foul-plagued Gudy against Johnson City and exploded for seventeen points, nine rebounds, three assists, and two steals. Jimmy subbed for Connolly at off-guard, while P.K. spelled Jenkins at point, helping to keep the starters fresh. They played tough defense, took care of the ball, and ran the motion offense like they had been playing it for years. Tompkins, McElroy, and Pitman (Attorneys at Law, Cheyo nicknamed them, the three juniors joined at the hip, a team within the team) gave solid if not numerous minutes. With fewer than two minutes to play against Jonesboro, Tompkins hit a pair of free throws that extended the Hilltoppers' winning streak to nine.

But it was the last game, the night before against Chicago Polytechnic, the clipping of the newspaper account in fresh black and white, that gave the best indication of how good the Toppers might be. St. Jude had never played the Dynamos, but Collins added them to the schedule knowing that if the Toppers were going to win a state title they would have to beat a Chicago public school squad. He would not allow his middle-class kids to be victims of the big-city black-superstar-streetballer mind games and trash-talking intimidation that kids from Chicago liked to lay on the small town downstaters.

The Dynamos were the perfect opponent to explode the myth for the Toppers. From the South Side, it was the school that Collins would have attended had his mother not enrolled him in private school, they were ranked ninth in Class AA. They featured an assortment of quick-handed, fleet-footed, tough city kids, who ranged in height between six foot and six foot five. Most were as black as Jimmy, athletic as Jack, and arrogant as Jenkins. St. Jude had seen the Dynamos lose a close game to Hassan Jones and Blooming Grove in the Rail Splitter Classic, and Collins was concerned with the comments and the looks he witnessed from his squad. A few seemed ready to succumb to the myth, while Jack and the Rams had seemed too eager to challenge it. Neither view, Collins knew, would lead to victory.

"OK, listen up," Collins said as they gathered on the bleachers in the Wreck before jumping on the bus for the two hour bus ride to Chicago. "I want to talk to you boys now so you've got time to think about what I'm telling you. Now, next to Blooming Grove, Chicago Polytechnic is the toughest team we've played. Agreed?"

The boys all nodded.

"And unlike Blooming Grove we won't be playing them on a neutral court. We're going to the South Side of Chicago, to the ghetto. Anybody nervous?"

No one said anything.

"Well, if you're not, you should be," Collins said laughing. "I am, and I grew up not far from there. My brother Rudy graduated from Polytech. It's a rough school filled with a lot of tough kids… But still kids, like you."

Collins paced in front of his silent squad.

"Now, we're not going there to fight them. And we're not going to make lifelong friends. We're going to play basketball, on a court with the same dimensions, same ten-foot baskets, same free throw lines fifteen feet from the hoop, no different from the Wreck. And you know what else? We're a better basketball team than they are. Aren't we Coach Lane?"

"No doubt in my mind."

"Scooter?"

"Absolutely, Coach."

The boys cheered.

"But we won't win," Collins shouted, quieting the boys. "That's right, I said we won't win…if we don't play our game."

Collins let the statement sink in as he walked in front of the boys

"And our game is not their game. They're going to run at every opportunity. They'll clear a side and go one-on-one. They'll turn the ball over a lot but just as fast turn around and score three quick buckets. Some of them will taunt you. So will a few of their fans. You think Black Hills is different than St. Jude? You haven't seen anything. The only white faces you're going to see in that gym tonight are your teammates, Scooter, Lane, parents who make the trip, and maybe the officials.

"The whole gym will try to get you to play the Dynamos game. Turn it into a high-scoring, streetball affair. Don't fall for it. As helter-skelter as their offense may be, their defense is disciplined. They will take the charge. They'll trap. You will have to force yourself to stay in our offense. Press 'em whenever you can on defense. Fast break when you get a chance. Dunk in their face to show them you're not intimidated. Rain down jumpers. But don't taunt them back. Don't go one-on-one. Don't play their game. Play ours, and we'll win. It's that simple."

And that is what we did, Jack thought, as he looked at the headline of Carmody's column in that morning's *Harbinger*, "Toppers Spin Dynamos out of Top Ten." At first, like Collins said they would, the crowd had yelled and screamed at the St. Jude players, skeptical of the hype about the downstate team with so-called streetballers.

"C'mon white boy," one shouted at Jack as he held the ball on the wing in the first quarter, "what you got?"

When Jack passed the ball to Jenkins, staying within the offense, remembering what Collins told them, the guy hollered: "Yeah, that's what I thought. You ain't got shit. Great white hope my ass. If you were black the press wouldn't say shit 'bout you."

Despite Collins' talk, nerves got the best of them and the Toppers fell behind by six halfway through the first quarter. But after weathering the initial storm, the combination of the press and the motion offense turned things their way. The nonstop offense caused foul problems for the overeager Dynamos, who leapt at every fake. When the Toppers pulled even, then took the lead in the second quarter, the Polytechnic players panicked. Anxious about the damage getting beat by a hick town would do to their street rep, they tried too hard to get back into the game, and piled up turnovers.

At the half the Toppers led by nine. Midway through the third quarter, the Dynamos put on a spurt that closed the lead to three, but Polytechnic began to tire. They stopped fighting through or switching on the endless screens St. Jude threw at them. By the end of the third the game was not close. St. Jude led by twelve, the full-court press leading to easy buckets. Jack dunked three times, the last drawing a few cheers from the crowd as he soared above two Dynamos and slammed the ball home.

"That boy can play," Jack heard a thirty-something black man in a burgundy leisure shirt, gold chains dangling from his neck, say to the woman beside him.

When Collins pulled the starters with two minutes to play, scattered applause followed them to the bench. And when the final buzzer sounded, the Dynamos and their coaches all walked to the Toppers bench and shook hands, if not with smiles, at least with grudging respect.

"You know," Jack said to Sam, looking up from the scrapbook, "those folks up at Polytechnic were decent fans. Better than Black Hills. It wasn't nearly as bad as Coach made it out to be."

"Coach Collins was preparing you for the worst, that's all. People are people. There's a few jerks in every bunch."

Sam and Mary Lou followed the team bus to the game, caravanning with the Jacksons, Brewsters, Gudy's folks, the Jenkinses, and the Keinos, but the majority of St. Jude fans stayed home, scared to travel to the Polytechnic neighborhood.

Sam took a drag from his cigarette and exhaled gray smoke. "Then again, it was that first Black Hills game that pulled you boys together. 'Specially you and Jenkins."

"Randy's OK. Don't think we'll ever be best buds. He said a few things about Mom.... But I don't think he meant it. Just pissed off. It's cool, now."

"Probably bitter, and a little jealous."

"Of me?"

"In a way. More so about your having such a great mom. Randy's mother died when he was two. He never really knew her. Sally, the Mrs. Jenkins you know, is his stepmother. Good enough gal, but not Randy's mother. And she sure doesn't hold a candle to your mom."

"I didn't know that," Jack said, closing the scrapbook. "Didn't know Randy lost his mom...that he never knew her."

"No reason you should. You were two years old when it happened. You and Randy went to different grade schools and junior highs."

Jack stared at the fire and saw Jenkins and his actions in a different light, as if he had met the real Randy. He placed the scrapbook on the coffee table, realizing as he did so that his mother had stopped playing.

"Sam," Mary Lou said as she slipped up behind Jack and rubbed her son's shoulders, "shouldn't you be flipping those steaks?"

Sam glanced at his scratched Timex wristwatch.

"Oh, damn... yes, yes."

He knelt in front of the fire and turned over each steak.

"I'll get the salad out of the 'fridge and the baked potatoes out of the oven," Mary Lou said, squeezing Jack one more time.

"Sounds good, hon," Sam said as he slid back into the chair and his scotch.

Jack tossed a questioning look at him as Mary Lou sang her way to the kitchen. Sam waved his left hand and shook his head at Jack, waiting for Mary Lou to be out of earshot.

"I'm hoping she's simply in a good mood," Sam said in a low voice, bending toward Jack as Mary Lou walked into the kitchen. "But I'll count her pills tonight..."

"That doesn't mean anything, Dad. She could be flushing 'em down the toilet. Not like she hasn't before."

"I know, I know. I'll call Musselman Monday and see what he thinks of her behavior lately. Hell, maybe he'll tell me she's getting better."

Mary Lou's footsteps returned, and they leaned back, Sam lighting a Lucky, Jack sighing as he laced fingers behind his head and stretched his legs to the fire.

After dinner the family gathered in front of the TV to watch the CBS sitcoms *Rhoda* and *Good Times*, spinoffs from the *Mary Tyler Moore Show* and *Maude*.

"*Good Times* is funnier than *Maude*," Becky said, continuing a conversation they had every Saturday night, as the opening credits rolled, "but *Rhoda* isn't as good as *Mary Tyler Moore*."

"Yeah," Jack said, "and this lineup isn't close to what they had with *All in the Family, M*A*S*H, Mary Tyler Moore*, and *Bob Newhart*. We'd laugh for two hours, then tell the jokes at school on Monday. Everybody watched those shows. Spinoffs ain't as good as the originals."

"I miss Mary," Maggie said. "She was so pretty. She reminded me of Mommy."

"Well," Sam said, "we'll have to be satisfied with reruns."

When *Good Times* ended, Mary Lou and the girls made fudge, and the family moved into the living room to sing, Sam leading with a soft, natural tenor, while Mary Lou alternated between solos and duets with Becky on the piano. Jack wrestled with Maggie, tickling her until she Spocked him. Squeezing his shoulder with a tiny hand, like she had seen the emotionless Vulcan from *Star Trek* do a hundred times to immobilize hapless foes. Jack always dropped like a ton of bricks, pretending to be passed out.

It was a Saturday night like many they had before, just not the last few years. Jack struggled to embrace it. The idea of his mother skipping meds clouded his mind, casting doubt as to whether they were spending an evening with her or her manic counterpart. Like the Dynamos from the night before, Jack felt she was pressing too hard.

Later, after everyone had gone to sleep, Jack awoke from a dream in which his mother was playing the piano downstairs. Drowsy, Jack pulled himself out of bed and walked to the edge of the steps, half-thinking he would see her playing like when he was a little boy. He heard nothing, but saw a glow in the living room and a shadowy motion crisscrossing the wall. He crept down the steps to see Mary Lou in the rocking chair in front of the fire, head tilted toward the ceiling.

Awake but not present.

Silent but not still.

The unfinished scrapbook lay open on her lap, fingers drumming on the plastic covered photos. Not wanting to startle her but unwilling to leave her alone, Jack slipped his grandmother's lavender and white quilt off the oak blanket rack, stretched out on the couch, and watched Mary Lou by the fire, mother and son alone with their thoughts. Jack, strong at seventeen, his mother, middle-aged and fragile, her body a few feet away, her mind adrift.

He would not awake tomorrow with the scent of Chanel N° 5 on his pajamas, but somehow, in some way, Jack sensed he was still in his mother's care.

It's a Long Way to the Top

Two days later Jack lined up along the sideline with the rest of the Toppers in the home gym of the Elmwood Cardinals, listening to the national anthem, right hands on thumping hearts, before the tipoff of their opening game of the state tournament against Mount Pullman. Billy McGuire and Centennial had won the first game that night against Holyoke, setting up a possible Regional final with St. Jude on Friday.

A few minutes earlier Collins had quoted Carmody's column from the day before: "'The Illinois State Class AA Tournament,'" Collins read, smoothing the paper flat, "'is for schools with enrollments greater than 750 students. Its beauty is in its simplicity, cruelty and joy. The opening Regional round is played in high school gyms across the state. Victors advance to the Sectional Championship with three other Regional winners. The sixteen Sectional winners—the Sweet Sixteen—face off in the Super Sectional, played at a larger arena, a nearby college or junior college gym, to accommodate the bigger crowd. The teams who win in the Super Sectional advance to the State Championship—the Elite Eight—and play in the Assembly Hall at the state university in Blooming Grove.'

"Pretty simple, right?" Collins said glancing at the boys. "Carmody continues: 'Yet no St. Jude team has ever advanced past the Sweet Sixteen; only two, the 1942 squad and Radar Gene Lane's, have made it *that* far. The Toppers are up against both history and Hassan Jones and Blooming Grove, who they are slotted to play in the Super Sectional if both teams advance. The Regional and Sectional games will be played on Tuesdays and Fridays for the next two weeks, with the Super Sectionals the third Tuesday, the Elite Eight the following week at the Assembly Hall and the semi-finals Saturday afternoon, with the championship game later that evening.'"

"'It's a nineteen-day sprint to the finish that, if it does not always culminate in the best team in the state winning the championship, rewards the toughest, hottest, and most opportunistic. Regular season records mean nothing. Undefeated teams lose in the Regional. Teams without a regular season victory win for the first time. Simple, cruel, joyful and, most of all, unpredictable. That's why they call it March Madness.'"

Collins folded the paper and paced in front of the boys.

"Couldn't have said it better myself," Collins said. "We win or we go home. So don't look ahead. The only team you need to be concerned about right now is Mount Pullman. We won't play Centennial if we don't beat Pullman. Stay focused. Be patient. Run the offense. Execute the press. Beat Pullman. That's it. Let's go."

After their ten-game winning streak at the end of the season, hopes at St. Jude ran high. Three busloads of students and a string of cars followed the team in a driving snowstorm, the two-lane road leading to Elmwood drifting-over so heavily in spots that the half-hour drive took an hour. Played in the regular season, a Mount Pullman versus St. Jude game would not attract a huge crowd, with St. Jude being a heavy favorite. But because this was the tournament, neither Mount Pullman's nor the Toppers' fans took it for granted.

Jack felt nervous in a good way, ready to play, his concerns about Mary Lou relapsing had relaxed after a conversation with Sam the day before.

"Talked to Dr. Musselman about Mom," his father said, picking Jack up in the rusted Plymouth after Monday night practice.

"And…" Jack said, reclining the seat and rolling his neck. Collins laid off the washboards, but ran the starters through the offense the entire practice, honing their timing.

"He thinks Mom may be skipping her meds from time to time. But she's made good progress in therapy and he always emphasizes to her that she must take her meds. If she admits to not taking them, he has her take one right then and there from the supply he keeps at the office. He says 'bout the best we can do is keep an eye on her. And he told me—now this is me, Jack, not you—to not be afraid to ask her. Could be she forgot, he says."

"So, she's getting better? Not going through an upswing before she flips out again?"

"He didn't say that, exactly," Sam said, hands on the wheel. "Goddamn shrinks won't ever commit themselves to anything definitive....I guess they can't. But, yeah, I think he feels better now than a few months ago."

Jack stared out the windshield of the Plymouth, view blurred by the smoke from Sam's Lucky.

"But...she's gettin' better?"

Sam lifted his hands off the wheel and shrugged. "That's the gist of what I got from Musselman, yeah. I don't think we need to be anymore concerned about her now than we have been in the past. Just need to keep an eye on her, as usual."

Jack realized that was about as good an answer as he could hope for. And though it did not satisfy him, and knowing it frustrated his father as well, he stayed silent for a few minutes.

"That's what we're always gonna have to do, isn't it Dad? Keep an eye on her?"

"Most likely. But what the hell, that's the way it is for all of us, isn't it? Watch out for each other, try not to shoot ourselves in the foot, and hope God cuts us a break once in a while. What the hell? We're all day to day, Jack. We just don't like to admit it."

Sam bowed his head and shook it, his upper body rippling from shoulders to rib cage to stomach. Jack thought he was crying.

"I mean really," Sam said, raising his head and chuckling, crow's feet crinkling around tired eyes. "Think about it. What the hell you gonna do when the best you can get from a doctor—a guy nationally respected in his field, mind you—is a *Keep an eye on her*? I mean, what the hell?"

Father and son both laughed at the absurd truth.

"Keep an eye on her, Sam," Jack mimicked Musselman. "Thanks, Doc," he said imitating Sam. "Thanks a lot. Whatta I owe you for that one, Doc? Maybe I should hire a private eye. Be cheaper.'"

They joked all the way home, each every once in a while advising the other, *keep an eye on her*.

And so Tuesday night Jack stood calm, ready to play, listening to the anthem with his parents, sisters, and grandparents in the stands, the St. Jude fans fidgeting, players shifting from foot to foot. Jack smiled and thought, "What the hell... we're all day to day."

He proceeded to play the best game of his short varsity career, scoring sixteen points, grabbing eight rebounds, dishing out four assists, stealing the ball twice and blocking a shot—by half time. He capped the performance with a rim-rattling dunk in the third quarter, the crowd rising and leaping with him, the cheers soaking him like a hard, cleansing rain, his heart racing, but his mind clear, immersed in the moment.

Collins pulled the starters a few plays later, the blowout in full force. St. Jude won going away, 70–46, setting up the third and final rematch against Billy McGuire and Centennial on Friday.

The Pretenders

"Where's your daddy, bro?" Jimmy shouted at Billy McGuire after slamming home a dunk in the fourth quarter of the Regional Finals game, sending the redhead sprawling. "You look confused."

McGuire shot a glance at Jack standing next to Jimmy, the two Toppers looming over him for a moment while the ref retrieved the ball from the stands. Jack shrugged his shoulders at McGuire, smiled, and offered a hand up. The fired-up Jimmy raced down court.

"Screw you, Jack," McGuire said slapping the hand away.

"Hey, man. Jimmy's my friend. Thought he should know how you felt 'bout things. That's all."

"He know you feel the same way?" McGuire shouted as he jumped to his feet and shoved Jack.

"Screw you, McGuire," Jack shouted, fists clenched at his sides, chest bumping against McGuire's. "You redneck bastard. I'm not like you."

"The hell you aren't."

"Break it up," the ref said, stepping between the two boys. "Play ball. Play ball."

Jack stared at McGuire for a second, spun around, face flushed, and ran back on defense, missing Jimmy's offer of a high-five at half-court. With a ten-point lead in the fourth, the Toppers did not apply the press.

"You OK, Jack?" Jimmy shouted, catching Jack by the arm. "What'd McGuire say?"

"Nothin'," Jack said, pulling his arm away. "Screw him."

"Let it go, Jack," Jimmy said, giving Jack a pat on the butt. "It's cool. It's cool."

Jack nodded and found his man for defense. A few minutes later, Collins pulled him from the game, the Toppers lead large enough to rest the starters. Although not a blowout like Mount Pullman, the Centennial game had not been as close as predicted. Jimmy had played his best game of the season.

Elmwood had let the Centennial and St. Jude teams into the gym early, and Jack had watched Billy and Jimmy joking around at the pregame shoot-around. He hadn't thought too much about it. Kids from both teams knew each other from Y ball, little league baseball, and various activities. But when Jimmy started telling Jack what a cool guy Billy seemed to be, Jack spoke up about what Billy said at Cheyo's New Year's party.

"Hey, man," Jack said as Jimmy dribbled a ball out by half court, "I'm not sayin' Billy is a bad guy, but there is somethin' you should know, Jimmy. I mean... Ah, hell, it probably ain't as big a deal as I'm makin' it sound."

"What, Jack?" Jimmy said picking up his dribble. "He say somethin' about me?"

"No, not you in particular. But he's got an attitude about black people."

"What'd he say?"

"Oh, well, he told that old joke about the definition of confusion..."

"Father's Day in East St. Louis. Yeah, I know. Cruel, but some hard truth to it."

"Yeah, I know, not cool but not the KKK. But he also went off about Hassan Jones and the 'Blooming Grove bro's' and their 'Black Man in America' summer team, then the Black Muslims. I don't know, the usual shit some white guys get riled up about. Made me uncomfortable, that's all, you know what I mean?"

"Yeah, I know," Jimmy said, looking toward McGuire.

"I'm sorry, Jimmy. I shouldn't've brought it up."

"This type of thing happen much? White people sayin' shit about blacks and you not sayin' anything to me about it, tryin' to protect me?"

"Man, I don't know about often, but, yeah, it happens."

"They ever say things about me? Like about me and Sandy, for instance?"

"No man, no way. They know better than that. They know you and I are friends. They know I wouldn't put up with that."

"Yeah, but they seem to think they can talk this shit around you, Jack. You know, about blacks in general. I mean, what'd you say to Billy that night?"

Jack looked at Jimmy but did not speak.

"It's OK, man," Jimmy said, laughing. "Man, Jack, you should see the look in your eyes... I had an idea of what Billy said. Couple of brothers from St. Jude heard him getting loud. Told me you looked like you couldn't get away from him quick enough. You know, we do talk about y'all. You white folk make for good conversations."

"Why, you sonuvabitch," Jack said, smiling.

"Careful, Jack" Jimmy said, laughing louder. "I think somethin' bad about 'blacks in general' almost slipped out."

"You knew? All along?"

"It's cool. Look, I don't think Billy is all that bad a guy. I mean, when the time is right, I'm gonna let him know I know what he said. Make him think twice next time. But you know, man, there's black guys do the same shit. Chinese, Mexican, you name it. None of it's right. Doesn't matter where it's coming from. But it's not like Billy, or white people, got the market cornered on that bullshit."

The Toppers won by fifteen, and the court filled with players, coaches, cheerleaders and fans. Jack watched Jimmy run up to McGuire and offer his hand. But the boys did not laugh like Jimmy and Jack earlier. McGuire, his freckled face crimson, slapped Jimmy's hand and flipped him off before stalking away. The blue-black Jimmy, Afro spiked high, hands on hips, stood frozen in the sea of surging, smiling white people.

Jostled into motion, Jimmy turned and walked off the court alone.

Breakdown

The following week in the Sectionals proved uneventful for the Toppers, who followed their Regional dominance with two more wins against McKinley and Havana, neither game close. The press, the motion offense, the athleticism of Jack, Brewster, Gudy, and Jimmy, along with the strong guard play of P.K., Jenkins, and Connolly, and the Toppers deep bench was proving overwhelming for the typical high school team with a seven- or eight-man rotation and two or three above-average players to contend with. Most were gassed by the half. When the final buzzer sounded against Havana on Friday night, the fans, the press, and any-one who had any interest in Illinois high school basketball and March Madness started talking about the Super Sectional matchup of the Hilltoppers against Hassan Jones and Blooming Grove the following Tuesday.

"Possibly the only team left," wrote Art Carmody in Saturday's *Harbinger*, "that has the talent and the depth to match up with the Toppers, who handed Blooming Grove its sole defeat of the season at the Rail Splitter Classic in December. It is not an exaggeration to say that whoever wins this one is the odds-on favorite to take it all at the Assembly Hall. These two teams are that good."

The local radio shows ran lengthy call-in segments for the next three days about the upcoming showdown. The *Harbinger's* letters-to-the-editor page on Sunday dripped with supportive comments and praise for the boys and the coaches, the beer bust and the suspensions long since forgotten, the coffee shops, bars, and barbershops abuzz about basketball.

"Wish I was up for reelection," Sam joked on Monday night at dinner, the night before the Super Sectional showdown. "Thanks to Jack and the Toppers, I'd win in a landslide."

"Unless Jack or one of the boys ran against you," Mary Lou said, voice tight, words clipped, no hint of humor. Eyes fixed on her chipped, lime-colored plate, she cut off a piece of the T-bone Sam grilled in celebration of the upcoming game with a stabbing slice of her steak knife.

While Maggie chattered on about a frog that escaped from its container in Mrs. Yale's classroom and the chaos that followed, Jack glanced at Sam while Becky looked at Mary Lou.

Following Dr. Musselman's directions at the start of the tournament two weeks earlier, Jack and Sam had kept an eye on Mary Lou. During Regionals she had maintained the same upbeat demeanor they had remarked upon that Saturday night, as if she had a couple of drinks and was buzzed—not herself but not transformed. At the Mt. Pullman blowout Jack watched her from the bench. She moved with the crowd, cheering when appropriate, eyes on the game, perking up at time-outs when the pep band played, perhaps too enthusiastic with her rooting. Late in the fourth quarter, the game long since decided, Mary Lou was the lone person who stood and applauded a takeaway layup by P.K., his parents and Luke not rising for the garbage-time basket. Glancing about she took a seat, aware of her exposure. The other Regional and Sectional games revealed more of the same as far as Jack could tell. Mary Lou *a little manic*, as she had come to say about herself, a result of the sessions with Dr. Musselman and his attempts to get her to recognize the stages of her illness so she might take the appropriate action. Meaning she should take her meds, talk to Sam, or call Musselman before things spun out of control.

Toward the end of the Sectional championship game against Havana, Collins called a timeout and pulled the starters. Jack turned to see his family and the rest of the St. Jude fans applauding, Mary Lou among them. The pep band played the school fight song. Jack stood on the outside of the huddle, drinking water, wiping himself dry with a towel as Collins talked to the kids entering the game. He watched as the St. Jude fans stood to sing the school song and danced in place to "Sweet Georgia Brown." The buzzer sounded, the band stopped playing, and everyone sat, including Jack on the Toppers bench, as play resumed, boys and ball zipping around the court.

"Jack," Gudy said, with a nudge, pointing towards the stands.

Mary Lou stood, shimmying and swaying, Maggie next to her, clapping hands and grinning.

Jack waited for a few seconds, praying she would take her seat, his mother the model of decorum and good manners, not one to disrupt an event or detract from a performance. The game decided, the stands stayed packed with people from both sides hanging around in support of the kids and wanting to see the trophy presentation. A bald man with a thick, black mustache and his stout wife, seated behind Mary Lou, said something, waving a hand in a downward motion, but Mary Lou did not sit. Sam, a few feet to the side on the same bleacher, watching the game with Becky as always, attention on play at the far end of the gym, swiveled his head when he heard the man's voice. Sam motioned to Mary Lou and Maggie to sit, pointing at the folks behind them to indicate they were blocking their view. Maggie sat, but Mary Lou waved a dismissive hand at Sam, turned and spoke to the mustached man and his wife, and stayed up, smiling and swinging her hips.

The man glared at her, then at Sam, who again motioned at Mary Lou. But she ignored him, avoiding eye contact as she followed the players on the court.

The couple, realizing Mary Lou was not going to sit and nobody could make her, grabbed their coats and walked down the bleachers, the wife stopping to speak to her. No longer smiling, Mary Lou stuck out her tongue at the woman and gave the man a light shove in the chest before waving them away with a flourish, like a queen dismissing a pair of serfs.

Sam rose and crept towards Mary Lou. He paused for a moment in front of his wife, who glared, daring him to make a scene, eyes no longer playful but bulging. Sam shook his head and chased after the couple. He caught them as they made the turn at the end of the bleachers, Sam sliding an arm across the shoulders of the mustached man, apologizing, Jack knew, smoothing things out.

Color flooded Jack's face and he tossed the towel over his head.

"Don't mean nothin', Jack," Gudy said. "Look... She's sittin' now. It's cool."

Up in the stands Mary Lou sat, talking and laughing with Maggie as Becky stared. Etta slid to where Sam had been and put her arm around Becky.

That same stare that Becky had flashed at the game she now directed at Mary Lou across the dinner table.

"Sure are good steaks, Dad," Jack said. "Where'd you get 'em?"

"From the freezer of his other family, more than likely," Mary Lou said.

"Mary Lou," Sam said.

The children stopped eating, Maggie looked at Jack and Becky for guidance, not certain what she heard, none of them sure what to do. Jack was familiar with the "other family accusation," and Becky knew because Jack told her. But as far as Jack knew, neither Mary Lou nor anyone else had breathed a word of it in front of Maggie.

Mary Lou glared at Sam across the circular kitchen table, fork in one hand, knife in the other. The girls to her left, Jack to the right.

"What? The children don't know about their brothers and sisters?" Mary Lou said, a fake smile crossing her face.

"Becky," Sam said, voice steady as he slid the paper napkin from his lap and wiped his mouth, his movements slow and deliberate as he eyed the knife in Mary Lou's trembling right hand. "Why don't you and Maggie take your plates into the TV room."

"OK, Daddy," Becky said, no longer eyeing her mother, afraid of the look on Mary Lou's face. "Let's go Maggie."

Jack nodded at Maggie.

"It's OK, Mags. I'll join you in a minute."

As the girls left the kitchen Sam rose and took an ivory-and-gold-checked towel off the oven door.

"Maggie spilled her water," he said as he sat where Maggie had been, next to Mary Lou, wiping the table, the towel wrapped around his right hand.

"Mary Lou, you've never spoken like that in front of Becky and Maggie before. Have you been—"

"Taking my meds?" she said with a smirk.

"Yeah," Sam said, steady and quiet.

"Guess not," she said as she cut a piece of steak and plopped it in her mouth. "But what's it matter? Why shouldn't the girls know the truth?"

"The truth?"

"Don't start with me Sam. Don't play this game in front of Jack. He knows the truth. He knows about the blonde...."

"Oh, well, if Jack knows, then it's OK. Let's talk about my other family. Which one is it again? I get confused."

"Don't patronize me, you sonuvabitch," Mary Lou said, waving the knife and fork while scowling at Basker who had padded in from the living room.

"OK, OK," Sam said, catching himself. "I'm sorry. I just get frustrated with all this...this..."

"Wait, wait..." Mary Lou said, tilting her head toward the ceiling, ignoring Sam.

"Mary Lou..."

"No, no, I could never..."she said, face twisted, neck muscles tight.

"Mom..."

"There must be someway else," she said, head upturned, hands balled, resting on the table, clenching the knife and fork so tight her knuckles turned white, shoulders rising, as if she were about to jump.

"Mom?" Jack said and leaned forward, lifting his left hand but not extending it toward her, afraid to touch her, as if an invisible shield might shock them both. "Mom?"

"OK, OK," Mary Lou said with a sigh, head dropping, shoulders sagging, knife and fork tilting sideways in her hands, away from the plate. "OK."

She rolled her neck, straining to relax, and settled her gaze on Jack, who dropped his left hand onto the table.

"It's going to be OK, Jack," she said with a smile, brown eyes tearing then bulging. "I know the answer now. It's going to be..."

FLASH—the knife whizzed past Jack's eyes as Mary Lou swung her right arm high, twisted, and threw her tiny body like a rag doll.

CRASH—the lime dinner plate cracking on the white linoleum.

FLASH—again, the steel blade glinted at the top of her arm's arc before she slashed down at Sam.

Sam jerked his right hand from under the table, gold-checked dishtowel folded and wrapped tight around it, and caught the blade in the cloth, clutching Mary Lou's thin wrist with his left hand. The point of the knife pierced and scratched the green tabletop as Sam ripped it out of Mary Lou's clenched fist, the blade clattering to the floor. Enraged, Mary Lou threw lefts and rights at Sam, striking him in the chest and head as he struggled to his feet attempting to grasp her, dish towel turning crimson.

"Grab her Jack, grab her," he shouted.

Jack rose from the table and seized his mother from behind, wrapped her in a bear hug and forced her face down to the floor.

"Goddamn you both," Mary Lou screamed. "Goddamn you both!"

"Stop it, Mom!" Jack shouted as Mary Lou thrashed beneath him. "Stop it!"

Becky came running from the TV room, covered her mouth with a hand, then jerked it away when she saw Jack with his right knee buried in the small of Mary Lou's back, her arms and wrists pinned behind.

"What's happening? What's happening?" Becky screamed.

"Becky," Sam said kneeling, taking her right hand into his left. "Becky, honey, settle down. Settle down."

Becky averted her gaze from Jack and Mary Lou and looked at her father, his touch calming her.

"That's a good girl," Sam said. "Listen to me now, honey. I hurt my hand. I need you to go the phone, find the number for the ambulance on the emergency list next to it, and call it. Should be right at the top. Give them our address and tell 'em to hurry.... Can you do that, honey?"

Becky glanced at Jack and Mary Lou, nodded at her father, and raced to the black wall phone by the refrigerator.

"Keep her down, Jack," Sam said as he stumbled to the sink, turned on the faucet, unwound the towel and rinsed the wound.

Mary Lou, tiring, stopped squirming and screaming. Jack heard her gasping for breath and lifted his knee but did not remove it or loosen his grip.

"Dad..." Jack said. "Dad..."

"Keep her down, Jack. The ambulance'll be here in a minute."

"No...Dad...Dad...look."

Sam turned to see Maggie standing next to Jack, squeezing his shoulder, Spocking him.

"Oh, honey," said Sam.

He wrapped his hand with a second towel, ran to Maggie, kneeled down and hugged her. Becky, phone call made, joined her sister in her father's arms next to Jack. As the girls sobbed, Jack held his mother down, Mary Lou moaning, "Damn you all, damn you all."

After a few minutes, Basker, standing nervously beside Jack, began to howl and raced through the living room to the front door, his canine ears the first to hear the wailing siren of the approaching ambulance.

Life During Wartime

Jack opened the back door, wiped the gray, slushy snow off his shoes, patted Basker, and hung up his coat. It was 6:30 a.m. the morning of the Super Sectional. Sam sat slumped at the knife-scarred kitchen table, cigarette smoke drifting up from Jack's grade school clay ashtray, a pile of bills on the left, checkbook in front of him, stack of envelopes to the right. Jack watched his father's familiar routine as he examined a bill, took a drag from the Lucky, and, if he could pay it, wrote out a check and slipped it in an envelope. If he did not have the money, he slid the bill to the side and scratched a note to call the company or person he owed to tell them he would pay them next month.

Jack knew medical insurance did not cover mental illness, but at seventeen did not understand the ramifications. His father not telling him about the second mortgage on the house to keep the cash flow steady, and even then, not able to keep up with the bills. Many of the people the Hendersons owed were local, which in one way was a blessing. They knew Sam and worked with him on payments. But it was humiliating for Sam to have to ask, and small town gossip hurt.

"Hear about Sam Henderson? Judy down at the electric company told me he was late on the bill…again," leaving Sam to wonder who knew what about his finances.

They had dropped their membership at the country club the previous year, attending the New Year's party as guests. He did not have time for golf anymore, Sam told his friends. He had not bought a new suit or sport coat in three years, nor had he purchased anything for Mary Lou, reserving the money exclusively for the kids' clothes. The Caprice needed tires, the house a new roof, and Becky braces. But after paying the mortgage, utilities, and buying food, it seemed all the cash went to doctors, the hospital, or the pharmacy, with nothing left at the end of the month but more unpaid bills and mounting debts.

Seeing Jack, Sam glanced at one more bill, this one to Musselman, and thinking about the doctor's latest advice and the catastrophe in the kitchen a few hours earlier, he scribbled a note and tossed it to the side.

Musselman could wait a month.

Jack shuffled in and sat across from Sam who, like Jack, wore the same clothes he had on the night before. Sam took a sip from a cold cup of black coffee.

"How's Mom?" Jack said, looking at the stack of bills.

Sam set down the coffee cup, slipped off his bifocals and rubbed his eyes with both hands, the right one wrapped in white gauze.

"Not good. They've got her drugged and in restraints. But she's safe. Not a danger to herself or anyone else."

"Sorry I left the house last night, Dad. I should've stayed with Grandma and the girls."

"Yeah, probably," Sam said, sliding his glasses on. "But I can't blame you for wanting to get the hell out of here. I'm sorry you and the girls had to go through that. And you told Grandma where you were. How's Luke? Don't see him once college starts."

"He's good. Wrestling season's about over."

"You guys drink some beers?"

"Yeah, more than I should've. Didn't sleep much."

"Did the boys come over?"

"No," Jack said, thinking of how he and Luke sat in silence watching TV, taking turns grabbing Old Milwaukee long necks from the fridge. "Luke was gonna call 'em, but I told him not to. Not like there's anything new to tell 'em. Mom's in the mental hospital. They know why. Might as well let the guys get their rest. Jones and his buddies kicked our asses last summer in the Y-league after we'd been partyin' the night before. No need to repeat that."

Sam drank his coffee, lifting it with his left hand.

"How's your hand?"

"Ah, its fine. Got nicked when I grabbed the knife."

"Dad," Jack said, leaning forward, "how'd you know?"

"Know what?"

"How'd you know she was gonna stab you? Wrappin' your hand in the towel like that. How'd you know?"

"Didn't. Just thought I better be prepared if she did."

"I've never seen her so crazy. Never thought she'd try to hurt any of us. I mean, I knew it was possible...but I didn't think she'd actually..."

"Don't beat yourself up, Jack. Why should you think your mother'd try to stab me?"

"You did."

Sam set the coffee down and stared into its blackness.

"Well, it isn't because I'm smarter than you, Jack. And I'm not proud of the fact that I sometimes think the worst of people. It's just that I've seen things most folks haven't...because of the war...I know what people are capable of when they've been pushed too far. Seen how quick civilized people turn into animals when they've seen enough horror. Seen people kill for a few bucks... for food... for water."

Sam slipped the Lucky from the ashtray and took a drag.

"Hell, one night me and Ollie were waiting for a transport train in a small town in France. We'd dropped off a POW at a detention center nearby. Had to point our rifles at a dozen Frenchmen—people we GI's liberated from the goddamn Nazi's for chrissakes—who surrounded us at the station 'cause they were starving. They were gonna steal the K-rations from our packs. Kill us if they had to. For the food. They'd been through too much, Jack. Been pushed too far. You could see it in their eyes...I saw that same look in your mom last night. The illness has pushed her too far. She's been through too much...just like those folks in France during the war."

"But, this thing with Mom, I mean, well, hell, Dad...at least the war ended."

"The war ended." Sam nodded, bloodshot eyes gazing into the coffee. "The war ended."

He tamped the Lucky out and picked up a bill with his bandaged hand. This one he would pay. "Better go shower and get ready for school, son," he said, looking up and cracking a small smile. "Somebody said something about a big game tonight. Onward and upward, buddy." He opened the checkbook and clicked his pen. "Onward and upward."

Tenth Avenue Shoot Out

Conklin Field House, the site of the Toppers season opener a few months earlier at the intercity tournament, was packed with 8,000 high school basketball fans, not an empty seat to be seen, small kids squeezing onto the concrete aisle running between the upper deck on either side of the court, as close to a home game as a team could get in the tournament. But Blooming Grove was an hour away and they bussed in their student body, cheerleaders, and pep band. As far as school support went, the teams were evenly matched.

The same held true on the court. Except for Hassan "Go-Go" Jones, the Toppers matched up well with the Bombers. Brewster would face an almost mirror image at center, Connie Hairston, a six-foot eight, black-muscled, rebounding and shot-blocking beast, with a full beard. He did not have Brew's offensive skills but kept close to the basket and around the ball, his strong hands snatching it from the scrums underneath the hoop for put-backs and garbage buckets. At one forward was the six foot six Jones, who Jack would guard, hoping for an angel on his shoulder and plenty of help from teammates. At the other, Joey "Monty" Montgomery, a junior and the lone white kid in Blooming Grove's starting lineup. A step slow and weak on defense, he did one thing well: He could shoot the lights out from anywhere on the court. Gudy would guard Monty and was told a hundred times by Lane not to leave him alone.

"When Go-Go drives," Lane said, "you have to stay home with Montgomery. You drop down to help and Jones is goin' to kick the ball out to that skinny kid, and he's gonna knock down the jumper. Kid's a pure shooter. But that's all he is. Stay with him and he can't hurt us."

Johnny Simpkins and Ronnie Booker were Blooming Grove's starting guards and Jenkins and Connolly matched up well with them. P.K. might have a problem with Simpkins' size when he subbed, but he was quicker; Jimmy could play with either one of them.

As Lane had predicted months earlier, it might be the Toppers' bench that made the difference. As tough as the Bombers' starting lineup was, they had only a seven-man rotation, two interchangeable six foot three swing players, both seniors, Barney Ross and Eric Barnes, and no backup for Hairston. But that was where Jones made the difference. He had the physical ability to play any position on the court, from point guard to center, and the basketball sense to stay out of foul trouble, even while playing aggressive defense, averaging three-plus steals and several blocks a game.

"In high school basketball," Carmody wrote in his pregame column, "more than at any other level, it is the stars that make the difference. Coaches can't recruit like in college, you can't draft and trade like the pros. You have to live with what you have, design your system to make up for your players shortcomings, and count on your stars to step up when the time comes. Hassan "Go-Go" Jones has stepped up for three years of varsity ball. In a few hours we'll find out if the Toppers have a player, or players, who can answer him."

Jack knew the last comment was directed at him and, to a lesser degree, Brewster and Gudy. But it was Jack who hit the game winner against Blooming Grove at the Rail Splitter classic. Jack had sunk the final shot against Black Hills and had been suspended when they lost the first game. Carmody had a point. Stars made the difference. It was a question of who would shine brighter this Super Sectional night.

As the two teams walked out to center court for the opening tap, Jack looked into the stands where he had spotted Sam, Becky, Katy, Maggie, Etta, and Roger during warm-ups. The girls waved, Etta and Roger clapped and cheered, and Sam, cracking the same half smile from earlier that morning, gave him a nod and a thumbs-up with his bandaged right hand. A vision of Mary Lou doped up and strapped down in the hospital flashed across Jack's mind, but vanished with the scoreboard buzzer's boom.

"Onward and upward," he thought, glancing at his father again. He shook his head, tucked the bright white jersey with the royal-blue trim into his shorts and slapped hands with the Blooming Grove Bombers as the boys jockeyed for positioned at the tip.

Hassan Jones, his wild, high-right Jimi Hendrix Afro bushier than ever, gold headband stretched across his forehead, was the last guy Jack greeted, the two boys soul-shaking and nodding. Jack had forgotten how young Jones' face looked up close, his black cheeks dotted with pimples, his attempt at a Fu-Manchu spotty at best. But his body, if not filled out like a full-grown man, was hard and sleek, muscles running like rope down arms and legs, veins popping from forearms and hands. Silky, smooth strength and power oozed from Jones's pores as he pranced like a thoroughbred racehorse around the center-court circle looking for a starting spot.

"Play our game," Jack thought, repeating Collins's pregame advice from a few minutes earlier in the locker room. Collins, dressed in a royal blue three-piece suit with an indigo and white striped tie and starched, buttoned-down, ivory dress shirt, kept it brief, going through the match-ups, repeating the things he had been telling the boys for months.

"There's nothing else to say." Collins set his clipboard down and motioned the boys to bring the circle in. "We are…" he said as the boys extended right hands, stacking them high…

"HILLTOPPERS."

"We ARE…HILLTOPPERS…WE ARE…HILLTOPPERS…WE ARE HILLTOPPERS…"

"OK, OK," Collins shouted. "LET'S GO WIN THIS THING."

As Jack replayed the locker room scene in his mind, the ref tossed the ball in the air, and Hairston tapped it to Jones, who batted it in front of him and broke past a flatfooted Jack on his way to the basket, going airborne six feet from the rim, leather ball perched in his black suction cup of a right hand, and slammed it through the hoop.

"Game on, Jack!" Scooter stood and shouted from the bench as the Blooming Grove fans exploded and Jones high-fived with his teammates. "Game on!"

The first quarter was all Blooming Grove. Having practiced regularly against the Toppers press since the December loss, the Bombers' starting five zipped the ball around, dribbled furious and fast to the center of the court and avoided the sideline traps. When all else failed, they found the all-everywhere Jones, always racing like a bridegroom late for his wedding, challenging Brewster at the far end, forcing Jack and Gudy to drop back to help. The Bombers had no more breakaways after the opening tip, the Topper press holding firm, but neither did the Toppers. Blooming Grove gave up no turnovers in the first quarter, the Toppers unable to steal the ball off the dribble, intercept a pass, force a five- or ten-second count, not even a traveling call. When the horn sounded, the Toppers trailed 15-9, Brewster and Gudy scoring the only points on put-backs and foul shots.

When the second quarter started, Jack found himself on the bench with Jenkins, Lane between them, Jimmy and P.K. subbing.

"You see that, guys," Lane pointed as the Bombers broke the press again, Booker faking right off the inbound pass, dribbling to his left and firing a pass in front of Jimmy down the middle to a breaking Jones. "Booker's a lefty. Hasn't gone right yet. Only fakes. Don't go for the fake, Randy, force him right. Tell Frank. I bet Booker turns the ball over."

Jenkins nodded.

"Jack," Lane said, putting a hand on his shoulder. "You gotta maintain your position in the press while keeping an eye on Jones. Where he goes, the ball goes. Hell, every time Montgomery touches the ball, the first person he looks for is Jones. That goes for all of 'em. He's their security blanket. Look at 'em, Jack. They're all searchin' for Jones."

That may have been OK strategy against an average team, but the Toppers were not average. They were more athletic than any team the Bombers faced during the season, and, as good as Jones was, he could not go one-on-five. So, if they were going to get beat by Blooming Grove, Lane said, make the other guys beat them, not Jones.

A lesson learned, Jack thought, when Lane lost in this same Super Sectional. Lane, the Hassan Jones of his day, unable to win the big game by himself.

After two minutes passed on the clock, Collins returned Jack and Jenkins to the game, along with Cheyo and Tompkins, who substituted for Brewster and Gudy. Lane grabbed the two starters and sat with them on the bench as he had with Jack and Jenkins. The Toppers trailed by six, 21–15, but Hairston had picked up his second foul, and the Bombers brought the shorter Ross in to play forward, moving Jones to center.

With the Bombers' ball out, Jack and Jenkins told Cheyo and Connolly what Lane said. The ref blew his whistle, and Simpkins tossed the ball to Booker on the right side. True to Lane's word, the guard faked right and tried to go left. But this time Jenkins cut him off and forced him right. Rattled, Booker dribbled up the sideline, Connolly sticking with Simpkins. Jack, playing his left middle position, saw Jones angle toward Booker, waited a split second for Booker to commit, and when the Bomber guard lifted the ball to pass, Jack flashed in front of Jones, slapped the ball down and dribbled toward the basket, the middle of the court left vacant when Booker went up the sidelines and Simpkins lagged behind. Jack bounced the ball twice more and exploded for the hoop, soaring over a step-too-late-Simpkins for a rim-rattling dunk and drawing a blocking call.

The St. Jude crowd erupted, rocking the rafters, cheering until the ref handed Jack the ball at the free-throw line. The Bombers fans filled the silence with boos to distract Jack, who swished the free throw. The Toppers trailed, 21–18, but the complexion of the game changed instantly. Blooming Grove turned it over two of the next three times they took the ball out, Booker traveling once, Simpkins getting a five-count. Cheyo scored one hoop on a put-back and Jack hit a jumper on the wing over the shorter Ross. Jones answered quickly with a bucket of his own, but, by halftime, Jack had another steal off the press, scored six more points, and the Toppers led 30–28.

With Hairston returning at the start of the third quarter, the two teams traded baskets, neither team going on a run, and neither Jack nor Jones dominating. At half the Bombers made adjustments and now handled the ball better on the press, but they got no breakaways and Collins kept shuffling players in and out, keeping his guys fresh, hoping to wear down Blooming Grove's seven-man rotation. Early in the fourth quarter Hairston picked up his third and fourth fouls within a minute, reaching in on Brewster for one and going over Jack's back for the other, signs of tiring. The Bombers gave him a seat, saving him for the end of the game. With Jones guarding Brewster, Jack took advantage of the match-up with the shorter Ross, sinking a pair of jumpers off the wing and one from the corner.

The Toppers' motion offense clicked, and the press wore on the Bombers. But Jones kept Blooming Grove in the game, sinking jumpers or driving to the hoop. Gudy twice slid down the lane with Jones, who did as Lane said, kicking the ball out to Montgomery who drained the open the shot both times. With two minutes to go, Hairston returned, the Bombers' first five now on the court, and Collins followed suit, replacing Cheyo with a rested Gudy. The two team's starters now matched up like at the opening tip, stars aligned, Jack on Jones.

The two teams had played to almost a draw since halftime with the Toppers holding a one-point lead, 58–57, the difference a Jones three-point play off a windmill dunk over a hacking Connolly. While Collins substituted for the other boys, he spelled Jack only once in the second half, for one minute, not wanting to lose his presence on the press or scoring on offense.

Jack was used to playing the whole game but not hung-over. The beers and lack of sleep hit his legs more than the rest of his body, a half step slow by the fourth quarter. With the slower, shorter Ross guarding him it hadn't mattered, but now, with Hassan Jones in his face, Jack felt the weight of the night before crashing down.

Not just the boozing with Luke, but the violence of his mother, her insanity sucking away his energy, leaving him flat, forced to create an artificial excitement, an exuberance that should have been natural. But after last night, after the many nights like it, Jack felt anything but young.

Still, with the clock at a minute-forty and Collins signaling for the boys to run the offense, no stalling, Jack shook it all off, knowing his teammates needed him now. Everything else, even Mary Lou, could wait. He squared his shoulders, jab-stepped Jones off-balance, and slid off a Brewster screen as Go-Go hit the big man with a thud. Brewster's bulk created space for Jack to take a pass from Connolly and sink a fifteen-foot jumper from the left wing, making the score 60–57. Jones responded thirty seconds later with a slithering drive past Jack and through the Toppers' middle, a play Jack could not have stopped had he been fresh, Jones's first step so swift and long after a jab fake he slid past Jack and into the lane in one stride.

With the Toppers lead at one, 60–59, and sixty seconds to play, Collins shouted for the boys to go into their version of a stall: run the motion offense but work for a layup. With both teams in the bonus any foul sent the other to the line for a one-and-one. Make the first, you shoot the second, miss it and your opponent can rebound and go on offense. The Toppers zinged the ball around like a pool hustler shooting bank shots, the ball hopping from player to player, none holding it for more than a few seconds, running the Bombers ragged. As the clock dropped below twenty-five seconds, the crowd on its feet, roars bouncing off the walls, Simpkins turned and fouled Brewster when he caught the ball in the post. Simpkins knew the big man was the Toppers' weakest free throw shooter and did not want his own center, Hairston, to foul out to stop the clock. The Bombers called their last timeout to let Brewster think about the free throw and to set up the next possession.

"OK," Collins said to the Toppers, thorough as ever, "don't assume anything. If Brew makes both free throws do not press, drop back to half court. We'll have a three-point lead, and we don't need to foul. If they get a three-point play and tie the game, do not call a timeout. Run the offense and get a good shot. If we miss, we're in overtime. If Brew makes one or none and they get the rebound, hustle back on D and get on your man. If they don't score and we get the ball, run the offense, layups only. Force 'em to foul again. If they score and take the lead, run the offense, make a basket. We win. Whatever happens, do not foul. Do not call a timeout. Do not give them a chance to set up their defense. Got it?"

The five starters, spread out on the bench, made eye contact with Collins and nodded.

"It's final exam time, boys" Collins said. "Bring it in."

"TOPPERS," all the boys shouted, Collins's prompt completely drowned out by the din around them.

Twenty-three seconds remained on the clock when Brewster stepped to the line and took the ball from the ref. He wiped the sweat off his right hand onto his shorts, dribbled the ball three times, set, and shot. From where Jack stood, in between Jones and Simpkins on the right side of the lane, it looked good, the ball spinning in a lazy, comfortable loop to the hoop.

Nothing but net, Jack thought.

But the ball landed long, ricocheted sideways and into the outstretched hands of Hassan Jones, who turned in mid-air and fired it to a back-pedaling Simpkins, the ball at half court with Brewster, Gudy, and Jack standing in the lane.

But Connolly and Jenkins cut Simpkins off as he passed the midcourt line, stopping the breakaway, allowing the two forwards and center to catch up. The clock stood at eighteen seconds as the Bombers went into their offensive set, running the play called during the timeout. To no one's surprise the ball ended up in Hassan "Go-Go" Jones' hands, the All-Stater dribbling the ball at the top of the key. Jack crouched, eyes on Jones' chest, ignoring the jukes and ball fakes, his goal to keep Jones in front of him and force the long jumper. A shot he would drain, Jack realized, but better that than a dunk or dunk with a foul and a two-point lead.

Jones bounced the ball a few more times, crouching like a black panther ready to pounce, the speed and height of each succeeding dribble quicker and lower, arms and hands pumping like pistons—THUMP, THUMP, THUMPTHUMPTHUMP. Then Jones paused and straightened, the ball hesitating with him like an extension of his hand, rising higher than the last dribble, the clock at thirteen seconds.

He's gonna shoot the jumper, Jack thought, leave time to follow the shot if he misses.

Jack edged forward.

And when he did, Jones slipped past on the right, getting to the free throw line in a single step.

Gudy, guarding Montgomery on the right wing, slid down to cut Jones off, his body doing what his mind knew he should not, reacting, not thinking. But if Jones took one more dribble he would be called for the charge. Gudy had position. Jones, too smart to be hit with a charging call, bounce-passed the ball to a wide open Montgomery, sixteen feet from the hoop, leading the junior forward enough to make him take a step, putting him in rhythm to shoot instead of flatfooted and frozen. Monty caught the ball clean and in stride, came to a jump stop, went straight up and swished the jumper.

Blooming Grove led, 61-60.

The crowd cracked like thunder. The players on the Blooming Grove bench leapt and shouted. Montgomery jumped towards Jones, the skinny white kid beaming at the black superstar. But Jones pointed at Connolly in-bounding the ball and screamed at his teammates to get on defense as he searched for Jack.

Eleven seconds remained by the time Connolly snatched the ball, stepped out of bounds, and fired it to Jenkins, who raced past half court.

Nine seconds. Jack ran down the right side line on the Toppers' offensive end, his legs turning to lead when Montgomery canned the jumper, muscle memory now hustling him along. He saw a flying Jones angling toward him, "Go-Go" for damn sure, the guy never tired, Jack thought. Jenkins dribbled the ball at center court, no breakaway available, allowing teammates to catch up and run one last set of the motion offense, the clock ticking down.

Seven seconds. Jones now at his side, Jack ran toward the right corner as a racing Gudy hustled to the lower right block and planted his big body, Montgomery trailing.

"Pick, pick, pick!" Montgomery hollered at Jones, straining to be heard above the frenzied fans.

Five seconds. Jones spotted a flash of Gudy's white jersey as Jack cut across the lane. Jones staggered as he fought his way past the solid Gudy and lost a step along the way. Atop the key, Jenkins saw Jack's cut and fired the ball to Connolly on the left wing, who turned and winged it to the corner, the play unfolding as it had against Black Hills, Jack open in the left corner for the game winner.

Three seconds. Jack caught the ball, slammed to a stop, and turned his body in one fluid motion toward the hoop.

But this time, instead of a slow-footed, blond-haired Swedish center stumbling toward him, a sleek, Jimi-Hendrix-Afro'd ballet dancer of a ballplayer flew at Jack's face. Go-Go's lean right arm scraped the sky, pink-palmed hand spread wide, shouting at the top of his lungs, the mass of people jammed into the gym joining Jones, electrified and surging to their feet as one.

One second. Jack jumped, ball in shooting position, and let it fly, the brown leather clearing Jones's fingertips by a fraction, flight unobstructed, spinning true and clean toward the hoop.

The buzzer blasted. The ball reached the top of its arc. The entire crowd watched, as did all the players, even Jones, who twisted his body and completed a perfect pirouette, landing lightly next to Jack, the rivals now side-by-side, gazing together as the ball fell toward the basket, the net ready to catch and release, the shot pure and certain and dead on...

Who Are You?

Jack sat by himself in the bleachers of the Wreck, navy blue pea jacket on but unbuttoned, knowing he should go but not prepared to leave, craving quiet. The gym, lit by back-up lights, a single, weak one above, dim and hush as a church sanctuary on a Saturday night. The team returned to the Wreck to drop off their gear. Jack wanted a moment before driving home with Sam, who waited in the parking lot in the beat-up Plymouth. Chaos reigned after the game, fans pouring onto the floor, the PA announcer calling on security to clear the court for the trophy ceremony, students and parents alike celebrating.

Jack shook his head in wonder.

The locker room door opened, a pocket of light in the dark gym, and Collins walked across the floor, heels clicking and echoing on the hardwood, coming to a stop in front of Jack.

"It's time to go home, son."

Jack sat silent as tears rolled down his cheeks, thanking God for the semi-darkness.

Collins sat down next to Jack.

"I'm sorry, coach....I was drinkin' last night. Hung-over and tired today. My legs were gone by the end of the game. That's why that shot fell short, hit the front of the rim. It's my fault we lost. I'm sorry."

Collins stayed quiet, Jack's sobs echoing in the empty gym.

"I heard you had a rough night. How's your mom?"

"Better," Jack said, wiping his cheeks, tears slowing at the mention of his mother, wondering who had spoken to Collins. "But the same. It's kinda hard to explain."

"And your dad's hand?"

"Fine. The old man's tough."

"Yes, he is."

Neither spoke. Collins waiting for Jack to gather himself, Jack struggling to do so.

Collins reached into his back pocket and removed his wallet, fishing out the faded and tattered piece of paper he always kept wrapped inside the game program. He set the wallet on the bleacher, unfolded the single sheet, and held it under the faint overhead light.

"This is a letter from my brother, Rudy. He was a great player. Much better than I ever was. *You* could give him a game, but not me... He was drafted and sent to 'Nam. Sent me one letter...this one. He was not one for writing, couldn't write all that well to be truthful. Regardless, I carry it with me and read it from time to time. He doesn't say a lot... typical letter from a soldier overseas, I suppose. Talks about the miserable weather, the night patrols, guys getting killed and wounded. Tells me to stay in school, keep playin' ball, do the things he didn't so I wouldn't end up in 'Nam myself someday. You know, kind of stuff big brothers tell little brothers...stuff your Dad probably tells you."

"Sure," Jack said, looking at Collins.

"So, anyway, he's dealing with all this, but thinking about me. And then at the end, dig this, pure Rudy, making the best of a bad situation..."

Collins lifted the letter and read.

"'But, hey, little bro', they got a couple a patched up balls and a court at base camp. Ain't much to it. Packed dirt, metal backboard and a rusty rim, no net. But we play. Even in the rain. Just don't dribble, 'cause of the mud...but it's cool. Cool just to play. Ain't nothin' cooler than just playin'. And you best believe your big brother owns that piece of dirt. 'This is MY court!!!' I holler at them grunts and jar heads...'"

Collins paused and smiled, picturing Rudy in his prime, black and beautiful as they used to say, then finished.

"'Keep the faith, bro! Love, Rudy.'"

Collins cleared his throat.

"Few weeks after I got this," Collins said, waving the letter, "two Army officers came to my mother's door. Rudy had been killed in action. He was nineteen."

Jack stared at Collins and then dropped his eyes to the floor, no longer crying.

"The thing is, Jack, we all have things we have to deal with. Crosses to bear. Some heavier than others. But we get one shot at this life. Some of us are blessed to get a better look. Rudy didn't get much of one. His letter reminds me of how good of one I'm getting."

"I'm sorry," Jack said. "I mean, about your brother."

"Just one of those things, Jack. Nothing we can do."

"And I'm sorry about tonight. I blew it...for you... and the team."

"We all blew it, Jack. You...me.... Maybe I should've called a timeout, come up with an inbounds play, gotten us a better look...Brewster missing the one and one....Gudy leaving Montgomery open—Lane is still cussing about that. Talk about someone getting drunk right now."

They laughed.

"Life is what it is, Jack," Collins said, patting Jack on the shoulder as he stood to leave, putting the letter into his wallet. "Now you best get on outside to your father. He's waited long enough to take you home."

Take the Long Way Home

"Jack," Sam said, "let's get this pile of trash into the cans and call it a day."

It was late in the afternoon of May 1, six weeks since the Super Sectional loss to Blooming Grove. Hassan Jones and the Bombers went on to win the state championship, none of their games as close as the one-point win against the Toppers. Jones was named Mr. Basketball for the second consecutive year and accepted a scholarship to Notre Dame. A Catholic, it said in the paper, an altar boy, the Black Muslim rumor as false as the pregnant girlfriend in Detroit and the summer-in-jail stories. Turned out Jones carried a 3.7 grade point average, mathematics his strength, and wanted to be an engineer.

Somewhere Billy McGuire scratched his red head in confusion.

In the Class A tournament, the Black Hills Miners and Coach Patton ran roughshod over the small-school field and won the state championship game by twenty points, adding to the "General's" legendary status as a "winner."

St. Jude's graduation was in three weeks and the Rams had made plans for the fall. Cheyo and P.K. headed for the local state university, roomies in a dorm, living on campus per university regulations as freshman, then planning to share an apartment with Luke during his senior year.

"Party hearty that year," Cheyo said.

"Let's make sure we don't flunk out," P.K. said, looking ahead too, but from a different perspective, taking charge, directing Cheyo off court like he did on.

"Goddamn points," Cheyo said. "You're all the same."

Jimmy received an academic scholarship to Georgetown in Washington D.C., off to study political science and prep for law school.

"Knew it," Luke said, "you're already plannin' your political career. When's the revolution?"

"Changin' of the guard is coming, Sarge," Jimmy said with a laugh. "But don't worry…We aren't lookin' to replace anyone, just join 'em."

Gudy and Jack enrolled at the state university in Blooming Grove. Since Jack did not play varsity until his senior year, the four-year schools did not have him on recruiting lists. A few called as the season progressed, but given Jack's history as a streetball player and disciplinary problems in high school, they hesitated to offer a full ride. For the best, Jack thought. He did not want to play organized ball at the next level, unconvinced he had the ability or the desire. Playing against Hassan Jones and surviving a season with Coach Collins made him realize how good Division I jocks were and how hard they worked to get that way.

Jack turned eighteen in April and registered to vote and for the selective services. Mary Lou played and sang "Happy Birthday" to him on one of his visits to the mental ward. Nurse Decker allowed her to play a few hours a day, at Dr. Musselman's orders.

The Rams, eligible for one more summer in the eighteen-and-under division in the Y-League, added Jenkins, Connolly, and Brewster to the team. The junior trio of Tompkins, McElroy, and Pitman formed a squad to carry the St. Jude varsity banner.

"Does this make us Rams?" Jenkins asked Jack as they leaned against the front counter at the Y, submitting the roster.

"You're on 'double-secret probation' through the summer," Jack said with a serious tone. "Then, yeah, if you memorize the lyrics to 'Old Black Betty, bam a lam' and pledge allegiance to Barney Fife, Jethro Bodine, and Clint Eastwood, we'll put it up for a vote and see if you can survive the induction ceremony."

Jenkins stared uneasily at Jack.

Jack laughed.

"I'm messin' with you," Jack said. "Bein' a Ram's a state of mind, man, not a club. Play ball, be cool with folks, have fun, and you're a Ram. 'Sides, we wouldn't of asked you to play if you're weren't already a Ram. Just lighten up a little, OK Randy? Life's too short."

Jenkins smiled.

Mary Lou returned home at the end of April, having stayed in the hospital since the night she broke down. Dr. Musselman would have released her after four weeks, but Mary Lou said no, sensing she needed more time, uncertain the medication was at the proper level. The voices had betrayed her, threatened her family, and Mary Lou was determined, if not to mute them—unsure that would ever be possible—to counterbalance and lessen their influence.

Mary Lou spent the first day of May in her garden. She took a hoe to the weeds, yanked and cleared all the lifeless growth, then turned over the brittle, grey soil, revealing its yielding and fertile black side. She dug holes and planted fresh flowers, a mix of geraniums, daffodils, and petunias, the multihued petals that had been missing for three years blossoming once again. Gaps existed, but Mary Lou thought the full range of colors would reemerge. She saved the rose bushes for last, kneeling in front of the three weathered yet sturdy sticks, gloves on to protect from the prickly thorns. Mary Lou wrenched the roots of the dead red and white roses from the dirt, making room for the new plants with bright pastel blooms, two medium-sized pale pink bushes on either side of a larger yellow one.

"Better," she said to herself, standing to examine her work.

"We better get busy," Sam said to Jack as the two of them watched Mary Lou work that day. "Our mud puddle of a yard is gonna look bad next to your mother's new garden."

They made a trip to the hardware store to replenish supplies and tools, buying fertilizer, grass seed, two new rakes, and a bright green garden hose. They raked the front, back, and side yards, separating the leaves, branches, and twigs from the garbage and burning them in the gutter. Sam loosened the dirt in the bare patches of grass, smoothed it out, sprinkled seed, and then soaked them in with water, dragging the garden hose from spot to spot. Jack rolled out the spreader from the garage and filled it with fertilizer, running it across the established grass, the next good rain certain to turn the faded yellow lawn a lush green. When they finished the yard, they grabbed two hedge clippers, Sam working oil into the hinges and sharpening the blades with a file. Father and son trimmed the evergreen bushes growing next to the front of the house. It took them a few hours, but by the end of the afternoon, the yard, not green yet, at least looked well kept for the first time in years.

Jack stooped to help his father gather the bottles, bags, and pieces of paper they had stacked in the wheelbarrow and hauled them to the aluminum trashcans by the garage. They dodged the girls on the court, Becky shooting hoops, Maggie riding her bike. Sam smashed the trash down and bent the dented lid into place on top.

"Think I'll go take a bath, then see what your mom wants to do about supper. Maybe I'll grill. Nice day for it."

"And a scotch?" Jack said.

Sam lit a Lucky and watched the girls play. "Not today, I don't think. Not sayin' I'm done drinking. Gonna be days I'll need more than one scotch. But today's not one of 'em."

"Kinda thinkin' of cutting back myself, spending more time with Katy. Not sure what the Rams might think, though."

"Well, spending more time with Katy is a no-brainer. They're not gonna object to that. As for the boozin', those boys are more than drinking buddies, Jack. They're your friends. They won't care."

"Hope you're right."

"If any of them razz you about drinkin' less, tell 'em it dovetails with your Grandfather Weller's theory about believing in God: *it sure as hell can't hurt.*"

They laughed.

"I wish I'd a known him," Jack said. "Sounds like a character."

"He was. Had his faults...like we all do. But when it was all said and done, Wally was a good guy."

Jack walked to the court, expecting to see the girls, but instead heard them in the TV room laughing and joking with Grandma Henderson, Basker barking. Etta was visiting this time, not caring for Mary Lou, who arrived home in better condition than after previous stays in the mental ward.

Jack grabbed the basketball Becky left in the middle of the court and bounced it from side to side. As he did, he heard Mary Lou begin to play. He picked up his dribble to hear if she sounded tentative, groping for notes, mind and memory in a fog, play muddled and lurching.

The opening bars of Mary Lou's bluesy version of "Over the Rainbow" slipped through the windows, notes and chords ringing clear, downbeat slow and heavy. Her husky alto tenor voice soon followed, cracking on the high notes.

As his mother played the piano, running slim fingers up and down its black and white keys, Jack dribbled the red, white, and blue basketball. Working it from side-to-side, up and down, juking and jabbing against an invisible opponent, an inner voice whispering: "Wait for it, wait...wait."

He circled and stalked around the concrete, momentum building with each jackhammer dribble—THUMP...THUMP...THUMP... THUMPTHUMPTHUMP—until the beat reached crescendo and the voice shouted—"NOW!"

Jack pounced, leaping toward the hoop as he had done so often. A boy of seven, an adolescent of thirteen, a young man of eighteen, the only constants his love of the game and desire to play another day. Jack rose to the height of his jump, slammed the ball through the rim, and landed on the concrete, keeping an eye on the ball until it came to rest against the rock border guarding his mother's flowers.

He admired the revitalized garden as Mary Lou sang, the music sounding almost the way he recalled it from childhood—"Yes, Mom, I remember you from before"—but knowing in his heart neither she nor her music would ever be the same.

Jack shrugged. He walked into the kitchen, poured cold water into a clear, clean glass, and sat at the table Mary Lou painted forest green when he was a boy because it was his father's favorite color. He drummed his fingers on the table-top to the bluesy beat, tapping along the jagged knife scar left from Mary Lou's breakdown.

And he listened again, and for the first time, to his mother play.

Made in the USA
Lexington, KY
28 February 2012